After the Flood

Alec Marsh

2.10.24

'After the Flood.'

Very best wishes

Alec

Copyright © Alec Marsh 2024.

The right of Alec Marsh to be identified as the author of this work has been asserted by him in accordance with the Copyright, Designs and Patents Act, 1988.

First published in 2024 by Sharpe Books.

For Elizabeth Witney

AFTER THE FLOOD

Chapter One

May 1938

For the past twenty minutes or so slivers of the distant terracotta city had been visible in the cracks between the woodland and steep rocky hillsides as Thrace raced by. Then, through the broad windows of the Orient Express, the impossibly blue waters of the Sea of Marmara appeared, flashing in the early morning Levantine sun, like fish glinting in the shallows of a stony stream. Since departing Paris on Tuesday evening they had crossed a continent and now Constantine the Great's New Rome, *Nova Roma*, was but puffs of smoke away. The intervening four days had vanished in a blur; Ernest Drabble was on top of the world.

Being in love had rather taken him by surprise. Yes, he had read about it, and, yes, he had brushed up against its peculiar intoxications before. But with Charlotte, it was altogether different. And with the heady festivities of their marriage just behind them and then their honeymoon begun, the delicious sensation had not just been sustained but intensified. It was, in turn, a heightened emotional state that coloured everything – even the tone of voice in his head with which he read the dry correspondence of Oliver Cromwell – and perhaps less surprisingly – the poetry of Andrew Marvell, a volume of which he had brought with him on honeymoon.

Well, of course, he would. That's the sort of thing you expected of professors of English history.

Not that he'd spent much time reading yet.

Instead, as their train had travelled through the nations of the Continent, crossing borders and passing between tongues, he and Charlotte had persisted in their own state of blissful, insular ignorance. Their world was each other — not the broad rivers, dreamy plains and medieval spires or smoky cities of *Mitteleuropa*. As a result, it was as if they had woken up in Sofia, which is when they started to notice the outside world again. Or indeed Drabble's old friend Percival Harris, who was somewhere else on the train and probably waiting for them to emerge and keep him company. Drabble checked his watch and decided he wasn't going to leave their bed just yet.

'Poor Harris,' he announced.

Charlotte looked over.

'Do you think we should get up?'

'No way!' The sharpness of his contradiction was softened by a smile. 'It was his own stupid idea to come with us in the first place.'

'Yes, but we could have said "no".'

'Have you ever tried saying "no" to Harris?'

She cocked an eyebrow inquisitively at him.

'It's harder than you would imagine.'

She laughed and rolled onto him, her mouth finding his, and he immediately forgot his social obligations to Harris – or indeed Harris's existence at all...

Charlotte giggled incredulously.

'Again?'

In a while they were both propped up in bed, watching the landscape drift by through the window. Married life had a lot to commend it, Drabble thought again as he reached for his cold cup of tea. His eye caught the cream face of his wristwatch.

'We'll be there in no time.'

'I can't wait to smell it.'

He smiled, and pulled her closer to him.

'I can't wait for breakfast.'

The four wagon-lits of the Simplon Orient Express had been robbed of their restaurant car the night before at

AFTER THE FLOOD

Belgrade. Apparently, this was what happened, owing to customs or some other bureaucratic obstacle. It meant that the satisfaction of their gastronomic appetites, as well as the splendours of Byzantium and the former Ottoman capital, awaited them in Istanbul inside the hour. First there would be the tedious formalities of the station to overcome. They would also have to get out of bed and get dressed, of course. Drabble spoke without taking his eyes from the impossibly blue water of the Sea of Marmara.

'What would you like to see first?'

'The Hagia Sophia.' Charlotte laid aside her Turkish phrase book. '*Lutfen.*'

'*Loot-fen?*'

'*Lutfen*,' corrected Charlotte. 'It means "please".' She smiled. '*Tesekkur ederim* is "thank you".'

'You're such a swot,' he said kindly.

'Not everyone's as clever as you, you know...'

She broke into laughter, his mouth found hers, and they rolled over onto the bed... there was world enough and time yet to get dressed.

Harris halted outside the door of Drabble and Charlotte's compartment, his hand raised, poised to knock. He heard a faint noise from inside that made him stop and he leaned his ear closer to the door.

He immediately recoiled, emitting a low growl.

Once more unto the breach dear friends? Really? He hurried along the corridor and rather portentously checked his pocket watch, a performative act of disapproval that he alone would relish. It was gone ten. What self-respecting couple – even newlyweds – rutted like demented rabbits at this hour? And for Christ's sake, they'd been married for almost a week... Surely it would start to wear off *soon*?

Harris started for his cabin, feeling gloom descend. When he had invited himself along on Drabble and Charlotte's honeymoon, he had anticipated a modicum of reluctance on their part. It was to be expected, after all. As it turned out they narrowly avoided causing offence, but then – as Harris explained, he was literally unoffendable – he recovered from it fast enough. By which point, Charlotte, to give her her dues, had come round to the idea – perhaps she had half-expected it anyway – and agreed. Certainly, if she had had any reservations, she had kept them to herself, which was jolly decent of her. Drabble had been less circumspect. 'Are you ruddy well off your chuff?' he barked, with insulting incredulity. 'Why in God's name would I want you on my honeymoon? Should I invite my mother along as well? Perhaps my aunts? Shall we share a cabin?'

That, Harris didn't mind admitting, had cut him pretty severely. And he hadn't known quite what to say in reply – which was unusual for Harris. After all, Drabble knew well enough that Harris had been to Constantinople before, and so his local knowledge would come in handy. And it would, wouldn't it?

Still frowning, Harris let himself into his cabin, becoming faintly aware of the passing landscape outside – not to mention the juddering of the tracks (the Turkish portion of the line was decidedly iffy, even worse than the Greek stretch). He poured himself a broad whisky and flicked in soda water before settling into a seat.

If it was early enough to be doing *that*, then it was surely early enough to be doing *this*. Hah! He raised his glass and took on board some of the scotch and felt his torso loosen with relief. Next, he fished out his pipe and prepared it. Soon clouds of smoke filled the small compartment, occluding the glittering Sea of Marmara which stretched out smooth and silky in indefinite shades of bluey-grey. The heat of the day

AFTER THE FLOOD

was already beginning to penetrate the glass and Harris' mind began to fill with fresh possibilities. Constantinople, recently renamed Istanbul – almost certainly at the hands of joyless modernist technocrats – was imminent. He sighed and drew on his pipe: the seat of the Roman empire for longer than Rome itself. And here he was, a native-born Englishman in an immaculate brilliant white Fowler & Larman suit, with just enough linen in it to take the edge off the oppressive Levantine sun, and just enough cotton to stop the creases. Here he was in the prime of life. By Gad, there was nothing Harris couldn't achieve if he put his mind to it.

The train had been in Istanbul's Sirkeci station for some time when Drabble and Charlotte stepped down from the carriage and into the shade of the platform. They were immediately aware of various uniformed stewards and officials waiting for them, not dissimilar to a celebrated personage arriving at a sleepy provincial English town. Just as they were set upon, through the din, Drabble became aware of the approach of a generously proportioned white pith helmet. Beneath it he saw the Harris's face, a little puce. He was hurrying towards them, being assailed by a swarm of cheerful hawkers.

'Welcome to Constantinople,' boomed Harris over the top of this jostling halo of followers. 'Come on!' He snatched at Charlotte's hand, half-dragging her away and ignoring her own attempts to evade his grasp as well as Drabble and the objecting voices of the assembled Turks. 'Our carriage awaits! Your bags are loaded, and breakfast, and the glories of the fabled Pera Palace are but moment thither!'

As Charlotte wriggled from his hold, Drabble drew level and they exchanged a vexed glance. Drabble scowled but her face was written with a quizzical look. The pith helmet stormed off ahead through a doorway.

'Yes,' sighed Drabble, as he caught a refreshing blast of salty air. 'You're right. Drunk already.'

They arrived at a broad forecourt of green lawns and fountains feeling the heat of the day after the tepid shade of the station. Hectored by Harris, they departed in a small convoy of three hansom cabs, one for them and two more for their luggage. White and yellow passenger ferries streaked with rust jostled at the shore, black smoke tumbling from their funnels. Beyond a broad body of blue water crouched a low landmass.

'Asia,' bellowed Harris, importantly. His hand swept towards the far shore, where houses dotted green hillsides covered in trees.

So, this was the mighty Bosphorus. White caps crested the dancing waves in the breeze. Drabble gazed out, sensing a widening horizon and with it a broader canvas to life.

A bell chimed loudly and a scarlet-painted tram – positively Ruritanian in appearance – paused under sagging electric cables in their path, cutting off their progress. The driver halted the cab, avoiding a collision, and then spurred his horse out onto the rails. They fell in behind a tram and then headed up past a vast mosque on their left, from which worshippers were pouring out in great numbers. A crack of the whip and a flick of the reins had them careening right – crossing another tramline regardless of an oncoming motorcar – and up over the water.

'The Galata Bridge!' Harris leaned forward. 'In ancient times, the Byzantines stretched a great chain across the mouth of the Golden Horn to prevent marauders from getting in.'

Before them an urban hillside of great antiquity opened up. Countless structures and roofs competed for their attention. Amid the architectural cacophony rose a tall Romanesque tower with a conical roof.

AFTER THE FLOOD

'The Galata Tower.' It was Harris again. 'Built by the Genoese in the 14th century... this is the old European district. Our hotel's just by it.'

Leaving the bridge the cab melted into a traffic jam of cars, cyclists, carriages, lorries belching black smoke, taxis and horse-drawn cabs. A red-painted tram was marooned at the centre of it, its driver ringing its bell futilely.

Their driver threaded his way through this Gordian knot – a glance told Drabble that their luggage was still following, too – and they began to climb; away from the noise of the cars and the muddle of white ferries at the shore, the hooves of the horses clattering noisily on the paved road. Tall, substantial stone buildings in neoclassical style stood either side. They were faintly familiar...

Harris bobbed forward. 'This is the banking district. Look –'

He pointed to a sign declaring 'Bankeler'. They turned a corner, passing a hotel, and a vast structure resembling the country seat of a British aristocrat – it could have snatched up from Oxfordshire – loomed above them. 'Pera House, the British consulate,' announced Harris. Drabble saw a Union Jack flying from its high roof, above a vast Latin inscription which declared: 'British Embassy built for Queen Victoria in 1844'.

They were now climbing steeply and turning, tighter and tighter around an ascending spiral, the horses working hard. And then they stopped.

Without waiting for the driver Harris kicked open the small door of the cab and stepped down from the carriage. 'We're here!'

A uniformed doorman – broad moustache waxed to points, ornamental turban and crimson piping on his coat – stepped forward and shepherded them into a broad, milling lobby. Here among the attentive bustle of staff, Drabble saw a wiry

Anglican priest, perspiring in a tatty linen suit under the loop of his dog collar. He appeared to be taking his leave of an ornately attired cleric of an Eastern Church. A pair of well-dressed women – they looked central European – waited in a clutch of chairs by a fireplace and were adorned with a rich floral plumage and tufts of fur. Next to them, an observant-looking Turk in a black suit sat browsing a newspaper and smoking. Another man in a dark suit sat reading a newspaper with Arabic script in the other corner, underneath a Greek goddess holding up an urn filled with lilies. At the counter Drabble spotted the uniform of a British Army officer – the cut of the suit and precise sandy shade of khaki were unmissable. More luggage swept in and brought more guests in its wake – a pair of middle-aged Americans, bickering over something. Then a voice boomed out.

'Ernest Drabble, while I live and breathe!'

Drabble turned. Andrew Streat stood grinning at him from ear to ear as if not a day had passed since they last laid eyes on one another. But it was a decade or more since Oxford. In the interval Andrew's hair had surrendered the top of his head and retreated to the safe ground of his chin, where he now possessed the world's least convincing beard. But he still had that runner's frame which had seen him perform a flat mile quicker than anyone Drabble had ever met. Nor had he lost that hint of mild doubt in the lift of his eye.

'Andrew!' Drabble shook his hand warmly. 'You haven't changed a bit.'

Drabble introduced Charlotte before Harris, who had been distracted at the counter, arrived.

'Streaty!' He slapped Streat lustily on the shoulder and beamed. 'What the devil happened to your hair?' He broke into a cackle. 'It slid onto your face!'

Streat smiled awkwardly – he and Harris had never quite hit it off, and this sort of comment from Harris never helped.

AFTER THE FLOOD

Not that Harris knew.

'So you're still teaching out here, what?'

'At Robert College.' Streat smiled, taking them all in. 'It's a little slice of Oxford overlooking the Bosphorus. You must visit – *all* of you.' He appended this comment with a glance at Harris before handing his card to Drabble and popping on his hat. 'But now,' he glanced at the clock on the wall, 'I must fly, otherwise my students will be in up in arms!'

They watched Streat depart and step into the sun.

'Curious fellow,' pronounced Harris. 'I remember distinctly you telling me that he was the most gifted historian of his generation. What's he doing out here at some dusty hole no one's ever heard of?'

Charlotte caught Drabble's glance and half smiled.

'Come on Harris.' She took his arm. 'I think it's time we had our first Turkish breakfast.'

A voice interrupted their progress: it belonged to a nattily attired Turk of late-middle age who stood behind the broad counter; a pince-nez resting on the conurbation of his nose and moustache.

'Sir Percival?'

Harris turned expectantly.

'You are *the* Sir Percival Harris of the *London Evening Express*?'

Harris beamed majestically.

'I cannot deny it.'

The Turk swept off his pince-nez and, rushing around the side of the counter to address Harris, bathed him in the sunshine of his smile.

'In which case, sir, on behalf of the Pera Palace Hotel, it is my great pleasure to insist that you take our very finest room – the Presidential Suite – at no extra charge over the standard room rate. It will be an honour to have you to stay, sir.

Correspondents of the *London Evening Express* are most especially esteemed in this establishment.'

'Goodness –' Harris grinned, momentarily wondering if he should offer the room to the honeymooners before deciding that it might appear ungrateful: 'Thank you, I accept.'

'My pleasure, *Effendi*. Lord Axminster is a most important guest…'

AFTER THE FLOOD

Chapter Two

After the sort of breakfast that almost took them until lunchtime, they went sightseeing. Their first destination was a short carriage journey back across the Golden Horn and up the hill from the terminus of the Orient Express: the Hagia Sophia, the cathedral of Emperor Justinian, built in the sixth century and somehow still standing despite everything man and geology could throw at it.

Their Turkish guide spoke practically no English, but smiled, and adverted their arrival at any important feature during the tour by coughing savagely, like a Yorkshire terrier on the cusp of an attack, and pointing in the direction of that which was to be viewed.

In this way crossed they Byzantium's Imperial doorway – the one once used by Justinian himself – and into the cool, gloomy nave, surrounded by enormous ancient pillars and the hint of incense, and above distant windows that admitted piercing light. They gazed towards where the altar would have been and, above it, the apse adorned on each pillar with dramatic Arabic calligraphy displaying Koranic exhortations. At its centre, the Madonna with her oddly distended Christ child surrounded in gold, looked down at them through the web of hundreds of flickering candles suspended by great chains from the high ceiling. Before the enthroned Madonna was a great Romanesque dome, with its curious, martial-looking Orthodox winged angels painted on each of its four supporting pendentives. They were, plainly, a very long way from Canterbury or Westminster. Drabble had seen photographs but they had not prepared him for the scale or sense of being of the actual artefact itself: this earthy composite of East and West, of the ancient and...

The guide's cough heralded another observation.

'Dome is a hundred and eight metre –' he jerked a finger heavenward. 'Highest dome for thousand years until cathedral in Seville built.'

He nodded again towards the distant ceiling and then abruptly moved on. In the upper story they were shown a name inscribed on the stone balustrade.

'Wiking,' he coughed, before Harris filled in the rest from his guide book. Next were taken to a slab on the floor – inscribed with the words: 'Henricus Dandolo.'

'The dog of Venice…' announced the guide.

The tourists smiled.

'He led the Fourth Crusade in 1204,' explained Drabble, nodding towards the slab. 'When the Christians sacked Constantinople – on the way to liberate the Holy Land.'

Harris shook his head. 'What an absolute rotter!'

'Yes.' Drabble nodded. 'Constantinople never really recovered from it, either.'

Charlotte smiled.

'Oh for one hour of blind old Dandolo!
The octogenarian chief, Byzantium's conquering foe.'

The guide led on, nodding towards a narrowing along which the wall was adorned with mosaics showing several Byzantine emperors – faintly emaciated-looking heads protruding from enormous golden checked robes. Drabble knew the images well enough, and their purposes – they memorialised gifts to the cathedral by various rulers, the cornerstone of a bargain that saw the city through thick and thin from the fall of Rome until the coming of the Ottomans in 1453. As they listened Drabble found Charlotte's hand. They interlinked fingers as the guide continued.

A flash bulb exploded behind them – *whumfp!* – and Drabble turned; a diminutive, grey-suited gentleman lowered his camera from his eye, revealing a carefully trimmed beard and square tanned face that could have belonged a Swiss financier on vacation. A signet ring glinted from his left

AFTER THE FLOOD

hand. He wound on the camera – *zzz-zzz-zzz* – and met Drabble's offended gaze with a bland smile. Then he raised this camera…

Click!
Whumpf!

Drabble winced as the world went white…

He was about to protest when the Continental banker stepped aside and looked down at his camera, winding on his film. Drabble turned back to Charlotte and Harris, neither of whom had quite registered what had happened. Instead they were engrossed by the mural of John Komnenos 'the Good', ruler of Constantinople during its glory days in the 1100s. The little man stepped forward, and now pointed his camera more obviously at the mosaic. The flashbulb went off.

That was enough. Drabble was about to protest when he felt the gentle pressure on his arm. It was Charlotte.

'What's wrong?'

'Oh, nothing.' He shot her a reassuring smile, but glanced back at the photographer, who was winding the film again on his Leica. Her gaze followed, but then Harris broke into a coarse chuckle.

'According to William of Tyre this Johnny was small and damned ugly,' he looked up from his book. 'And despite making donations to this place, he indulged in pagan sacrifices to cure his impotence…'

Drabble didn't catch the rest. Instead he observed the tanned Continental banker complete his circuit of the upper landing and head off in the direction of Henricus Dandolo and the Viking inscription. Drabble sighed, gazing over at the man's brown shoes, Leica camera and his impeccably tailored dove-grey suit. And then, just like that, the little fellow disappeared from view.

Drabble returned his attention Charlotte and Harris, who was still gawping up at John Komnenos the Good.

'I think you'll find that the impotent one was Emperor Alexander...'

They returned to the Pera Palace Hotel. The heat had built convincingly and they were still rather exhausted from the journey. But it wasn't the heat that was bothering Drabble: he was annoyed with himself for not having confronted the man with the camera in the Hagia Sophia. Yes, it was probably nothing, but there had been something so brazen about the fellow. At the time he had been so taken aback by it that he almost doubted himself, but looking back it was undeniable. The fellow had patently taken at least one photograph of *them*, if not several. But why? Was he so enamoured with Charlotte that he felt compelled to break with convention and commit her face to celluloid – without permission? Drabble gazed at Charlotte's face, just inches from his, on the bed. She was utterly perfect. Momentarily he forgot his irritation.

'It's strange, it's it?' she announced, as she turned onto her back to face the ceiling. 'You spend four days principally sitting down, eating and drinking or sleeping on train and despite having ostensibly made no physical exertion whatsoever, you're still floored by it.' The windows were open and a decent breeze was making a plausible effort to reduce the impact of the Orient on their unacclimatised bodies. The May they had left behind at home had been fine, but was a very different kettle of fish from the climate that had greeted them in Istanbul. Drabble stirred from his thoughts.

'I'm pretty sure the temperature doesn't help. But I don't think you ever really sleep well on a train.'

He certainly didn't, especially since his experience aboard the Penzance sleeper all those months before in December 1936.

'I'm sure you're right...'

AFTER THE FLOOD

Charlotte rolled onto her side and broke into a smile. 'Especially on honeymoon.' She paused and he realised she was watching him. She had a warm, settled expression on her beautiful, honeyed face, but there was also something amused about her.

'You're not still thinking about that peculiar little man at the Hagia Sophia are you?'

'The guide, you mean?'

Charlotte shook her head and cast him a sideways look.

'You know I don't mean him.' She realised she didn't have his full attention, or rather, he was looking at her breasts, visible through the gap in her unbuttoned blouse. It pleased her, but she brought her hand to her chest – closing off the sight – and added meaningfully: 'I saw how you looked at him.'

Drabble smiled and found her waist with his hand.

'I'm sure it was nothing.'

But he wasn't. He kissed her and she laughed as she returned the pressure on his mouth, pulling her hand away and rolling on top of him...

Down in the hotel's bar, Harris had taken the top off his first sidecar of the day and was contemplating lining up a second. After the first taste he knew already that he would need the barman to up the dose of Cointreau. I'll have him trained in no time, Harris thought, as he surveyed the room.

He sighed. He felt ghastly. It wasn't a physical thing. No, it had gradually dawned on him that it really wasn't as much fun as he had hoped being on honeymoon, particularly somebody else's. In fact, it was rather sick-making. Yes, he sighed, nauseating was the word. And it wasn't only the gratuitous fornication. It was the offensive proximity to two people so obviously in love. It was unbearable. Every glance they threw at one another was a standing reminder of what his life so transparently lacked; it was a mirror of the evident repulsion he elicited in the opposite sex. Why else had his personal life been such a disaster?

Harris shook his head and sipped his sidecar.

He set down his glass and turned to the window. The terracotta-coloured roofs melted into the distance. In the infinity he arrived at a decision. It was time to get married.

He was thirty-two years of age, and life was marching on. The previous five or six summers had been a blizzard of weddings: all the chums from school and university had trotted down the aisle. Now even Ernest was gone, too. And now he had got the hint.

The thought prompted a pain in his heart... like someone had punched him in the sternum. He found himself rubbing his chest.

Harris stifled a sob and took a tilt of his sidecar. Oh Lord, his eyes were watering. Why did that always happen? It must be the heat. He experienced a sharp intake of breath. Or a breakdown. He set down his drink decisively. Was this how it begins? With thoughts one couldn't prevent from obtruding... with voices talking to one at all times of night or day? With waves of self-pity breaking on a barren shore of bleak solitude? Harris gazed up at the ceiling, hoping that gravity might prevent further moist excretions from his tear ducts. Almost. He took a deep breath. It could be worse. It was time to order another sidecar.

He attended himself to the bar and its patrons, a largely expat crowd. The place seemed busy for early afternoon, but, in truth, he had no idea how busy it ought to be. Moreover, this was, he reminded himself, the warmest part of the day and how better to endure the heat than in the well ventilated bar of the Pera Palace Hotel, sipping cocktails under the energetic gyrations of its electric ceiling fans? In a city such as this, you could hardly pass your time lying on a sun lounger reading gloomy American novels written by half-literate dipsomaniacs. Who would do that?

AFTER THE FLOOD

Harris affirmed the nod of the barman, who immediately began preparing him another sidecar. He turned away, his mind suddenly filled by Princess Padmina, she who had become everything to him during their sojourn in India the year before. He stared back out towards the window, but the blaze of the sun did not penetrate his unseeing pupils. An onlooker might have deduced that something was afoot because of the mildly imbecilic expression on his face; Harris didn't care. He was flushed with the joy of glimpsing her, of feeling her almost present. She was an incredible specimen of womanhood. Too good for him, by far. He exhaled. No sooner had she appeared than he felt an immediate, pending collapse approach: the knowing that he was without her, and always would be. For whatever reason, Princess Padmina had eluded him, just as his charms had somehow, ultimately, eluded her. Harris shrank, the air suddenly let out of him and his chest sinking, followed by his chin. The mental image of Padmina faded from his mind. She was gone. And always would be.

He reached for his sidecar...

A man pushed his way to the bar next to him and was presented with a whisky, deluged with ice. From the fit and condition of the suit, Harris knew exactly what he was dealing with – a press man, almost certainly of American extraction, given the cut, and since he was dressed too well to be the Fleet Street variety. (British journalists do not, and never will, wear tie pins except in RKO productions.)

They nodded at each other, sizing each other up like a pair of new boys. The newcomer, whose close-cropped hair was receding to the point of metaphor, lowered his gaze at Harris's orange-hued libation.

'What in God's name is that?'

The drawl was unmistakable. A wire man, had to be.

'An Englishman's orange juice.' Harris smiled. 'Three parts Cointreau, one part orange liqueur and a dash of lemon juice to take the edge off. Or at least that's how it ought to be.'

The American smiled and half-raised his glass.

'Cheers.' A distracted expression visited his face and he stared over Harris's shoulder as if looking at someone, before sipping his drink. 'Rye whiskey,' he announced, afterwards. 'I'm Fisher... *The Times*.'

That would be the New York version, of course, so not the real *Times* at all, which was published in London. Harris let this pass. People didn't always like having such things pointed out. 'I cover Turkey, the Balkans and a bit of provincial Soviet stuff that my revered colleague in Moscow can't be bothered to do.' The American gave Harris a fast once-over with serious, appraising eyes. 'I used to do the Soviet beat full-time so it's easy enough to pick up. You?'

'Harris; the *London Evening Express*.' He waited as the other acknowledged the prestige of his publication. 'Diary correspondent and writer-at-large.'

Fisher chuckled and took out an agricultural-looking black cheroot, which he lit in a rapid action. 'Well, you're smack bang in the middle of the right place for gossip in Istanbul at the Pera Palace. You know they used to hang a sign on the wall here asking spies to give up their seats for proper patrons of the hotel.' He cracked a smile. 'Can you believe that?'

Harris wasn't sure he could, but now that Fisher had remarked on it, it dawned on him that the room was rather well-stocked with suited men, sitting alone at tables or the bar, none of whom were quite giving their newspapers convincing attention. Case in point was a lugubrious-looking Turk in a creased black suit, whose neglected moustache shadowed a starched collar. He was at the bar, smoking a pipe and was patently doing nothing else but watching the room. Then there was a blond-haired man, mid-thirties and smartly attired, reading the *International Herald Tribune* by an upright electric fan. And then there was a thick-set fellow – more neck than anything else – with pale, pock-marked pinkish skin in a coarse suit like sackcloth that shouted Comintern chic, earnestly neglecting the crossword on a folded newspaper in the far corner. If he wasn't a Commie, Harris was Mata Hari.

Harris beamed – the Pera Palace was going up in his estimation. A glint flashed in Fisher's eye and he broke into another chuckle. 'The Brit I usually see here is missing.' He scanned the room. 'But over *there's* the guy from the US Consulate who I see here a lot. He's called Heinz.'

Harris spotted another man close to window and nodded in his direction.

'That's Laurent,' whispered Fisher. 'Ostensibly a geography master at the French lycée.'

Harris grinned and took a swerve at his sidecar.

'Who's that?' He nodded towards the severe-looking grey-haired man in the corner by the doorway leading to the lobby.

Fisher replied without turning. 'Hesse. More approachable than he appears, and excellent English. Interestingly, I've never seen him or Laurent exchange a word. Apparently it's personal.'

'Well, of course.' Harris raised his glass. 'Cheers!'

'Cheers...' Fisher all but finished his whiskey. 'As I never tire of telling my editor, Istanbul isn't just the place where east meets west, it's also where north meets south.' He chuckled. 'There's a sea of shit that moils and rages here; it's the eye of a human storm.'

Harris grinned. 'Wonderful. Well, I'll drink to that!'

Unbidden, the barman splashed some more whiskey into Fisher's glass before turning away to another customer.

'You know that Leon Trotsky lived in this hotel for four years? That's right. After Stalin ran him out of Russia. I wouldn't be surprised if each of these guys haven't been all over his room like a rash, just to see what he might have left behind. They won't find anything. I'm convinced of that.' Fisher poured the rest of his drink into his mouth, letting the last drops drain from the ice. 'Leon was many things but he wasn't a fool.'

Harris noted Fisher make a discreet three-sixty of the room. Whoever or whatever he was looking for wasn't here.

'Well –' Fisher stabbed out his cheroot and rose from his barstool. 'Nice to meet you Mr Harris. How long did you say you were in town? So long.'

Fisher hurried out, leaving Harris to relish the room of spies. How priceless!

He celebrated with another sidecar, but sipped at it slowly. It was knocking on four o'clock, so the afternoon tipple might yet knock on into predinner sharpeners, though he would need time to change. No hurry. Not yet, anyway. He took out his pipe and began to fill it, dwelling on Fisher, when he became aware of a new presence at the bar beside him, materialising at first with the arrival of an unseen cloud of musky scent.

The girl had the exquisitely fine jawline of a Russian prima ballerina. Her complexion – formed of that contest in the female of the species between the precise hue of skin-tone, lips and eyes – was so far from the ordinary and beyond his scope of experience that Harris did not know if she was a Turkess or from the Balkans – or Llanelli. But the eyes *were* green, and brilliant English racing green at that. Dark smudges adorned her eyelids, emphasising large eyes and a beauty spot favoured the corner of her mouth, alerting the onlooker to the otherwise flawless symmetry of her face.

She removed a silver cigarette case and lit a cigarette as the barman placed an effervescing glass of champagne on the marble slab before her. The green eyes found Harris and she raised the broad fizzing rim to her mouth – where it paused...

'Good health, Monsieur.'

AFTER THE FLOOD

'Santé,' replied Harris gamely, as he tried to place the accent. It might have been a Bulgarian playing a Frenchman for all he knew.

The girl smiled, showing teeth and laughed to herself, throwing her head back, revealing her throat and the smooth triangle of skin under her chin. For the first time since arriving in Constantinople, Harris found himself bursting into nervous laughter.

Drabble bathed before dinner in their suite, the bath an enormous marble job with absurd caryatids in each corner, like a sultan's mausoleum. If the intention had been to make the bather feel imperial, it failed. Rather, the egregious domestic opulence made Drabble feel a bit ridiculous. Certainly, when compared to the chipped, pinched bath he had the use of in college it was in a different league – deeper, wider and with an ample supply of hot water, this was an immersive experience that was in itself almost worth travelling two thousand miles for. Well... He sighed. Like it or not, the limitations of Sidney Sussex's plumbing were behind him for good. Now that he was married, he would need to find a house, a house for him and Charlotte. This thought warmed him and he looked over at her through the open door and her outline on the bed. She lay naked, facing him on her side, with just a sheet drawn up to her hips. She was looking at him silently. He met her eyes and wondered what she was thinking. She smiled and he returned it. His focus shifted to her breasts, one cushioned over the other, and then his eyes acknowledged her hand which gently stroked her lower stomach. She shifted on the pillow.

'What will we call him?'

'How do we know it's a "him"?'

'We just do.'

He grinned. This was now a standard refrain. 'I see.'

'I was thinking about Andrew.'

Andrew? Her last suggestion was Horatio... His first thought was of Andrew Marvell, which pleased him. Andrew was an apostolic name, too, so most people could spell it, and it was unostentatious. A cloud drifted in as Drabble remembered the cumbersome figure of Andrew Catchpole, a Tudor historian from Brasenose. No, Andrew wouldn't do. Then, coming thick and fast, there was Andrew Tey-York from school, a contender for its most odious character, a bully and a liar. Then Drabble remembered something else – which more or less closed the account; his first cousin, on his father's side, was an Andrew, and so was his son. Oh yes... had he missed his birthday?

Charlotte turned onto her back.

'I still like Horatio... but I just feel it's a little fussy.'

Drabble looked over again, feeling some relief.

'I think you're probably right, darling.'

The truth was, that when it came to names for boys – or indeed girls – his mind was essentially blank. Perhaps somewhere or other he was still coming to terms with the imminence of fatherhood, and therefore the inventive power of his imagination was arrested by shock. Not that he didn't want to be a father. On the contrary, it was simply a prospect that filled him with the sort of wonder and excitement that hitherto only a crisp, Alpine mountain or a seventeenth-century archive could have achieved. Charlotte interrupted his deliberations.

'Shall we tell Harris at dinner?'

He looked over; her hand still lay protectively over her midriff.

'Do you think that's wise?'

'Well, he's your best friend.'

'True,' replied Drabble doubtfully. Unusually, his concern wasn't what Harris would do with the information, rather it was what the information would do to him. Harris had had to put up with rather a lot of change already in the past few months, and Harris, he knew, didn't always do well with change.

'Mightn't it be a little early to tell him?'

She propped up on one arm, her face caught in a frown that indicated curiosity but perhaps mild irritation.

'It's been three months.'

'Has it really?' Drabble smiled. 'Goodness. Well, isn't it still too early to tell anyone, let alone Harris?'

Charlotte's expression hardened – and then her faced cracked, and she sank back onto the bed, giggling.

Her laughter faded to a deep sigh.

'Darling, one day you really are going to have to help Sir Percival Harris grow up. You do know that.'

Drabble laughed and pulled himself down under the warm water, feeling it suck in above his head. He then opened his eyes and looked up at the world through the surface of the water.

And that's when it came to him.

He broke from the water and found himself speaking as it cascaded off his face.

'The man in with the camera — I've just realised what's been troubling me about him. His eyes. They were different colours!'

'What?'

'The man in the Hagia Sophia,' he repeated. 'The one who took the pictures of us. One of his eyes was yellow. The other one was green.'

Back in the bar of the Pera Palace the girl kept her gaze on Harris and blew a funnel of blueish smoke to one side through pursed, highly kissable lips.

'What brings you to Constantinople?'

Harris grinned.

'I'm on honeymoon!'

There was a pause. Then there came a small detonation in her nose as she snorted her cocktail, the translation having taken a moment to come through; 'Honeymoon', after all, was rather specific vocab. Just then, she emitted a strange noise, like the excited bark of a feral dog of indeterminate ancestry. It was laughter.

'You are funny,' she declared, raising her glass to her lacquered lips. She took a deep tilt and eyed him coolly. 'My name is Yasmin. Tell me Harris, do you like to dance?'

It was very late. The warm night air was scented with woodsmoke and spices and somewhere, among the lights dotted across the cityscape before them a band could be heard playing a jaunty tune accompanied by a wailing female singer. It drifted in through the open windows, above the hubbub of the city. Charlotte, removing an earring, remembered what it was that she had been meaning to say earlier in the evening.

'You know it has a name.'

Drabble paused in the act of undoing his tie.

'What does?'

'The eye thing. It's called *Heterochromia iridum*. And, actually, it's relatively common, particularly in cats.'

'Cats?' He resumed removing his tie. 'It's still rather striking, though?'

'But not as striking as the brazen fashion in which he went about taking photographs of perfect strangers in the Hagia Sophia. Who on earth behaves like that?'

'I'm not sure,' replied Drabble. He could have added 'still'. He poured a drink and took it over to the Juliet balcony, where the doors were open, and gazed out over the city, an indecipherable mosaic of darkness, interspersed with blobs of yellowy lights from distant windows or doorways, and the occasional glimpse of neon or red from hotel or restaurant. Smoke filled with unfamiliar scents – sweet, aromatic and

AFTER THE FLOOD

bitter – drifted up through the air. He caught the cry of seagulls over the sound of the motor taxis.

Harris had not joined them for dinner, an unexpected if not unpleasant surprise after the enforced intimacies of the Orient Express. Having had three dinners in his company since Paris, a break for one night was welcome and if Drabble felt that then he knew Charlotte must have, although she was generous enough not to say so.

Given that such tact or sensitivity was not among Harris's traits, there could only be one explanation for his absence, perhaps two. Either he had been distracted by a woman, or he had found a story. There was a chance of both, but if he was asked to put money on it, Drabble would have said it was the former. He could only pray that Harris had made a better choice than last time.

Charlotte plucked off her shoes and lay back on the bed. She closed her eyes and grinned. 'What a day... *what a day...* I'm still breathless about the Hagia Sophia...'

Drabble lay down next to her.

'Yes. And there's a whole new day of discovery tomorrow.'

She turned to him, her eyes wide. 'I'd like to get the ferry up to where Byron swam the Bosphorus. We could have a picnic and then return in time for sunset.'

'That sounds perfect.' He took her face in his hands and kissed her. Her mouth returned the pressure...

Chapter Three

Harris's eyes creased open. The scorching sensation in his skull warned him against this rash action – and no sooner had his eyes admitted daylight that he slammed them shut again. That was enough. Lightning bolts lanced through his grey matter as if Thor himself had been unleashed on his cerebellum. More than this, the pain was tinged with paranoia and uncertainty. He had no idea where he was.

The air, he noticed, was pungent with incense and tickled the nose, like a high-church Sunday. Low, grey light entered the room through the open curtains, a tasselled blind swayed back and forth in the window. Outside he could hear a car idling and he supposed that he must be on the first or second floor above a road. The high ceiling, cornicing and set of tall double varnished doors told him he probably in a mansion flat, which was reassuring. At least it would have been if he was in London, although it probably signified well here, too. The breeze did little to relieve the stifled atmosphere; he recognised his clothes lying on the floor in a jumble just as he became self-consciously aware of his own nakedness. What had happened? He turned to see the back of a girl lying beside him, a neat triangle of shoulder blade shading her spine. His eye travelled down to the cleft of her bottom.

Well... he might not remember much – how about a big fat 'nothing'? – but he couldn't fault his taste. From this perspective at least, impeccable as ever old man. Which was something, but it didn't eradicate the unease he felt. Then, gradually, the fog began to recede. Oh yes... It was the strikingly pretty girl from the bar with the green eyes and the voice of Serbo-Croat paint-stripper. Oh yes.

So it was.

There had been a short, somewhat confused, walk along the Grand Rue de Pera down the hill into Galata. He had slipped on the cobbles in the dark, which she had found uproariously hilarious. Then they had descended down to the dockyards where the liners come in. That's right. That had led to a dim, smoke-filled dungeon of a bar with thumping, fast-paced tunes thrashed out on screeching, unfamiliar instruments. There was champagne, cigarettes and an exotic dancer. Oh... his throat felt like someone had been using it as a knife-block. What *were* those cigarettes? They certainly weren't Craven As. Harris looked at the feminine back beside him. It could be a Canova, he told himself, except the sleeping girl's skin had more velvet to it than even the coiffured marble of that Italian genius. Harris swallowed. Glimpses of the night before flashed before his mind: the stumbling return, the stairs, reaching the room, the first delicious touch of her lips, the hasty removal of clothing...

Harris felt himself awakening. Oh, God. His hands found her hips, and she stirred. The girl slid towards him, her fingers entwined in the brass bedstead. Harris exhaled regretfully, this wasn't going to agree with him, but he was stuck between a rock and a hard place...

Then another cloud passed over him.

What was her name?

He hesitated and then thought better of it. What, after all, was a name? And having started he couldn't stop. Not now. No, the sensation was too delicious, too intoxicating, too...

But what was her name?

In fact, who the dickens was she?

Harris opened his eyes, breathing hard, trying to force the nagging questions out of her mind.

He looked about the room for a clue – seeing knick-knacks, multitudes of bottles and jars, bowls of assorted trinkets and candelabra draped in wax. Was that an invitation on the mantlepiece? No, no... Had he ever known her name, now he came to think about it? Had he even asked? Had he... the thoughts and doubts rained down on him.

Harris froze and emitted a low, bovine groan. He rolled on his back and stared up at the ceiling, sweating profusely, blinking. He felt like he was on a ship that was moving; his chest was about to explode from heartburn and to top it all, a searing pain now stabbed the top of his brain. Was it the beginning of a stroke? Or an aneurism? He'd heard about aneurisms. Harris squeezed his eyes and held his breath – hoping the pain would pass.

Yet the questions refused to go away.

Who was this girl?

What precisely had happened over the preceding ten to twelve hours? Memory lapses weren't that uncommon for him – *true* – but a whopping blackout like this, was a first. And whatever it was it stole the moment of conquest – not that that was the word – from him utterly.

And part of the 'who', of course, was the 'what'? What was she? He saw a blonde wig on a mannequin's head and various necklaces draped from the points on the mirror at her dressing table. Why would she have a wig? She liked to dress up?

A gloomy suspicion began to rear its head in his imaginings but he scarce permitted himself to use the word – just as his eye alighted upon a red, lacy piece of underclothing hanging from the arm of a chair. But there could be no other explanation. Why else would this beautiful young woman pick up a strange man in hotel bars in broad daylight? Why else would any of what followed have transpired without… His mind returned to the preceding moments; perhaps she was a sympathetic nymphomaniac, one who preyed upon the priapic needs of visiting Englishmen? Or perhaps he was the unwitting collaborator – or facilitator? – in a psychological condition to which she was the victim? His gaze travelled back to the wig. Perhaps she was just rather keen on amateur dramatics?

AFTER THE FLOOD

'Sir Percival Harris,' she had said to him – a fragment of conversation appeared in his mind's eye... he remembered his surprise at her knowing his name, but no more than that. 'You are a celebrity,' she had slurred in her mostly broken English.

A celebrity. How thoroughly ridiculous. But of course, he hadn't minded. Not one little bit. To hear it had made him warm inside, and when a man has a woman like this giving him her full attention, he is surely fêted. Harris closed his eyes. Any sense of imperium dissipated; in fact, the reverse, and any lingering joy of sexual triumph evaporated. Nature abhors a vacuum, so as one emotion departed, another made its entrance; the newcomer being shame, arriving with a brass fanfare. Or was it guilt? Was it guilt – guilt at his own dissolute, shallow, pathetic pleasure-seeking behaviour?

Why was he cavorting with? – Harris paused, arrested. Why was he cavorting with? – he paused again... Come on man, he told himself, spit out. Why was he cavorting in the middle of the day with this woman, rather than doing something profoundly serious and improving with his life?

Britishers hadn't sired the Industrial Revolution and forged an empire upon which the sun would never set by spending their waking hours indulging in bouts of thoroughly unchristian, decadent, extramarital fornication.

Good God, man, look at yourself!

The insurgent voices of the counter-revolution in Harris's mind were relentless and he could not for the life of him stop them. They had captured the palace and were now seizing the radio stations and newspaper offices: he was corrupted and useless, an abject human failure of the most irretrievable kind. And what, after all, had he achieved?

The girl turned to him, her lips parted expectantly and her face flushed. Her breath warmed his face and her nipples brushed against his chest. The corners of her mouth rose and she spoke in a chocolatey, husky voice with that now familiar harshness of accent that could peel wallpaper at a hundred and fifty yards. Harris winced. She positively sounded like a Boche in a bad mood, but, *actually,* he didn't mind. He didn't mind because she was beautiful and her eyes, her face – the whole caboodle – glowed with a rare energy than made him forget everything else. Suddenly, the voices stopped.

'Do you remember last night?' she asked.

'How could I forget?'

She smiled at him, her eyes squeezing shut. Harris grinned. Really the hefty voice wasn't as bad as all that.

'Have you enjoyed *much*?'

'Rather.'

Harris grinned, though he immediately found himself wondering if his fears were true. Was she about to ask for a weighty tip? (In which case she'd earned it.) He sincerely hoped not, and he realised how crushing it would be. Harris cleared his throat:

'And how about you?'

The girl smiled, rather ambiguously, which made him fearful, and shifted herself.

'*Very much.*'

Her expression suddenly looked far less ambiguous and Harris's heart bounced with joy. Then he felt her grasp... and he gave a sharp intake of breath.

'Again?' he asked, breaking into a giggle.

The green eyes studied him mercilessly.

'Again,' she said.

It was coming up to ten o'clock when Drabble returned to the hotel restaurant to see if Harris had yet materialised for breakfast. He had not. That was not so very unusual; Drabble knew that Harris was partial to brunching – or even lunching – in bed after a protracted binge. So he went upstairs to check on his old friend at his room.

AFTER THE FLOOD

But as he arrived on Harris's corridor, Drabble saw immediately that something was wrong. A policeman stood outside his door and raised his hand at Drabble's approach. In that moment Drabble noticed that the woodwork of the door behind him had been forced at the jamb by the lock. There had been a break-in.

'What's going on?'

The policeman squared his shoulders. 'No enter, *Effendi*.'

'But where's Sir Percival Harris?' protested Drabble.

The man smiled apologetically – but held his hand up. Plainly he didn't speak English, nor was he going to let Drabble in.

'Where is Sir Percival Harris?' Drabble found himself repeating.

The man shrugged again, 'I not know, *Effendi*.' He had evidently cottoned on to Drabble's meaning. 'He no here.'

Drabble's eye fell on the damaged woodwork, his mind filling quickly with questions and possibilities. 'But what's happened?'

The policeman offered another apologetic bow, 'Small English, *Effendi*...'

'Oh for goodness' sake –'

Drabble barged past the policeman and snatched for the door handle. The policeman seized his wrist and dragged him back. Just as Drabble tore it free, a voice cut them both short.

'Professor Drabble, I presume?'

A tall, lean police officer with an Errol Flynn moustache stood behind them. A holstered pistol sat on the hip of his impeccable green tunic above flared breaches and gleaming brown leather riding boots.

'My name is Inspector Hikmet. You are wanting to know what has happened to your travelling companion and his room? First, your friend is not here, sir. Second, there appears to have been a burglary during the night.' Hikmet cleared his throat, weighing up Drabble's expression before deciding on his next course. He gestured to his underling to open the door.

'Kindly do not touch anything, Professor.' He led Drabble into the enormous room. 'Evidence of an apparent break-in was discovered by the cleaning staff this morning. Further, the bed had not been slept in.' He turned back and cocked an eyebrow. 'Have you any knowledge of Sir Percival's whereabouts, Professor?'

'No. That's why I'm here, looking for him.'

Hikmet nodded.

'And when did you last see him?'

'Yesterday afternoon.'

'Did Sir Percival tell you where he was going, yesterday afternoon?'

Drabble explained that he had not, although if he had to guess then it would have been straight to the hotel bar. But he kept his counsel for the time being.

Harris's bed didn't just look unslept in, it looked pristine. His clothes, however, were strewn about the floor – whether by burglars or Harris himself, it would probably be impossible to determine. Usually, Drabble knew, it would take Harris a few days longer to amass this level of disorder.

Drabble was aware that the policeman was watching him closely as he took in the room, presumably looking for him to betray something. Harris's leather briefcase had been broken into, he saw, the brass lock prized open and its contents distributed over the desk. Harris would be upset about that. Inspector Hikmet cleared his throat.

'Did Sir Percival have any items of value among his possessions?'

'Apart from some cufflinks, a watch, perhaps a travel clock – nothing much, I imagine. He would have had a few travellers' cheques and perhaps some sterling. But nothing worth going to all this effort for, I wouldn't think. I'm sure he would have deposited any significant sums of money with

AFTER THE FLOOD

the hotel.' Even as Drabble said this he doubted it was true. Harris was too trusting, too lazy.

There was a pause. Hikmet cleared this throat. 'I wonder if Sir Percival will be able to advise us when he returns?'

He left this ponderable hanging, doubtlessly inviting Drabble to offer some information or speculation in return. Drabble left it alone. He took in the room once more before heading into the adjoining bathroom. The contents of Harris's wash bag were dotted around the marble fixtures haphazardly, presumably as he'd left them. Several of the towels were on the floor, exactly where he would have left them. Should he be worried? He glanced at his watch. No, not yet.

But soon.

However, given the time it was still well within the bounds of possibility that Harris had simply got himself into some local difficulty, probably due to alcohol, from which he would emerge in due course with an appropriate story to go with it. That, after all, was Harris's way.

Returning to the bedroom, Drabble registered a mildly inquisitive expression on the Turkish inspector's face, which he ignored. Instead he asked a question.

'Have you searched the room thoroughly?'

Inspector Hikmet nodded curtly. 'All the customary steps have been taken. Sadly there are no fingerprints or anything of overt value from a police detection point of view.' He sighed. 'My assumption is that Sir Percival was not present when the break-in took place. I believe it would be useful for Sir Percival to see the room and let us know if anything in particular is missing, or out of place or strikes him as relevant.'

Just then a floorboard creaked noisily under Drabble's foot. He stepped back and trod on it again. The board groaned unhappily. Both men looked down. Drabble tried it again.

He dropped to his knees. Sure enough there were tiny, hairline scrape marks where the varnish had been worn away around the board, leaving the freshly exposed wood.

'Inspector…'

Harris lay gazing at the ceiling, perspiring heavily and grinning. The girl's head rested on his chest, her hand over his heart. A bead of sweat ran down his forehead and gushed down into the well of his eye and nose. It was hot and her skin burned against his. He had to slow down his breathing.

That had been sensational.

Incredible.

Seriously spiffing.

It also confirmed several pieces of information in Harris mind: one, that he would have to cut back on the Craven As – the mid-coital coughing fit had not been *tres amusant*. Second, he ought to introduce a little more squash into his regimen to promote his physical durability. Ah, well, he had kept up. *Just.* But goodness me, this woman was a veritable athlete. He closed his eyes…

Why had he not spent more time in Constantinople? Where he came from girls weren't like this. Well, *not nice girls*. This velvety Canova had embraced him with a level of game dexterity that did not fall within the worldview of the *Book of Common Prayer*. He sighed.

What it proved was incontrovertible evidence of the existence of a sublime physical bliss. That's right. Despite all that he had heard. Now he had eaten of the lotus-flower and there could be no turning back. What's more, if this fair maiden *were* – he hesitated – a prostitute, then she jolly well offered a thumping endorsement of the profession and quite possibly the greatest single vindication of the principle of the division of labour since Adam Smith put pen to paper. Harris gazed at her willing face. He had to know. Not because he

AFTER THE FLOOD

was worried about the fact, not anymore, but rather because Harrises just liked to know.

'I say,' Harris turned to her, his tone light. 'What is it you said you *do*?'

'Do?'

The flawless forehead approached a frown.

'For a living,' he added. This was met by a profoundly blank look. 'Um, what's your *job*?'

'My job?' The girl began to laugh.

To the sound of splintering wood, the police constable levered the floorboard up with his bayonet – and rather more brute force than finesse. It was immediately obvious that the narrow space beneath it was empty, but there was a crisp rectangular outline in the dust that showed where something had been until very recently. Something, perhaps a book. Inspector Hikmat stared down at it moodily before clearing his throat and flicking at a crease in his tunic with an air of mild irritation. He pulled a card from his pocket and presented it to Drabble.

'Tell Sir Percival that we need to speak to him urgently. Kindly ask him to telephone my office as soon as he returns.'

The inspector barked an order at the constable, replaced his cap and delivered a parting nod at Drabble before striding away.

As the police constable bent down to start putting the floorboard back, it struck Drabble that never in his wildest dreams could he have imagined his honeymoon as being like this.

But then, nor could he possibly have guessed that this was but the beginning.

ALEC MARSH

Chapter Four

Drabble and Charlotte arrived at the church during the first hymn and squeezed in to one of the last pews at the back. The vicar, his white surplice billowing behind him, was flanked by robed sacristans bearing candles, and progressing with dignified alacrity towards the Gothic Revival rood screen swathed in a shifting cloud of incense dispensed by a lad vigorously swinging a silver thurible. They arrived in formation and about-turned towards the congregation with a military precision as the assembled throng belted out the second verse of *Onward Christian Soldiers*, accompanied commandingly by the organ which, like almost everything else here, would not have looked out of place in the Surrey Hills.

Drabble could not see Harris in the congregation, but nor did he expect to. As a rule Harris was a great believer in the benefits of organised religion, *for other people*. So be it.

Amid the familiar – the grey stone pulpit and the brass, eagle lectern, were signs of their exotic location, such as the pale service dress of various army officers present. In other respects it was business as usual: the ladies wore hats, and the smell of shoe polish spoke of Sunday best. Drabble knew that the rows ahead would be filled with the great and the good of British society in Istanbul: the Foreign Office mandarins, the wealthy merchants and traders, the soldiers and various hangers-on who occupied desks at the palatial Italianate British Consulate that they had seen yesterday on their way in.

Numerous flags – the Union Jack, but also those of regiments and various Commonwealth nations – sprawled from the rafters or fell from staffs leaning into corners or niches. On the walls were plaques dedicated to the memories of Britons who had died well in far-flung scenes.

AFTER THE FLOOD

Their friend Andrew Streat was up in the choir stalls, looking strangely clean and out of place to Drabble's mind at least, his mouth moving in the exaggerated motion of song. Andrew had said he would see them at church, but not mentioned that he was in the choir. Still, Drabble smiled, a man must have his secrets. He saw that Andrew's shirt had been ironed but that his cream linen suit was a far cry from the military perfection of the other congregants.

The priest – a small, wiry man with hair greying at the temples – welcomed everyone in a strong baritone, which carried a hint of a Welsh accent. A trio of military medals on his chest included the MC. Suddenly, without introduction, the priest broke into song, his voice rising in volume and pitch, and the entire congregation stood.

The singing of liturgy reminded Drabble of Lancing, but the tune employed at the Crimean Memorial Church was rather different from the one used all those years before. It sounded monastic, and he guessed it probably was.

Drabble heard the clonk of the door and turned, hoping to see Harris. But it wasn't him. He turned back to the front, feeling a stab of worry, before reassuring himself that his old friend was almost certainly still sleeping off a hangover. That said, Harris would have enjoyed this heady combination of incense, sky-high Anglicanism and intense patriotism. Drabble grinned to himself. They were hallmarks of a theology in which the presentation of a dark blue passport bearing His Britannic Majesty's royal arms at the Pearly Gates automatically gains admittance, 'without let or hindrance'.

After another hymn, there were the readings, followed by a short sermon, in which the priest indulged in some etymology of the Greek translations of the Bible from the Hebrew, and soon the congregants were gathering outside in the shade of significant plane trees for coffee and tea served by a panel of military and diplomatic staff wives. Once again it could almost have been Dorking – but for the occasional palm trees and waxy, broad-leafed shrubs.

Drabble and Charlotte found themselves in the company of an enervated British Army major who did something nonspecific in the consulate and a mannish American woman swathed in wooden carved and beaded necklaces, who described herself as a teacher. Standing mutely beside her was her husband, a gaunt older man in a dark grey suit with snowy white hair who may or may not have taken a vow of silence. The woman was giving a forceful explanation of why the Drabbles ought to visit the Princes Islands – a nearby beauty spot of some repute – when on the far side of the throng, Drabble saw Andrew Streat in close conversation with the priest. Streat glanced over, catching Drabble's eye, and invited him over with the bob of his chin.

Drabble whispered into Charlotte's ear and slipped away, leaving her to field the earnest teacher, mute husband and yawning major.

Drabble was introduced to the vicar, the Reverend Douglas James, who nodded at him soberly and shook his hand firmly. 'Dr Streat has told me a huge amount about you, a little of it good.' He spoke without enthusiasm or evident pleasure. 'How do you like the Memorial Church? A little slice of home, is it not?'

After a few minutes' small talk, Streat was separated by an interlocuter and disappeared into the pale drill, hats and brass shoulder buttons. By this point Drabble and the Reverend James were onto the sung liturgy. 'It's Marbeck, sixteenth century,' he was explaining. 'They very nearly burned the poor bugger for heresy, but he escaped by a whisker, which is a relief.'

'I should say.'

'Well, we couldn't very well have a heretic's setting for the liturgy, could we? Not even the Anglican church would go along with that.' He drained his tea. 'I hear you're on

AFTER THE FLOOD

honeymoon. When I was married, we went to Llandudno. Mind you, there was a war on then.' He smiled. 'Are you going to introduce me to Mrs Drabble?' Drabble turned towards Charlotte but she was obscured from view. 'Let me fetch her…'

Drabble broke away, threading through the milling crowd, back to where Charlotte was.

But she wasn't there.

And nor were the teacher and her husband. He scanned the immediate surroundings of the gathering, which was starting to thin out, not seeing Charlotte anywhere. He turned sharply, and almost bumped into the enervated major.

'Have you seen my wife?'

'What?'

Just then he caught sight of the teacher and her husband ascending the steps of the church, heading for the lychgate. Looking the other way Drabble saw the forecourt around the tall doors of the church was now almost empty. Where was Charlotte?

He dashed inside the church, hoping to find her inspecting the interior. But she wasn't there and it was empty, silent saving for an elderly woman who looked up from a pile of hymnals.

Drabble returned to the threshold – Charlotte must have gone for a stroll in the churchyard. He slid roughly through the last of the crowd and took the shady path around the side of the building, striding past dense shrubs rising high on the banked earth of the churchyard. He knew at once that she was not amongst the graves or spent magnolias.

He turned around, telling himself not to worry. Where was she?

Drabble broke into a canter, retracing his route to the tall, arched doors of the church. He then bounded up the stone steps to the lychgate.

At the top he looked left up the hill and then right down it, but the cobbled lane was clear of her slim outline in either direction. He turned back, his mind dumbly failing to comprehend the situation, and looked down the steps at the entrance of the church at what was left of the gathering. Charlotte could not simply vanish. She must have gone with the teacher and her husband to see something. Yes, that was it. They would have dragged her away to see something. He rushed out into the road, following it till he reached the spot where it turned the corner. But the thoroughfare here was clear – save for a group of boys kicking a football. He dodged past them and out to towards the main road and the flank of the Galata Tower beyond. The teacher and her husband were at the end of this road – a third silhouette was with them.

Drabble shouted and broke into a run. He arrived with sweat pouring from his face; the mannish woman turned, and her expression darkening as she registered his alarm.

'What's wrong?'

'My wife. Charlotte. Have you seen her?'

The woman frowned and exchanged a glance with her husband, who spoke for the first time, 'She said she was going to join you…'

Drabble turned on his heel. Charlotte must have gone the other way. His footsteps rang out on the flagstones as he charged back past the church, through the rest of the milling congregants who were now arriving in the road. He clattered down the cobbled hill, passing stalls and scruffy boarded-up shops. A pair of urchins were taunting a dog with a stick in a piece of scrubland. In the distance a tram rattled by, its bell chiming, and on the far side of the lines a tall mosque gave way to the choppy waters of the Bosphorus, blue and suddenly ominous. Drabble scanned the road back and forth… It was hopeless.

Charlotte was gone.

AFTER THE FLOOD

Chapter Five

Drabble stood in the parlour of the parsonage, overlooking the churchyard, recovering his wits and breath. The Reverend James handed him a scotch and was speaking to him, but it was a mumble lost to the alarming traffic in Drabble's mind. The trouble was, he remembered almost nothing about the last moments before Charlotte vanished. Try as he might, it was a blank. All he could think of was ruddy Marbeck. Just then it came to him, and he felt a wave of relief. He set down his untouched whisky.

'She'll be at the hotel.' He looked at the Reverend James. 'Why didn't I think of that before?' He rushed from the parsonage.

Of course, Charlotte had been suffering occasional bouts of morning sickness for a week or two – or at least, that's what they assumed it was. So it was highly plausible that she had had to dash back. That's what would have happened. His footsteps pumped up the steps and out into the lane. Yes, Charlotte would be at the Pera Palace. Why hadn't he thought of this sooner?

But the first sign that this was not the case came from the doorman at the hotel, who declared that he had not seen her since they left to go to church. Nor had she requested their key from the front desk, and indeed it was still on its hook. Then Drabble found their room empty with no sign of her having been there in the interval since they had left.

Perhaps she'd been hungry?

He tore into the restaurant, where lunch was starting – and paced past the tables. She wasn't there. Of course, she wasn't. He arrived in the bar, of all the places he could think, about the least likely. Several men looked up – interested, momentarily – before returning to their newspapers. That's when he recognised a dishevelled figure at the bar.

'Harris!'

Slowly the face that he knew all too well turned towards him and, when it did, he saw it was haggard but happy. But the smile vanished the moment the watery eyes registered Drabble's expression.

'Good God, Drab. What is it?'

'We've got to go to the police. Will you come with me?'

Inspector Hikmet sat listening, his narrow fingers steepled under his chin. He had brought in a constable, who sat at the desk beside them taking notes, and reclined in his chair, his boots up on the corner of his desk. Meanwhile the Turk's cool gaze triangulated between Drabble, Harris and the fan that turned erratically below the nicotine-stained ceiling. Every now and then Hikmet reached for his cigarette and would ask a question, such as, 'You know she is "expecting" or you *believe* it to be the case?' or 'Has your wife been examined by a medical practitioner?' When Drabble finished they sat in silence, the only noise the whisper of the constable's pencil on the page and the uneven rasp of the oscillating fan.

Inspector Hikmet lowered his feet from the desk and squared his shoulders at Drabble. In light of their earlier conversation at the hotel, his tone was surprisingly sympathetic, for him.

'*Effendi*,' he said. 'You are understandably distressed. I ask you to return to your hotel. We will handle this... I will get word to you at the Pera Palace the moment we have news. You should understand that people go missing all the time in Istanbul – tourists especially – and with perfectly innocent explanations. Try not to worry. I am sure that even as we speak Mrs Drabble will be in the care of one of our police

AFTER THE FLOOD

officers. I have seen this before, *Effendi*. I will telephone to you at the hotel as soon as we hear *anything*.'

He rose from his chair and raised his hand towards the door, marking the end of their interview. But Drabble did not obey the social signal, and Harris, half up, plonked himself back in his seat.

The inspector remained standing and cleared his throat.

'What is it, *Effendi*?'

'We were followed yesterday, in the Hagia Sophia…'

Hikmet arched an eyebrow.

'I see.'

'And we were photographed…'

Drabble explained about the man with *Heterochromia iridium*. Hikmet lit another cigarette and listened and at length remarked, 'I cannot arrest a man for taking photographs, Professor Drabble, much as I might like to.' He turned and read the look on Drabble's face. 'However, I give you my word that we will make a note of this man's description; you never know, it may prove useful in this case. I never rule anything out.'

'Thank you.'

He nodded solicitously, as Drabble rose from his chair. Harris followed his lead.

'For now, Professor Drabble I strongly urge you to return to your hotel. You may not realise it but you are in shock.' He addressed Harris. 'Sir Percival, you and I have urgent business to discuss about the break-in at your suite. But that can wait… For now, I urge you to accompany your friend back to your hotel and to get him a drink – and then ensure he takes some rest.' Hikmet reached out and shook Drabble's hand. 'Before you know it, *Effendi*, we will have some positive news, I am sure of it. For now, I urge you to rest.'

Chapter Six

But there would be no rest until Charlotte was found.

Minutes later Drabble stood before a high wooden double gate, his knuckles aching from repeated attempts to gain the attention of anyone within. Above loomed the upper storeys of the imposing stone façade of the British consulate. The tall Italianate windows were all in darkness or shuttered. No one was at home, or was listening, it being a Sunday. Harris placed his hand on Drabble's shoulder.

'Come on, Ernest – '

Drabble turned sharply.

'And what do you suppose we do instead?'

'I'm not sure, but wearing out your knuckles on the door of the consulate won't do any good… We would be just as well taking the inspector's advice and getting a drink at the hotel. Christ alive. *It's a Sunday*. Diplomats don't work on Sundays: everyone knows that – they hardly work at any time but certainly not Sundays.' Harris leaned in. 'If it comes to it, we will have to come back in the morning, old chap. But by then I've no doubt that Charlotte will have turned up and we'll have forgotten all about this.' He realised his voice had sounded distinctly unconvincing so added, 'You'll see!'

Drabble regarded at him gloomily before replying.

'We can be certain of no such thing, Harris. I would be grateful if you could be slightly less accepting of this scenario. I can't sit down and sip a dry martini while my wife is missing in Istanbul.'

Harris growled.

'Oh you are being too dramatic, Ernest. Don't you see?' He sighed. 'She'll turn up, right as rain. You heard the inspector. This sort of thing happens all the time here. Waiting's the only rational thing you can do. For all we know she might be

AFTER THE FLOOD

back at the Pera Palace already – sipping a bloody dry martini herself.' He let the comment settle, and softened his voice. 'Look, we should go back and wait, and whether we do that with a martini in our hands or not is rather beside the point.'

Drabble glared and shook his head. Of course, he couldn't very well expect any better from Harris.

'Go on then,' he hissed. 'Go and have a drink, Harris. Get whammed. That'll help. I'll telephone you at the hotel to check in for any updates from Inspector Hikmet. Just make sure you're in a fit condition to take the call.'

Drabble began to stalk away, leaving Harris, pink-faced and stammering.

'B-b-but Drabble – ' Harris's eyes veered from the gates of the consulate before returning to his friend. 'H-hang on. Where are you going? STOP!'

Drabble did not know where he was going. But that didn't matter. At first he just walked and moving felt better than standing still. Arriving at the Grand Rue de Pera he saw the ornate wrought-iron gates of the Swedish consulate, and reached a resolution. If he couldn't raise anyone by knocking on the doors of the consulate, there would be other ways…

Withing five minutes he was standing in the black shade of the broad plane trees outside the front door of the parsonage by the Crimean Memorial Church. The Reverend James answered the door and took one look at him.

'Come through to the parlour.'

The dark, heavily carpeted room smelled fruitily of incense and fortified wine. Andrew Streat rose from a wingback armchair and offered a consoling smile.

'Hello Ernest –'

James appeared at Drabble's side with a glass of madeira – and handed it to him. He took a sip.

'I need to contact the Consul-General. Do you have his telephone number or an address?'

The parson and Streat exchanged a glance.

'The Consul-General won't like being disturbed on a Sunday.'

'I don't give a fig what he'd like. This is an emergency.'

'It is –' Streat agreed softly. 'But Greenhalge is the sort of cove that won't see it that way. It will only set him against you.'

'Which you don't want,' continued the Reverend James, pursing his lips. Drabble went to take a sip of the madeira and stopped short – his hands were shaking. He looked up and met Streat's gaze, but lost sight of him as and images and memories of Charlotte like photographs flashed up in his mind's eye. Turning, falling, her face was caught in a hundred different moments. Then he could smell her, and hear her laughter, and see the tender look she gave when she didn't quite agree with him. These swept before him. He caught his breath and set the drink down, before he dropped it, and reached out to rest his hand on a bookcase. This was the panic, of course. Drabble half-fell into a chair and exhaled. Through the window he saw the dark, tranquil churchyard. Beyond its walls lurked a vast city and somewhere within that was Charlotte. His Charlotte. His Charlotte with their child.

He pressed his hands to his face, feeling tears spike at his eyes. He had to find her. He couldn't sit here doing nothing. He needed a plan of action. Yes. He needed, above all, to take action. Streat placed his hand on Drabble's shoulder.

'You've had a dreadful shock, Ernest. You can't see it because you're in the midst of it. But there's no two ways about it.'

Drabble lowered his hands; Streat was telling the truth, of course. Perhaps Inspector Hikmet and perhaps even Harris

AFTER THE FLOOD

had been right. Perhaps he should simply return to the Pera Palace, sit tight and wait it out. Streat exchanged a glance with James.

'Ernest, my old friend. Would you kindly tell us exactly what happened, from the very beginning?'

Harris never made it to the hotel. That's because, as he walked, a new notion came to him. Notwithstanding his own vaunting self-regard, of which he was blissfully unaware, he had been wondering quite what the girl had seen in him. Yes, he was handsome. *But, of course, he was*. Yes, he was in the prime of life – thirty-two years of age and never better; *yes,* he was the very picture of a certain post-Edwardian British virility. Moreover he was professionally successful and talented, and, what's more, a knight of the realm (and let's not forget the Star of India either, old bean). But he wasn't exactly *rich*, certainly not in the way that rich people are, which is to say, monetarily. Nor was he precisely handsome in the way that precisely handsome men were, either. But he was doing all right. And while it was true that conversationally he could rarely be equalled this girl barely spoke English, so it couldn't have been that which sent the Turkish goddess's pulse racing.

So it begged the question. And that was a question Harris wanted the answer to, albeit he appreciated that it might mean he had to confront a disobliging truth. For in the absence of any other reason for her unbidden decision to hop into bed with him, there must have been something else afoot – an economic motive, for instance. Yet she had not asked for money from him. And yet, acts of human charity and kindness seldom manifest themselves in such a fashion. So since Harris hadn't handed over any money it might mean that *someone else* had parted with it. But why would they have done that? Certainly they would need a good reason, and might that reason be related to the coincidental break-in of his hotel room? That could not be entirely ignored. Nor could another notion that now came to him; that somehow it could be related to Charlotte's disappearance.

Harris shooed away a particularly dirty-looking street bootpolisher, as he tried to get his bearings.

He hesitated. Did all that stand up? Or was it all simply masking a latent desire to see the girl again? Well, he could hardly be blamed for that, could he? He obviously *wanted* to see her again; *all of her* in fact. He permitted himself a smile. That was only human. So, yes, there was that. But it was the truth he was also after. Because, like it or not, there must be a further explanation why this beautiful young woman – a saint with inverted morality – was cruising the bars and nightspots of Constantinople luring essentially unimportant strangers to bed, in order to give them the nights of their lives. So there had to be a reason, and he was jolly well going to find out what it was. He had decided.

He sighed morosely. If she'd only asked for money, it would have been fine. *Almost.* If she'd only asked for *anything* – to see him again, even. That would have made sense. But much as it hurt his pride to admit it, as it stood, it defied reason. Here, after all, was a gorgeous specimen of womanhood, the sort of creature that would make Picasso's paintbrush go limp.

And now he had to get to the bottom of it. Harris took out the small piece of paper on which he had written down her address and hailed a taxi.

The girl's apartment was on the fourth or third storey of a *fin de siècle* mansion block on a neat side street down the hill from Taksim Square. Havyar Sokak, read the sign. Harris paid off the taxi at the corner and smoked a cigarette at the end of a road, pondering his next move.

AFTER THE FLOOD

After all, suspicion was one thing, but knowing what to do about it was quite another.

After about a minute he checked his watch. Three-thirty. That explained the rumbling in his stomach. He contemplated going to get some food before refocusing his attention. No, that would never do. Now he was here, he was here. He could wait, he decided, see what transpired – and confront her when she left the building. That was an option. But it might take hours.

Harris tossed the cigarette to the pavement and started for the apartment. Forget waiting, he would take the direct approach. That's right, he would knock on the door and come out with it. He would put it to her. But what was she likely to say in return? Would he get a straight answer?

Of course not. It was not the sort of question people gave straight answers to. He halted. It was not the sort of question people asked either. Not people in their right minds. He suddenly felt a little sordid about it all. No, he shook his head, doubting himself. What was he doing?

…Bugger. He really oughtn't be here at all. It was all wrong. Harris glanced back up the street, prevaricating. Why was he doubting himself? He lit another cigarette and hung back a moment. He needed to take stock.

The secret was charm: find the girl, invite her out for a drink, and then – eventually, work the information out of her. What was the worst that could happen? Yes. That was it. Harris picked up his step.

Just then he saw the door of her building swing open and he stepped hastily from sight behind a tall, potted shrub. *There she was* — looking stunning, and so fresh… but who was that man? Harris inhaled sharply as recognition dawned on him.

It was the snap-happy Swiss banker from the Hagia Sophia: the double-eye coloured devil with the camera. And she was hanging on his very arm. Harris eyes narrowed; his teeth gritted.

The minx! The sluttern! The brazen harlot! His hands clenched into fists. Then Harris's mind switched. The coincidence was too great. Something odious *had* befallen them. They had been the victim of a plot – an unscrupulous machination that was beyond the pale because it trammelled on the sacred intimacies of a man and woman. And then there was that possibility of a connection with poor, vanished Charlotte.

This injustice needed to be challenged.

Before he gave it a second thought Harris stepped out into the pavement, just as the girl and the man with the fishy eyes were climbing into a waiting limousine. He bellowed with all his might.

'Halt!'

They turned, their blank faces creasing into frowns. Something about the expression of fear on the girl's face told Harris immediately that this had been a very serious miscalculation…

In the parsonage Drabble concluded his tale.

Streat and James, both of whom had remained silent, exchanged a meaningful glance. James spoke first, addressing a question to Streat.

'Do you really think we couldn't consult the Consul-General?'

The schoolmaster shook his head infinitesimally and James nodded ruefully. The parson heaved himself up from his armchair and returned with the bottle of madeira. 'We've got to do something to help this poor fellow.' He topped up the drinks.

AFTER THE FLOOD

'I'm thinking.' Streat's tone was cold and delivered with a surprising authority. It occurred to Drabble, and not for the first time, that Streat was no ordinary schoolmaster.

Streat rolled his small glass between his fingertips. 'Going back to the Hagia Sophia, Ernest – the man with the *Heterochromia iridum*... You say he was slightly built. No more than five foot five?'

He noted Drabble's confirming nod. 'And you think *he* may have taken Charlotte? Have you any idea why?'

Drabble wracked his mind – he hadn't a clue and admitted as much. He shrugged, 'How on earth could I possibly know?'

'And you've told the police of your suspicions?'

He nodded.

'Very well, gentlemen.' The note of authority was still present in Streat's voice. 'He won't like it one little bit. But I think we have no alternative but to disturb Sir Terence's Sunday evening.'

Chapter Seven

Harris froze, his gaze interlocked with that at the girl and the dodgy-eyed cove. Then something very peculiar happened. His jacket was yanked over his shoulders pinioning his arms to his sides and a sack was put over his head, plunging him into a dark, stiflingly hot void.

He was then bundled into a car and driven for five or ten minutes before being hauled out and led into a building, up several flights of stairs – all still without the use of his eyes. He was led into a room and then shoved into a chair and felt his hands being tied roughly at the wrists to its stout arms.

'Who are you?' he barked, addressing the unseen figures. 'Unmask me you curs!'

In that instant the fabric was torn from his head and he sat blinking in the glare, a little startled. Before him was a broad, open double doorway – and a balcony beyond, through which a dazzling light pained his eyes. Looking into the light he became aware of a figure walking into his eyeline, a sack dangling from his left hand

As Harris's eyes adjusted – grudgingly – the outline of the human silhouette became more distinct and then the background ceased to blanch and the whole came into focus. There was a broad expanse of blue water – the Bosphorus – and in the distance, a hillside covered in nothing but green woodland.

'Sir Percival Harris –' The male voice was gently accented in Turkish and curiously high-pitched. 'My name is Mr Osman. You are my captive.'

There wasn't much to say to that. Harris looked down at his wrists, seeing red ropes lavishly looped around them; this Mr Osman wasn't taking any chances, clearly. Either that or he had significantly overestimated Harris's muscular

AFTER THE FLOOD

capacity. His gaze returned to the lightly bearded face of his captor. It was stuck on top of stocky frame and had a puffy quality to it, like icing sugar on the top of Victoria sponge. The man wore a coarse-looking, three-piece suit that could have belonged a general practitioner in the Yorkshire dales.

The up and down voice of his gaoler continued.

'You are probably wondering what you are doing here...'

Harris sighed irritably as his temper broke.

'Oh *fucking* get on with it, cake-face. Actually, *don't*. Spare me! *Spare me* the self-aggrandising, speechifying pomposity, you jumped up, swollen gnome –'

Mr Osman stepped towards Harris nimbly – surprisingly so – and slapped him hard across the face. Harris fell silent at a stroke and the lights went out, his head lolling forward. A second or two later, a trickle of blood descended from the corner of his mouth where he had bitten his tongue. Mr Osman lifted up the head of the rebarbative Britisher before letting it fall. He grunted dismissively, as if somehow the quality of this prisoner was somehow beneath him, and walked from the room.

Drabble arrived at the Pera Palace shortly before five o'clock. The formerly bustling marble lobby was quiet except for two or three men reading newspapers. There were no messages waiting for him at the desk – there had been no telephone call from Hikmet. Drabble collected his key and started along the corridor for the stairs.

He knew that she was not in the room, but he could not stop himself from checking. Somehow, despite the evidence to the contrary, she might be there.

Arriving at their room, no sooner had his fingers touched the door-handle when it seemed to drift open of its own accord. He hastened inside, his voice cracking, 'Charlotte?'

Perched on the corner of the bed was a striking young woman. She smoked a cigarette through a holder between her lips and gazed at him with brilliant green eyes. Her demeanour evinced a serene insouciance that made him suddenly furious.

'What are you doing here?'

The answer did not come from her.

'This is Yasmin, Professor Drabble.' Drabble turned towards the dry voice – seeing the man he immediately recognised as the diminutive Swiss banker from the Hagia Sophia at the window. He was dressed as before in a well-cut suit of light-grey, making him an impressive, if slight figure. This time, however, instead of a Leica camera, the man held a semi-automatic pistol, a Mauser with a slim magazine, and it was pointed at Drabble. On the small table next to him was a dark green fez, its tassel tinged with silver, as though it had been dipped in paint. The man cleared his throat. 'Yasmin is a concubine of sublime capability, and extremely good at whist.'

His right, yellow-coloured eye twinkled.

'I suggest you close the door, Professor, and have yourself a seat.'

When Harris came to, he discovered that the human Victoria Sponge had gone, leaving him to his confinement. Discovering that he had been untethered from the chair, Harris performed a prowl of the estate: a commodious room – twenty-eight paces wide, so large enough to accommodate a squash court and a half, with a bed, a pot (presumably the loo!). There was also free access to a high balcony that they rightly assumed he had no opportunity of escaping from – not unless he wanted a one-way ticket to the afterlife, whatever that was. The first question was, what did they want from him? Cake-face had not given him a clue. The second was, how long was he to be captive for? Again, no clue.

God's teeth. Harris was far too tired and hungover and generally deflated to become a pawn in someone else's melodrama. He sighed despairingly, his gaze confirming his fears. And there wasn't even a bloody book to read. Not that he'd probably be able to read. He returned to the balcony and lit a Craven A. He only had another twenty-six of those in his primary cigarette case and his reserve (experience had told him never to leave home without a spare cigarette case). This meant that he would have to pace himself, and that wasn't good. But he wouldn't have to be overly Spartan about it.

On the positive side, the view wasn't bad. If you had to be a prisoner, far better to do it overlooking the Bosphorus, presuming that's what it was, rather than, say, the Piccadilly line. Some people would pay through the nose for this view, after all. Directly ahead were lush green hills, presumably the Asian side, so he guessed he must be well north of the city. But where, and how would he get back? He sighed, allowing the tobacco to linger. What did it matter? The girl had betrayed him; quite possibly all along. Therefore she was most likely an accessory in the burglary of his suite and her only reason for their night together – one burned on his cerebellum for eternity – was some underhand plot. Rage erupted within him and raised his fist in complaint; and then it subsided, the first lowered… Well, it didn't matter. Whatever the motive, he half smiled, yes, *whatever the motive*, it had been worth it. The girl was… his smile broadened as if the sun had found his face. She was his Circe.

He gave an enormous sigh, one that could have inflated a decent balloon if one had the wit to capture the expelled airs, and contemplated his position.

ALEC MARSH

Here he was, Percival Lancelot Augustus Harris; Knight Grand Cross of the Order of the Star of India; Knight Commander of the Most Excellent Order of the British Empire; owner of four-and-half decent suits, two sports jackets of superior quality, one tiger skin rug (personally shot), a shotgun, a typewriter, and about eight hundred books of assorted quality, mainly unread. It wasn't much to show for a life. Yes, he'd been to university – and failed at that admirably. Yes, there was no wife, no children that he knew of, no home to speak of, no great wealth, no substantial pile, no fame, and certainly no portcullis or grovelling retainers tending fields stretching into the distance. Nothing. His footprint was transitory: just like his rented rooms and the lovely old duck who came in and did for him. He absently tossed his cigarette end into the Bosphorus and lit another. What had he actually accomplished? Not nearly enough, that's what. He felt the heavens press down upon him. Nothing really, except … well. What was the expression? Ah yes. As the fellow didn't say:

It's not the tears in your life, it's the life in your tears.

Harris looked down at the waves below. What was it? Fifty feet? Sixty? Difficult to say… And how deep was the water? Again, hard to say. Would he survive the drop? It would depend on how deep it was. Unfortunately, there was only one way to find out. He swallowed. It was a long way down. Maybe later. Yep. Another cigarette first. Then action. Nicotine was excellent for action, he had always found, (but also inaction, curiously enough). Harris leaned forward over the stone balustrade and gazed down at the choppy surface of the water. Golly, it really was a long way away – when you thought about it. He located the tip of his cigarette between his lips and lit up, remembering what the old colonel in the cadet corps at school used to say: 'Time spent in reconnaissance is seldom wasted.' Quite right. More reconnaissance was needed.

The Swiss banker gestured towards the wooden chair standing in the middle of the room with the barrel of the Mauser.

'Sit.'

The man did not necessarily look like the sort who would put a bullet in you for refusing an order, but given that he was armed with a German military handgun, it would be foolhardy to presume that he didn't have it in him. He was old enough to have fought in the Great War, so he'd quite possibly shot at – and, who knows, accounted for – a few Tommies in his time. It all meant Drabble wouldn't be the first Englishman to be in his sights, and that was sobering. Drabble reminded himself that getting shot and killed in a rash act of defiance would not serve Charlotte or their secret life locked within her well.

So he sat in the chair, met the gaze of his interlocuter and waited for him to begin.

'My name is General Mehmet Siviloglu – I am known somewhat in my country, but little abroad, although that is where I have been living these past few years. You should know that I am a Turkish patriot, one who is deeply concerned for the security and safety of the Turkish state and her people.' The man let this comment settle, rather as if he was a part justification for a statement that might follow, or a part excuse, however incongruous, for actions leading to kidnap. 'I was born in a village outside Skopje to a Muslim mother of Albanian extraction in what we used to called Rumelia, the "land of the Romans". My father was a Bulgarian mariner from Odessa. Skopje is now in Yugloslavia but it then was Ottoman territory, as it had been for three hundred years.' He paused, allowing that fact to be given its dues, and continued, 'I worked hard at school and entered the military academy, thereby becoming a soldier of the Ottoman Empire, in whose service my military rank originates. As a result, if anything Professor, I suppose I'm belated Ottoman.' He smiled. 'But there are worse displacements...'

'There are General. I feel like I'm one of them. Where's my wife?'

The general's eyes narrowed. Plainly he wasn't accustomed to being interrupted. And he didn't like it.

'I understand that in addition to being an eminent historian you are also a highly adept Alpinist.'

'I've fallen off a few mountains, yes.'

Siviloglu nodded.

'In my experience men who have learned the hard way tend to have learned their lessons best,' he smiled.

Drabble's temper got the better of him.

'I'm not interested in your educational philosophy, General. Where's my wife?'

Siviloglu raised a gloved hand.

'Shh! All will be revealed…'

'So you have kidnapped my wife!'

'I said – *wait!*'

There was an arresting severity to Siviloglu's tone, one that caused Drabble to fall silent. The man adjusted the grip of the Mauser, his finger labouring on the trigger, and he grimaced. His square face was a collection of crevices and lines, ravines – of calculation and cruelty. The tensing muscles in his neck and jaw told Drabble that he had better keep quiet, or else the man would lose his cool. The realisation made Drabble afraid. Despite his bravado, he didn't want to die, especially now life was getting so good. He swallowed and lowered his eyes, waiting for the general to continue.

AFTER THE FLOOD

'I need you to climb a mountain with me. I need you to help me find something, something which will assist my country in its recovery from the pains and depths of the past two decades. You will do this for me, Professor, and then you will be reunited with your dear wife and your happy life will continue.'

Drabble looked down at the handgun and then up at Siviloglu.

'I need to see Mrs Drabble.'

The black gloved hand went up:

'Out of the question, Professor. But I give you my word that once you have helped me accomplish this small but important task, you will be reunited.'

Drabble looked at the yellow and green eyes, at the arrogant face so accustomed to giving command and receiving unquestioning obedience, and he wondered what the word it gave was worth. Quite possibly absolutely nothing.

Drabble felt sweat bead on his forehead. He knew he had little to play with in terms of bargaining chips, except for plain stubbornness. He swallowed.

'I need to see my wife before I do anything or go anywhere.'

Siviloglu nodded and the hint of a smile appeared on his lean face.

'I'm not in the habit of repeating myself, Professor.' The smile deepened and there was something sickening about it. 'But for clarity's sake, I am happy to point out to you that I have other means of enforcing your compliance, in addition to inflicting pain on you, or depriving you of your life. You're an intelligent man so I shouldn't need to explain further.'

Drabble already knew the truth of this statement; he had no choice but to comply. For now. He might yet discover an angle or opportunity, but right now, Siviloglu held all the cards, in addition to a seven-millimetre Mauser. The Turk read his expression; the small yellow and green eyes rounded with pleasure.

'Good. In which case I shall continue.' He paused, theatrically. 'Professor, I need to solicit your help in a matter of vital Turkish national importance. It's a particular matter, one which I believe you are uniquely qualified to assist in, and one which requires the utmost discretion.'

Siviloglu cleared this throat, an act which the girl interpreted as a command for privacy, because she immediately rose from her seat on the bed, nodded at the general, and gracefully strolled towards the door, leaving a fragrant trail of musky scent in her wake. She pulled the door to behind her. The general cocked his pistol.

'Tell me, Professor, what do you know about Mount Ararat?'

AFTER THE FLOOD

Chapter Eight

It did not take long for Harris to become decidedly ill-enamoured with incarceration. He had returned to the parapet of the balcony and was eyeing the drop, trying to estimate the distance to the water below. He was not brave, but he was indignant, *furious*. And sometimes indignation could overcome cowardice – even a bad dose such as Harris had – driving him to do things that others interpreted as brave, but were, rather, merely acts of vertiginous high dudgeon. There was also an emotion present that was far worse than indignation, too. It was boredom, and that was simply fatal for making Harrises do stupid things.

When he was five his parents had locked him in a first-storey bedroom of his grandparents' house in Radnorshire – a forbidding Gothic rambling lodge that had since been converted into an asylum for elite cases of derangement. Young Master Percival did not take kindly to this and took matters decisively into his own hands. He went to the window, climbed up and opened it, and slid down the steep slate roof before arriving at the gutter. Once settled, he had thrown Rufus, his teddy bear, down onto the lawn below and watched him roll to safely. Then he jumped after. Somehow he accomplished all this without injury. He then scampered around to the front door, knocked forcefully upon it to rouse the occupants, before berating his parents for imprisoning him. The following week, bars went up on his bedroom window.

That day Harris learned the first of many lessons in the law of unintended consequences. The episode also sealed his contempt for confinement.

He peered over the balustrade. On reflection the drop was probably fifty to hundred feet. In the fading light of early evening the dancing waves were grey-to-brown and didn't look half as friendly as when they were brilliant blue. Of course, there was still no telling how deep the water was, but it was probably deep enough. The truth was he didn't know how much water-depth you needed in the first place for sufficient aquatic cushioning. Moreover he had read something or written something somewhere about how above a certain altitude that landing on water became like landing on concrete. Not recalling the precise detail – or indeed any detail at all – and not being cognisant of his actual height from the water, all meant this was unhelpful information. Concrete sounded very hard. Yet balanced finely against that fact was whatever Cake-face and his acolytes had in store for him, not to mention the sheer boredom of remaining here ... When it was a simple case of stepping off in a controlled fashion and keeping one's feet together and holding one's nose. It would be over in seconds. Mind you, that was also what worried him.

Harris tossed his cigarette into the water and counted. One. Two. Three... after six seconds the fag-end disappeared from view. It had to be more than fifty feet.

He went inside to conduct an experiment. How long did it take a cigarette to fall ten feet? He stood on a chair on top of the dresser and clambered up – precariously standing upright before releasing a Craven A, and counted.

A split-second later it bounced on the floor. Half a second, he concluded, climbing down. Half a second at most. Therefore in six seconds it would fall forty-eight feet, at least, if one assumed it would speed up a bit. That was quite a long way.

Harris frowned. It was a long way. He gathered up the cigarette and contemplated smoking it. There was another problem, he hadn't yet considered. In the past two hours he had smoked a dozen Craven As. At the current burn-rate, therefore, he would be left high and dry before the night was yet young. And that was worrying.

He lit the cigarette and watched a ferry steam past, up the middle of the Bosphorus. The lights strung from bows to stern were dainty and pretty at this distance, which was probably a good hundred yards. He could hear its steam engines thumping away from deep inside its rust-streaked hull, the sound carrying above the splashing of its turning paddle wheels. He didn't like the look of them. They were far from optimal for bathers. No matter, if and when the time came, he would steer well clear of ferries and all pleasure craft. Oh yes, hadn't he come second in the under-thirteens' breaststroke at Lancing?

He looked down at the surface of the water. The shortage of Craven As was a significant problem. Moreover, he was already bored to tears and, what's more, there was – now he came to think of it – a distinct absence of booze in the room. Good Lord. How had that fact escaped him so far?

So there was nothing else for it.

He steeled himself.

Sir Percival Harris was not going to take incarceration lying down. He never had and he never would. He set his cigarette between his lips, and, puffing, tightened the knot of his tie. He would not need his boater, and as much as it pained him, he realised he should destroy it to put beyond the use of the enemy. There was no good to be had from handing Johnny foreigner a perfectly serviceable boater, after all.

Certainly he didn't want one of them walking around with it, especially with his college colours on it its ribbon. But he found he could not do it, so he decided to take it with him. Better to get soaked than sported by a Levantine rogue.

Harris prepared himself at the balcony. Now was the moment. He took one last, absolutely magnificent drag of this cigarette and then threw it into the waves – again counting as he watched it vanish. It was getting dark now, but he knew that that very darkness was ultimately his companion in arms, so long as he didn't get run over because of it by a boat. Presupposing he was lucky enough to survive the fall, of course.

The first challenge was the stone parapet. It was too high to get one's leg over it with ease, yet it was too narrow to stand on it with any security. Then another question beckoned.

Ought he remove his shoes first?

Probably. They would not aid his swimming. But they were from his favourite shoemaker on St James's and had been fashioned by dedicated artisans from lasts shaped precisely to his very feet. And assuming he survived the water, he would need them to walk with, wouldn't he? Moreover, if he didn't survive then he would rather his body was found properly clothed, feet included. Yes indeed. Given the choice, he would sooner die with his half-Oxfords on, than off.

Righty ho, he told himself again. He cleared his throat and took off his spectacles and placed them in their soft buckskin case in his breast pocket. He performed a perfunctory stretch of the arms, exhaled and heaved his left heel up onto the ledge of the parapet. He succeeded on the second attempt. Seizing hold of it – with some difficulty because he was also holding his boater – Harris hauled himself onto the narrow beam of the balustrade, so that he was now lying face down on top of it with a leg dangling either side. From this height the drop sent his head spinning.

My God, he thought. It's too far. *Far too far.*

What a clot! What had he been thinking? Had his wits deserted him? And what were *those*? Rocks – yes, right below him, sodding rocks right where the water met the retaining wall of a terrace or God knows what? Look, there

AFTER THE FLOOD

were faint splashes! Good lord! Harris began to panic – his breathing sped up. He had to get back, *fast*. He lurched with his hands to grip the balustrade and dropped his boater, which swirled through the air towards the waves. Damn it. No matter. He had to get back to safety.

Just then, the inside edge of Harris's left foot skidded from the sandstone lip of the ledge at the base of the balustrade, throwing his weight in the direction of the water.

And then he was falling. The moment he realised it, he hit the water…

For a moment General Siviloglu's question hung in the air.
'What do you know about Mount Ararat?'
Drabble's gaze met the waiting yellow and green eyes. Like the majority of the world's population, he supposed, he was well aware of the presence of Mount Ararat and of its place in our culture. Here, after all, was where it was fabled that Noah's Ark had come to rest after the Great Flood. Everyone knew that. That was its claim to fame – and not just for Christians and Jews, but to Muslims too, for whom Noah was Nüh. Drabble's gaze returned to the pistol, and the black circle of the barrel pointing ominously at him.

'What about Mount Ararat?'

The general stroked his moustache.

'I will tell you a story, Professor. In summer of 1916 in the midst of the Great War a pilot of the Russian Imperial Air Force was flying above Mount Ararat, when he and his co-pilot saw the outline of ship, partly submerged. It was in a vast lake on the mountain-top at an altitude of around four and a half thousand feet. They described the object as being several hundred metres long. About the size of a battleship is what they said. They went in closer and took aerial photographs, and then returned, sending word to St Petersburg of their discovery. Very soon, two companies of

Russian Imperial engineers arrived to investigate – each approaching the mountain from different sides. The company that found the structure first confirmed it to be exactly what the pilots had suspected: namely the remains of a wooden ship-shaped structure of immense proportions. They noted it had a six or seven-metre high doorway in its side, and inside was a series of room of varying sizes. The technical quality of the carpentry they saw was reputed to be of an extremely high standard. The structure itself was manifestly ancient and assumed to have survived because it is beneath the ice for nine to ten months of the year, or mostly submerged in frigid waters. What these men found was Noah's Ark. It could be nothing else!'

The insistent, exultant look on the Turk's face irritated him – not just because of what he had done to them, but also intellectually. What he was asserting simply didn't stand up.

'And why has it taken more than twenty years for this sensational discovery for this information to come to light?' But even as he said it, Drabble realised there were plenty of reasons to explain such a delay. Revolutions, wars, persecutions being just a few.

Siviloglu smiled.

'Just as the engineers returned with their report and photography the Tsar was ousted from power in the February of 1917. In the months that followed the Bolsheviks seized control of the government, and as you know, God does not form part of the Soviet cosmology…'

'So, the Soviets suppressed the discovery, because proof of the Old Testament's original founding myth was not useful? That's convenient.'

'It's also true, Professor. Don't forget that the Ark story isn't only part of the Judeo-Christian world either, it's important to Islam also.'

'And there's no shortage of Muslims in the Soviet Union.'

AFTER THE FLOOD

'Quite so. Moscow no more wanted their religious ardour stoked up any more than among the Orthodox Christians.'

Siviloglu frowned. 'I am not surprised that you are sceptical, so let me enlighten you. We know that in the April of 1918 the Ark dossier found its way to the desk of Leon Trotsky, in his capacity as head of the Red Army. He suppressed the information and kept the secret to himself. Then you can guess the rest, Professor – as I know you are a keen follower of Soviet affairs. When in 1929 Trotsky was expelled from the Soviet Union by Stalin, he came first to Istanbul: and he brought the secret with him.'

Siviloglu took out a small tin and slipped a slither of something into the corner of his mouth, like a snake surreptitiously devouring a mouse. 'You may be interested to learn that Trotsky was a long-term guest at the Pera Palace Hotel, which is where he concealed the Ark dossier – under the floorboards in the presidential suite where he stayed. It took longer than expected to find the dossier, but it is now in our possession.'

Drabble exhaled, feeling his stomach tighten. He had seen for himself the dust-free rectangle left by the very file Siviloglu was crowing about.

'Very well. So what's this got to do with me, my wife – and our honeymoon?'

Siviloglu cleared his throat.

'Aren't you curious to see the photographs?'

Photographs of Noah's Ark? Drabble suppressed a nervous laugh; it came out like a dry cough.

'Not really.'

'I find that hard to believe, Professor.'

'I'd rather see a photograph of my wife…'

Drabble saw Siviloglu's eyes shift to a tan leather briefcase standing beside the bed. His gaze followed hungrily. He cleared his throat.

'This is ridiculous. Before I have anything to do with this, Siviloglu, I need to see Charlotte here. I *demand* –'

The general calmly removed a whistle from his pocket and gave it a short blast.

The door of the hotel room opened and a burly figure stepped in. He stood at least a head taller than Drabble, was broad-shouldered and bulges of his muscular arms could be seen through his dark grey coat. The neutral expression on his flat-nosed face was reminiscent of a seasoned non-commissioned officer in the British Army, the sort that has seen it all before, and eaten most of it for breakfast. And doubtless this man was tougher than Noah's boots. By way of announcing himself he threaded his fingers together and cracked his knuckles, producing an impressive orthopaedic orchestration that lasted a second or more. A smile lighted up across the scarred lips beneath the stubbly moustache. His little eyes looked down at Drabble, working out how to hurt Drabble first.

'This is Celik, Professor. He is going to give you a lesson in Ottoman hospitality. After that we will resume our conversation.'

Siviloglu popped another sweet into his mouth, and jerked his head sharply towards Drabble — a gesture that could not possibly be mistaken.

Drabble sprang from the chair and snatched it up, ready to defend himself.

Celik grinned as he stepped forwards, his waxed moustache turned up at the corners and his eager wrestler's eyes weighing up his quarry. Drabble edged right: Celik mirrored him. Drabble skirted left, again the Turk countered. Drabbled edged backwards... then stabbed out with the chair.

Celik dodged left nimbly and tore the chair easily from Drabble, sending it crashing to the wall behind.

AFTER THE FLOOD

Drabble took another step back and edged to the right. Celik followed. There had to be a way out of this. But just as Drabble's eyes searched again for an exit, Celik growled – and lunged.

Drabble flung the tan leather briefcase at Celik's head and leapt onto the bed, which blocked his flank. But he didn't make it. Instead a powerful force stopped his body mid-air – an iron hand was clamped on to his ankle, and snapped it back with stony certainty. The impact jarred Drabble's neck. He spun round, kicking out desperately with his other foot – stabbing as hard at the other powerful hand which snatched at this foot.

Celik ignored Drabble's kicks and hauled him to the floor, again all too easily. The drop knocked the wind from him, and before he knew it, Celik had a meaty hand around his throat. The last thing he saw was fist coming straight at him.

Imagine, if you will, a heavily laden tray – the sort that a thoroughly good tea arrives on at a smart hotel with brass knobs on: pot, auxiliary pot containing hot water, cups, saucers, all in Staffordshire's finest. Now imagine it falling from a very great height. Next, imagine it hitting the surface of a river and everything upon it bursting forth and erupting on impact. That is what Harris looked like as he landed back-first, his arms still windmilling, onto the tossing waters of the Bosphorus.

He didn't get a chance to cry out. Instead, he vanished into a plume of water cleaner than a golf ball slicing into a pond. And he sank fast, his arms still swirling, becoming a creature of the green, blue and brown marine world, shafted by light.

Was he still sinking? Harris could see nothing, but the air bubbles cascading from his mouth told him he didn't have long. They also told him which way was up.

He had to get to the surface to replenish this air supply. Then he had to swim away as fast as possible, because there was no point going through all this aquatic palaver if he didn't manage to escape. But first he must live. And how his chest hurt…

Harris kicked with all his strength and reached up with broad hand strokes heading towards the shifting, shimmering, pale ceiling. That's it. More air bubbles shot out towards the light. He continued to swim.

But the ceiling wasn't getting any closer.

Just then Harris's face burst through the surface and he took a huge, greedy gulp of air…

But what was that sound?

He didn't have time to process the question, let alone answer it. He ducked into the water just as everything went black. A monstrous, crashing mechanical cacophony overwhelmed him.

The drone intensified. Harris had to move. Spinning around, he swam towards the light – bursting free from the water inches from the side of a boat.

Harris heard a shout – then another, and panicked. He began thrashing away from voices. Just then he found himself being dragged through the water towards the great vessel and lifted up its side, as if by greater power. He landed hard on the deck, water cascading from him, and a moment later his sodden boater arrived after. About him were babbling Turkish voices and consternation: a guard or such in a navy-coloured uniform and gold buttons stepped and barked, keeping them at bay, as Harris removed his blurry gaze from the ranks of women's and men's shoes and looked up at the ceiling, his chest heaving, still recovering his breath. Good God. His ears resounded with the din of the engine… the incandescent splashing and vibrations. So much for bravery. Next time he would leave *that* for the

AFTER THE FLOOD

others. How he wished all these people, all this noise would go away. He was cold.

Slowly his shaking hand made its way to inside breast pocket of his jacket and he teased out his cigarette case. Popping it open he saw a trio of crisp, perfectly dry Craven As. He smiled and stabbed one at his wet mouth. A lit lighter came into view...

'Teshir kelor,' puffed Harris, the fresh cigarette wagging between his lips.

Clouds of smoke forming above his face. A cheer broke out among the watching crowd but not before a voice he knew cut in.

'That's quite all right old man.'

Harris squinted through the smoke

'Andrew Streat! While I live and breathe!'

Drabble came to slowly. Then, abruptly. He immediately saw General Siviloglu standing over him, and then everything came flooding back. His interlocuter's mouth was opening but Drabble couldn't hear the man's voice, albeit he could *see* his mouth opening and closing in a pattern of speech. Everything was hazy as reality peered its way back through the drawn curtains of his consciousness.

On Siviloglu's commandDrabble was lifted – not quite to his feet, because they didn't know to what to do yet – and deposited into chair. A rope was looped around his waist and pulled sharply taut – and that was him. Siviloglu stabbed out his cigarette, and approached him.

'You are going to come to Mount Ararat, and you are going to help me find the Ark. If you refuse you will be killed – and after that so will your wife, and your unborn child. But,' he paused and raised a gloved finger, 'not before we have shown you photographs of the mutilated remains to your wife.' The Turk paused, letting his message land. 'For good measure I also give you my word that, if you refuse to co-operate, we will also kill your friend Sir Percival Harris, whom we also have in our custody. Do I make myself clear?'

Drabble looked up at the face before him. He could no longer see the Swiss banker in it. Now its smooth symmetry was invested with pure malignant evil. Drabble's chest was heavy so when he spoke his throat felt constricted, like someone was pressing their foot against it. On his second go he got his words out.

'Where's my wife?' he croaked.

'She's safely in our custody. That is all you need to know. You will be reunited once you have completed your work for us.'

'How can I trust you to keep your word?'

'You can't, Professor. But as a simple matter of incontrovertible fact, you have no choice. For now, you have orders, which I advise you to follow to the letter.'

Siviloglu shot him a steely smile that turned his stomach. There was no arguing with that, and Drabble knew it. But it didn't make adjusting to it any easier.

Several questions were assailing him, not least, why him? He could very well imagine why this Turk might want the help of an experienced mountaineer – as Siviloglu had remarked. It was early May, so well before the summit of Ararat would begin to thaw after the winter. That meant there would be plenty of ice up at fifteen thousand feet. But the Ark lay far, *far* outside of his field of study – he was a professor of medieval and early modern history after all. What possible use could be in that regard?

'Why do you want me on this jaunt, Siviloglu? Noah's Ark isn't my cup of tea and you know it.'

'I'm well aware of your academic credentials, Professor.'

'So what's it's all about? Why does this have to happen now?'

AFTER THE FLOOD

Siviloglu exhaled, like a man weighing up whether or not he had the energy or desire to explain a complicated matter in full or to offer a shortened version.

'Mustafa Kemal Atatürk is unwell.' Siviloglu let the statement stand for a second. 'You will doubtless have seen reports of the president's bout of influenza, the one that required him to rest at the end of March? Well, he did not have influenza.'

'They never do...'

Siviloglu cleared his throat.

'In point of fact the president has highly advanced cirrhosis of the liver and he has but days left to live. It is imperative that we locate the Ark before he exits from the scene. More than that I will not say. But be under no illusion, Professor, we must not delay.'

Astonishing as it was, this statement provoked rather more questions than it settled. This was not least because Atatürk had been president of Turkey for the best part of two decades and was the father of the nation.

Therefore his sudden demise would leave a gaping hole at the heart of the country. It was now to be supposed that Siviloglu and his unknown associates were intending to use the discovery of the Ark as a means of spring-boarding themselves into the national spotlight so that they could fill this void and seize control of the Turkish republic for themselves. That they needed to accomplish this before a rival claimant could get themselves established was likewise a foreseeable necessity.

A sneer appeared on Drabble's lip; he couldn't help it.

'Rather a dirty business you're involved in, General...'

Siviloglu stared hard at him.

'It needn't be, Professor.' His eyes glanced toward Celik. 'Unless you particularly want it to be?'

'No thank you,' Drabble cast his gaze towards the ceiling, as if appealing to God or the gods to deliver him from this situation. He found himself shaking his head. Was it resignation? Probably. He had no choice, after all. None whatsoever. 'Very well, Siviloglu. Let's get this over and done with…'

The General smiled, the corners of his multicoloured eyes even joining in for the first time.

'But we'll need proper equipment; crampons, decent ropes, ice axes…'

Sivilolgu held up his hand, 'Everything will be taken care of.'

'In which case, get your oaf –' Drabble tossed his head towards Celik, 'to pack my bag for me while you tell me what your manifesto for Turkey is?'

Siviloglu barked at Celik, who began loosening Drabble's ties, and slipped his Mauser into his overcoat pocket.

'Pack your own bag, Professor.' Siviloglu drew back his glove to inspect his wristwatch. 'You have three minutes.'

AFTER THE FLOOD

Chapter Nine

Harris was finally dry and warm. He stood at a high window overlooking a quadrangle. The broad lawns were in darkness but the odd light showed in the windows of the stone buildings which enclosed them. This was Robert College; it felt and looked all rather familiar. Pleasantly so. Any Oxonian would have felt at home here, that was certain – he might have even eyed up a nice plot by the cherry tree in the corner. Except, of course, it wasn't quite so, since Robert College had been founded by an American, though maybe at this remove, the Brits and the Yanks amounted to the same thing.

Harris sighed and had another go at his second brandy. He had bathed and his clothes were drying out before the fire in the kitchen. He was dressed – or rather, underdressed – in pyjamas and a cotton dressing gown belonging to Andrew Streat, who sat in an armchair.

He had just concluded the story of his captivity and his audacious leap from the balcony.

'It sounds to me rather like you've had a lucky escape,' remarked Streat.

Up to a point, thought Harris. He had escaped, that was true, but whether he'd been lucky – now, that was another story. He turned to face Streat. He had never been sure about him, but had never quite known why. It was nothing overt, nothing he could put his finger on. Perhaps, it struck him as he stood there, it was the *absence* of something. Maybe it was something withheld. Yes... something was missing from Andrew Streat, but quite what that was, well, that was anyone's guess.

Streat took a long, thoughtful drag on his cigar, then asked, 'What are you going to do now?'

'I've got to get back to the hotel,' Harris knew that much. He turned to the window. 'I've got to help Drabble find Charlotte, or at least do what little I can to help him.'

'And you're certain that the man you saw with this young woman was the same man that you and Drabble saw at the Hagia Sophia?'

'Absolutely.'

Streat nodded thoughtfully.

'When I saw Drabble earlier, he was convinced that the man also had something to do with Charlotte's disappearance.'

'Nothing would surprise me.'

'I don't suppose you know who the girl is, do you? The one you spent the night with?'

Harris sighed.

'Not really. I know where she lives, though I doubt she's there now.'

Streat regarded him shrewdly, 'Well, that might be helpful. If you were to pass it to the police…'

Harris looked over at the window. It was late. Probably, too late to be of use today. But he had to find Ernest and let him know that he was safe. He would be worried sick. He needed to get dressed and get back.

'Could I use your telephone again?'

Moments later Harris placed the heavy Bakelite receiver back in its cradle. There was still no answer from Drabble's room. Where had he got to? Presumably still out pounding the ruddy streets of Istanbul looking for Charlotte, if he didn't know any better? Or perhaps he had been rounded-up by the squiffy-eyed so-and-so too? Harris paused in the dark corridor and leant his face into his hands. What on earth was all of this about?

Harris took a very deep breath and told himself to get a grip.

AFTER THE FLOOD

Moments later he returned to the drawing room where Streat, calm as ever, was waiting for him in his armchair. In that second Harris's despair was replaced by a question: quite who or what was this fellow – this possessor of the largest brain at Oxford in his year? What was he doing as a schoolmaster in the back of beyond in Constantinople? Yes, it was surely a nice school and all that, but really... Andrew Streat? It didn't make sense. And just then, before he could govern it, Harris came out with it.

'Tell me Streat, are you a spook?'

His host smiled kindly, 'What a ridiculous thing to ask, Harris. Whatever makes you think that?'

'I mean it. Are you a spy?'

Streat chuckled. 'Tell me, Harris. Have your years in the Fourth Estate eroded all your appreciation of social norms? I'm not really sure that's the sort of question you're supposed to ask.'

'That's your second non-denial.'

'Oh is it?' Streat snorted, and then looked away. 'I did wonder if you would be curious. But I didn't think you would actually ask point blank. Ernest didn't. But, of course, that's how you two differ, isn't it? Drabble is happy to intuit something or make an educated guess and leave it unsaid. You, however, would sooner drag something into the open. Presumably it's a professional reflex.'

Harris picked up his brandy glass and took the armchair in front of the low fire, opposite Streat's. He met the schoolmaster's gaze and nodded, telling him to continue.

'All right. If you insist on knowing. Yes. I can confirm that in addition to

being a schoolmaster, I also do some work, *from time to time*, for His Britannic Majesty's government but strictly on an *ad hoc* basis. So I'm hardly a spook or agent, as one might imagine it. But I do consider it my patriotic duty to pass on appropriate information as and when it comes into my possession, particularly if I feel it will be of benefit to the British Empire and her allies.'

'Anybody know about this?'

'Of course not. Apart from those that need to.'

'So why are you telling me?'

'Because you asked. Because you're a very old friend. Because, actually, I don't see the particular need to lie to you.'

A very old friend. Well, that was overegging the pudding a bit, wasn't it? Harris let it go. All in all he was rather surprised to hear that Streat liked him at all, probably more surprised than discovering he was a ruddy spy. He'd certainly kept it to himself. But now was not the moment to quibble. Harris raised his glass.

'Cheers.' He grinned at his host. 'I'm beginning to like you, Streat.'

'Marvellous,' Streat smiled. 'It's only taken you twelve years.'

'More like fourteen ... anyway, this is probably the first time you've ever been truly honest with me. So did you spy at Oxford, too?'

Streat shot him severe look, 'Only on you, Harris.'

It took half a second for Harris to realise he was joking, and then Streat said, 'It's like the Church of England old man. They get you in young.'

Harris wondered if that was why Streat had buddied up to Drabble at Oxford. After all, back then, Drabble had been a raving communist at Oxford, although he wasn't the only one. Harris looked down at his drink, at the flames captured in the surface of his brandy.

'Very well, my friend' – Harris paused, and smiled. 'What else do I need to know?'

Streat arched an eyebrow at him.

'Now that would be telling.' He grinned. 'What I can tell you, Harris, is that I'm going to do my absolute best to help

AFTER THE FLOOD

you because, mark my word, there's nothing good about any of this.'

The two black Mercedes-Benz saloons swept through the night, their powerful headlights stealing glimpses of the great walls of Constantinople looming above them on their right. On their left, was the dark abyss of the Sea of Marmara with the occasional light of ship at anchor or underway. Inside, with mounting unease, Drabble sat silently in the rear car watching the Mercedes-Benz in front, the one containing Siviloglu and his female companion. Drabble's hands were bound at the wrists and seated beside him was Celik. In the distance was the illuminated control tower of Istanbul's airport, protruding above a high fence topped with spools of barbed wire. Several lonely aircraft were caught in the floodlights amidst an expanse of tarmac. The convoy began skirting the fence.

They swept through a gateway and out onto the tarmac. The scattered terminal buildings, the hexagonal control tower with its radio masts, and a trio of darkened fire engines were left behind as the cars headed on towards a dark corner of the airport. They passed the vast gloomy mass of a Handley Page transport plane, probably a derelict relic of the Great War. And then Drabble saw it, a small silver twin-engined aircraft. The steps were down, the cockpit lights on and pilots inside, busying themselves at the controls. Various attendants in boiler suits were removing pipes from the fuselage.

The Mercedes-Benzes halted at the foot of the steps. The driver and Celik exchanged a nod, as the door was opened by a man in military fatigues. Drabble was shoved towards the door.

A fresh breeze from the sea caught him as he emerged. Siviloglu and the girl were up the steps, bowing their heads as they entered the plane. Drabble followed, almost in trance, a sense of doom seizing him as he climbed up from the tarmac – a push between the shoulder blades from Celik reinforced the point. Inside the plane were six seats, closely configured. Siviloglu caught his eye and gave a terse nod, just as at Drabble was pressed down into his seat by Celik and tied to it.

Minutes later they were soaring over Istanbul – a landscape of tiny lights – and the dark ribbon of the Bosphorus. The loud hum of the engines helped shut out the chatter in Drabble's mind, and he focused his attention on the gentle sensation of the plane as it undulated through the sky.

Would he see Charlotte again?

Was she safe?

Would he ever see his child?

Questions such as these were daunting enough to ask, let alone to answer. Morever nothing could be achieved by imagining the worst. The next hour, the next day… these were what he needed to focus on now. He opened his eyes and stared ahead at the bulwark separating the cabin from the tiny cockpit, spotting the small manufacturer's plate. It was steel with black type, the text in German. Siebel Fh 104-A Hallore, it read, manufactured in Halle in Saxony. Drabble closed his eyes and turned his mind to the close din of the engines.

…Halle in Saxony, ruled for centuries by the prince-archbishops of Magdeburg, a hotbed of Lutherism and the very place where the Reformation began. His mind travelled to the famous portrait of Martin Luther by Cranach the Elder, showing the thoughtful face of an awkward if brilliant mind, one that brought the world crashing down around him for a century or more. Luther could not have predicted the consequences of his Ninety-Five Theses of 1517. Would he have published them if he had?

AFTER THE FLOOD

Probably. Sadly. Which was the problem with a certain species of maverick. They were always happy to put the point above the person. And where people spilled truths, blood was sure to follow…

Harris and Streat arrived by arrangement at the back door of the Pera Palace Hotel, where they were met by the general manager. He took them straight up to Drabble and Charlotte's room by means of the staff staircase and found no answer – as expected. The general manager let them in and a rapid survey showed that various items belonging to Drabble had been taken, but that neither he nor Charlotte had fully removed their belongings. Drabble's large Gladstone bag was now missing but their trunk was still there. A chair had been drawn out from the table and left in the middle of the room, facing towards the window, which was perhaps at best unusual but nothing more ominous than that.

Streat examined room with what looked to Harris like a routine thoroughness or practised ease. Having worked his way through drawers, under bedding and behind the headboard, the schoolmaster emerged from the adjoining bathroom with a discreet shake of the head.

'Wherever Drabble's gone, he would appear to have taken his washbag with him. All Charlotte's things are still here.'

'And it looks like some of his under-clothes have been taken.'

Harris shut the mostly empty drawer.

The general manager stood waiting, saying nothing. There were no obvious signs of a struggle or violence in the room. Several other items of Drabble's clothing were missing – his walking boots and perhaps a jersey – but not much more. Nothing of Charlotte's appeared to have gone. Even her diary was in her bedside table.

So, where were they? And were they together? Might they, for sake of argument, both be captive in the very building overlooking the Bosphorus that he had escaped from only earlier on?

Harris, still engaged in making his own circuit of the premises (aware that he was following somewhat redundantly in Streat's more efficient footsteps) continued going through the motions. His search arrived at the adjoining bathroom, somewhat smaller than his own. He took in the bath, its palm trees and surveyed the assorted bottles and jars.

'This is a bloody waste of time,' he barked as his eye fell on a toothbrush, presumably Charlotte's, leaning against the edge of the toothglass. Various odd bottles and squat glass jars containing mysterious feminine potions and liquids dotted the side, several obscuring a small book, a pamphlet really, which he gathered up. A bookmark fluttered to the floor as he opened it to inspect the title page. It was called, *Advice for Expectant Mothers*. Suddenly Harris felt his head spinning.

Charlotte was pregnant. Ernest was going to be a father.

He let go of the book and stepped back, his knees weakening.

And then he slipped. A black pen-shaped object spilled out from under his foot and shot across the marble floor. Harris went down – cursing loudly – before scurrying over to capture the offending item.

And then he couldn't quite believe his eyes.

'Streat!'

Low down on the wall, on the skirting board, in tiny black writing, was a single word scrawled in Drabble's unmistakable, copperplate. It was just one word. And after squinting at it for a second, Harris realised what it was: 'Ararat.'

AFTER THE FLOOD

Chapter Ten

The British Consul-General, Sir Terence Greenhalge, leaned back into his enormous leather chair, his smooth fingers fanned across an inlaid portion of walnut on his broad desk. Before him sat Harris and Streat, and to one side stood a secretary of sorts whose name had never been provided. Greenhalge was a warty fellow and wore an expression of studied hostility. Any thoughts he had – if he was having them at all – were concealed by a professional exhibition of lugubrious indifference, quite possibly his life's work. Within seconds Harris had decided that he thoroughly disliked the man.

After studying his fingernails for a moment, Greenhalge exhaled, apparently with supreme effort, like a lumbering Lewis Carroll walrus contemplating which oyster to have first.

'So all we have is a single word, correct?'

Harris nodded.

'But it's a word left deliberately by Drabble for me to read and respond to.'

'I'm sure it is, Sir Percival, but the fact remains that it's hardly decisive nor comprehensive.' Greenhalge spoke wearily and glared over at the secretary with no name, presumably for letting them in.

'But we all know what it means,' appealed Harris. 'It has to be something to do with Noah's Ark – everyone knows that's where it's meant to be. That's what it says in the Bible!'

Sir Terence cleared this throat and lowered his tone.

'I'm not sure we can take the Bible as gospel.'

Harris threw up his arms.

'Why else would Ernest vanish like this?'

'Who?'

'Dr Ernest Drabble,' intoned Streat deferentially. 'He's the man who has gone missing.'

'Yes, yes, yes. Along with his wife who has also vanished into thin air too, what?'

'Yes sir.'

Greenhalge eyed Streat sourly, rather as if he were to blame for these disappearances.

'So, Sir Percival. Your supposition is that he's been, um, kidnapped by a funny looking fellow with different coloured eyes?' He swallowed. 'Is that correct?'

'Yes!'

Greenhalge thoughtfully caressed the large wart occupying his upper lip. The room remained silent, except for the ponderous syncopation of an elegant glass domed clock on the stone mantlepiece. At last the diplomat spoke.

'What is it that you want from His Majesty's government?'

'Well… help. *Help* would be useful. We need to find out what's happened to Ernest and Charlotte, and jolly well get to the bottom of it. The police are looking into it but it all needs much more oomph! And then there's these sinister coves who locked me up on the Bosphorus – I could take you to them myself right now…'

Greenhalge raised his hand.

'I think that's probably going too far.' He changed his pitch. 'It sounds like a job for the local police, Sir Percival. He turned his attention to Streat. 'What do you make of all this, Andrew?'

Streat drew breath. 'When you hear the word Ararat, I agree that all the credibility goes out the window, because Ararat can only mean one thing. And we all know that that's bonkers. But that is what Drabble wrote and we do know that he is not, in fact, bonkers, Sir. Quite the opposite, in fact.'

AFTER THE FLOOD

'But he did try to climb the north face of the Eiger without crampons,' interjected Greenhalge. He glanced over at the minion with no name and nodded importantly.

'Is there anything else on Ararat – mineral deposits, that sort of thing – that might merit someone's attention? Apart from the Biblical associations we all know of?'

The secretary shook his head.

The diplomat sighed. 'So just bloody Noah, then?'

'I agree it sounds jolly far-fetched,' agreed Harris.

'Far-fetched. It's positively deranged.'

Greenhalge closed his eyes for a second and they sat watching him draw all the strands together. Harris and Streat exchanged a glance. At length, the Consul-General opened his eyes and brought the palms of his hands crashing down onto the walnut.

'No,' he pronounced. 'We're not doing this. This is abject, first-class bunkum. Absolute nonsense.' He rose from the desk, muttering, 'If you want help, Sir Percival, then I can certainly recommend a first-rate psychiatrist. My wife's brother is one as a matter of fact. Makes a fortune. Failing that, contact the police and let us know if they aren't being responsive. We can encourage them. But that's about it. For now, kindly stop wasting the Foreign Office's time!'

Back outside, standing on the edge of the vast lawn in the consulate's garden, Harris lit a Craven. He was furious.

'So that's that,' he fumed.

Streat made no reply and the two of them stood in silence. In the distance was the pointed witch's hat of the Topkapi palace and the great masses of the Hagia Sophia and the Blue Mosque, with its four imperial minarets. They stood against a creamy, brownish sky on the cusp of nightfall. In that moment Harris reached a surprisingly robust-sounding conclusion.

'I have no idea exactly where I'm going to go, or why. But I've got no choice in the matter.' He took a deep drag of his cigarette and the smoke billowed from his mouth. 'What I do know is that the sooner I get going the better.' He turned to Streat. 'I'm going to get the bloody train to Mount Ararat and find Drabble. So help me God.'

The Turkish State Railway service for Ankara departed from an ornate-looking Haydarpasa terminus building on the Asian shore of the Bosphorus, which they reached by means of a passenger foot ferry from Kadikoy. Streat accompanied Harris on the grounds that he had more chance of making the train successfully with his help. He had booked Harris a cabin in one of the sleeping cars, and Harris quickly realised he was in for a superior railway experience. Which was something.

After all, if he was going to be on the bloody thing for the best part of a day until he reached Ankara – some five hundred miles off – a few creature comforts were the minimum that could be expected. After reaching Ankara he had been told that he would take another train to the end of the line at a place called Erzurum, in deepest, darkest Anatolia. Then it was a question of picking up a car and driver that would take him to the mountains. 'All told you're in for two days minimum, just to get to the base of the mountain,' Streat had told him. 'Don't suppose you've got any Turkish or Arabic?' And, of course, he hadn't a word.

They hurried along the platform, following the flank of the new-looking electric-power train. On reaching the section of the train where the sleeping cars began, Streat exchanged some sharp guttural sentences with a silver-moustached railwayman. He promptly seized Harris's bag and started loading it aboard.

AFTER THE FLOOD

'I take it there's a restaurant car?' enquired Harris doubtfully, as Streat ushered him up the steps of the carriage.

'Yes. And a bar, too.' Streat smiled as Harris's face lit up. 'Have no fear, Sir Percival, the Anatolian miles will fly by.'

'Thank God!'

Streat extended his hand, and Harris shook it eagerly.

'Good luck, Harris. Send me a telegram if you need anything and I'll endeavour to do what I can.'

Minutes later, having deposited his bag and been shown his compartment, Harris was in the train's bar. Lined in polished wood, the aroma alone was deeply reassuring and the quiet drone of conversation, interspersed with the sound of falling ice cubes or the sloshing of intoxicating liquids was precisely the sort of thing that put his frayed nerves at ease. Sir Percival Harris understood himself to be a man of words, not action, so little of what lay before him came naturally.

As for climbing mountains, he shuddered. He'd had enough of that lark when they had gone to Austria for Drabble's Eiger trip. From what he knew. Ararat was similar in height but rather less pointy. He caught the waiter's eye and ordered a double gin and tonic. The place was beginning to fill up, he saw, so there might be some conversation in the offing. That would help pass the time. Streat had suggested that he keep a low profile but it was difficult to see what harm could befall him on the train. Well, unless he was being watched and had been followed. He stole a nervous glance over his shoulder. That seemed a rather improbable, but then... who could tell these days? What he knew for certain was that there was no obvious and immediate cause of alarm. That's right, nothing to worry about. He took possession of the cool gin and tonic, declining the ice-bucket, and lifted the glass up to the light, admiring the ascending bubbles. Ah, thank the Almighty for the wonder of carbonated mixers.

Did Harris even add a silent prayer? He might. It had been quite a day, when all was said and done. A couple more of these and he would be in Ankara before he knew it. Then it was just another hop, skip and jump to the bounds of Armenia and the mountain.

He was savouring the first mouthful, the taste equivalent of the joyous Red Sea deluging the malignant forces of the Pharoah, when he heard a familiar voice.

'Sir Percival!'

He turned, meeting a broad smile that belonged to a friendly face that took him but a second to register.

'Fisher!'

'Would you look at that,' declared the American as he flagged down the barman. 'And there was me thinking this was going to be long night.' He clapped Harris jovially on the shoulder. 'Now it will be, but for all the wrong reasons!'

AFTER THE FLOOD

Chapter Eleven

Drabble awoke as the plane began to descend with a mild pain in his ears. He didn't know how long he'd been asleep for but it was pitch black outside the window, and they were coming down at steep angle. Through the crack in the curtain, he glimpsed two rows of lights of a landing strip through the windscreen. They were approaching it fast.

The Siebel touched down – it's wheels squealing – and taxied across a bumpy airstrip before coming to an abruptly stop. The engines cut out and the co-pilot was up and had the hatch open quickly. Hot, dry air invaded the cabin, immediately making the interior feel almost damp and acrid. Everyone was moving. Celik levered himself out of his seat, and then began untying Drabble, before signalling for him to exit.

Drabble emerged into the dark void of a remote aerodrome, feeling the warm breeze hit the moisture on his face. They were in an expansive dark landscape, surrounded by dirt and black hills dotted with trees and lonely farmsteads, shown only by singular lights in their distant windows. Then he noticed a small hangar close by.

That's where they were going.

His hands still tied, he made his way carefully down the metal steps – his legs still unaccustomed to movement – and felt the hard ground underfoot. He checked the time; it was coming up to midnight, confirming his guess that this was a refuelling stop, rather than an arrival. The other passengers emerged from the plane and began to move towards the hangar. A rustic-looking van with a rusty tank on its flatbed and curling rubber pipe on its side came growling towards them from the opposite direction, presumably on its way to refuel the Siebel.

The terminal wasn't much more than a single-storey barn, it turned out, but not before Drabble glanced back. Just in time to see the dim headlights of the arriving tanker stroke the smooth silver fuselage of the Siebel and come to rest on its broad tailplane. Which was when he saw it – a red band containing a white circle emblazoned with a black swastika. Siviloglu, pausing beside him, broke into a chuckle.

'That's right Professor. We are in very good company. In fact' – Siviloglu leaned in – 'the Führer assures me personally that he is taking a very close interest in our assignment.'

'So, what takes you to Ankara?'

Under all but these circumstances Fisher's question was entirely reasonable, but it hung there between them, waiting for an answer. In response Harris took another slug of his gin and tonic. It was working wonders, truth be told. Fisher had already volunteered the purpose of *his* trip east – a fertiliser conference taking place in the capital – and Harris, for better or for worse, suddenly decided that he would steer closer to the truth than might otherwise be cautious. After all, he could trust a newspaper man like Fisher, one of his own kith and kin. Harris glanced over his shoulder and then lowered his voice.

'Not for reporting, but I'm going to Mount Ararat on a clandestine mission.'

'Is that so?' Fisher grinned and scrutinised him through narrowed eyes. 'You're not a crazy Ark-hunters, are you?'

'I'm looking for my friend. He's been kidnapped.'

'Kidnapped? Who?' Fisher leaned in, his mind checking he had heard correctly. He took a careful look over his shoulder. 'Not Professor Drabble?'

AFTER THE FLOOD

Harris told Fisher the story so far. Most of it, except for the girl with the voice like paint-stripper and the body of a warm Canova.

'Did you go to the British consulate?'

Fisher read Harris's expression. 'I guess you did...' He shook his head. 'Greenhalge doesn't have a great rep.'

'I'm not surprised.'

'Any idea where Drabble is now?'

Harris shrugged, 'Presumably on his way to Ararat, if his scrawl on the wall means what I think it does.'

'And you no idea why he might be going there?'

He read Harris's blank look, 'I think I might know some people who can help. If you're looking for help, that is?' He drained his glass. 'There's a few people in government I know, I can make some calls when we reach Ankara.'

'Thank you.'

By the time the next few gins and tonic and whiskies had materialised, Harris had burned through a heap of Craven As and the train had gently rocked onwards towards Ankara. It was gone two o'clock in the morning. Fisher lit another cigarillo.

'So what's this great pal of yours really like, Harris? I've read about his Alpine exploits, obviously. Is he still a dangerous subversive?'

'I wouldn't say so. I think these days he's more subversive than dangerous.' Harris punctuated the reply with a slow drag on his cigarette. It was only as he exhaled that he wondered how Fisher knew of Drabble's former political sympathies, though they were hardly a secret. 'He tore up his party card in 1934.'

'Did he now?' Fisher issued a guffaw, 'That's what they all say.'

'Everyone sees the light in the end, don't they? To be a

Tory at twenty is to have no heart, to be a Communist at thirty is to have no brain…'

'And who would be unwise enough to disagree with Oscar Wilde?'

'Quite. Not I.'

'But is he still a committed socialist?'

'Probably, but he's not a member of the party, as far as I know. What I do know for certain is that Ernest is almost entirely wrong on almost everything you can be wrong about when it comes to politics. Whereas I'm usually right – or at least right-wing.'

Fisher snorted silently and smiled.

'What about you?' asked Harris. 'You've lived in Moscow, so you've seen it for yourself. Did you discover any sympathy for our Soviet friends when you were there?'

The directness of the question drew an arch of Fisher's fair eyebrows. They settled back in their proper place, as he smiled and emitted a warm, mahogany, smoker's chuckle.

'Harris, I couldn't lie to you if I tried. Look. I'm as staunch a supporter of Uncle Sam as you will find. However, I am not *totally* unsympathetic to human condition as perceived by our Soviet friends. In fact, like Professor Drabble, I tend to think that the Reds get a little more right than we often give them credit for.'

Harris mulled Fisher's answer as he stubbed out his cigarette. It seemed reasonable, surprising as it was. 'The way I see it,' he grinned, 'is we've got the Wops, the Krauts and the Japs all on the one side and then you've got the Frogs, the Brits and – if it comes to it – the Yanks on the other. The Ruskies, as ever, are a law unto themselves. The best that can be said of them is that they and the Jerries are like fire and water.' He levered open his cigarette case and took out a Craven A. 'The problem is in identifying which one's the fire

AFTER THE FLOOD

and which one's the water. I expect we'll find out soon enough, don't you?'

Fisher snorted and shook his head.

'Alas, Harris, I think it'll be all too soon.'

When Harris awoke the next morning, he was aware of an unfamiliar sense of stillness, or at least the absence of constant movement. There was pain too. Yes, his eyes hurt. He creased them open, like the reluctant doors of a Pharoah's tomb after a sleep of several millennia. The thin brown cotton curtains were wide open and searing morning sunshine filled the tiny compartment, transforming it into a greenhouse. He shaded his eyes as he retreated, whimpering, towards the shade. Good Lord. His head was pounding.

'Ooowh…'

He sent out his hand foraging blindly for the ledge, and braced himself as his stomach performed a series of unforgiving twitches.

'Uhhh, agh, ooowph!'

That was close. He lay back, panting, feeling utterly wretched. What time was it? He touched his stomach gingerly and located his pocket watch. He pinged it open and obliged an eye to admit enough light for vision and then focus to occur. Oh, bugger. The watch had stopped at five forty-four. He hissed, and immediately felt a sharp pain in his stomach. The dip in the Bosphorus must have disagreed with its inner workings. He slid his torso into a perpendicular position, one which removed his face from the reaches of the sun's baleful rays, and also gave him a better advantage on the outside world. Well, it was plainly much later than five forty-four on the basis of nothing else apart from the height of the sun. He could see multiple dusty railway platforms – not quite Clapham Junction, mind – but plenty to be going on with. As well as that there was a monumental station building that was attempting to make a Modernist architectural statement but failing. So this would be Ankara. He lay back and groaned.

Bloody Fisher. He was to blame for leading him astray.

Harris rubbed his face; his moustache was waxy and matted with something unpleasant. *Ugh…* He needed to shave. But given the violence with which his hands were shaking that might be too hazardous. He groaned again as another pain shot through his stomach. It was simply all too much.

And look at that! He was still wearing a shoe. The other was… Where was his other shoe? And where were his spectacles? Oh Lord… Without his glasses he was toast. He began patting various surfaces within reach, the pace of the search increasingly frenetic until he felt the fragile metal and glass object in his hands. He exhaled, and lowered himself to the bed, moaning. It was too much. Too much gin. Far too much gin. How many cigarettes had he smoked? His tongue was greasy, thick and metallic-feeling, as though someone had been using it to clean silver. Perhaps brass, as well. O Lord!

Then he remembered. He'd told Fisher about Drabble, Charlotte and Ararat. He told Fisher all about it when he'd distinctly set his mind on not telling a soul. Not a soul! Streat had told him on not account to tell anyone. 'Trust no one,' he'd quite clearly said. Oh, God! Could he never keep a secret? What sort of unspeakable fellow was he? Harris let out a long piteous sob, like a dog on the brink of vomiting. Tears pricked at his eyes and tumbled down his cheeks. He was useless… less than useless. And how his body ached.

He levered himself up, becoming breathless through the effort. There was only one thing to do in a moment like this: have a pipe. It was kill or cure. He reached for his bag and rummaged blindly until he had located the item in question

AFTER THE FLOOD

and its supporting cast of materials: most importantly his tin of Empire Star Broad Flake. He felt himself wilting in the face of the effort. But he needed a pipe. It would restore his constitutional equanimity or at the very least assist with its recovery. Then he would shave, and clean his moustache. And with luck, at some point he would find his right shoe.

As he finished preparing his pipe he remembered that he had to get off the train and find the Eastern Express. He squeezed his eyes shut as he set the match into the bowl of the pipe. Wondrous clouds of combusted Empire Star Broad Flake swirled in great masses in the sunlight. Oh yes, that was better. Harris managed a smile and broke into exhausted laughter. The bloody 'mountain of pain' – now that was a joke and a half. The railway journey was bad enough!

The pipe worked its magic. Soon he was standing and feeling much surer on his pins. The egg-frying Anatolian sunshine didn't look quite so intimidating anymore and he'd just clocked his shoe, poking out from under the unused, folded blanket, no less. Marvellous. A shave, a pint of black coffee, some baked Turkish eggs served with a bit of that lovely cake-like bread they had… and bob's your uncle, Sir Percival Harris KCSI, KBE, would be right as rain. As right as bloody rain on a wet Sunday afternoon in Merthyr Tydfil. That's right, he told himself, Merthyr Tydfil.

And so it was. An hour and a half later, Harris boarded the Eastern Express bound for Erzurum, a city that would lead to Ararat. He was welcomed aboard by a Turkish guard, one possessing the generous moustache of a brigadier in the Lancers c. 1890, and who spoke impeccable English. He deposited him at his cabin with his bag, before serving a glass of strong, piping-hot black tea. The guard's final act had been to point him in the direction of the bar and the restaurant car. Harris hung up his hat and drank the tea which he rinsed down with a Craven A, his strength returning. He then headed to the bar. It was another five hundred miles till they reached Erzurum and he wanted to be sure of a good seat. He hurried into the narrow corridor and found himself face-to-face with Fisher, who clapped him jovially on the shoulder.

'Harris! What d'ya know, I'm in the next cabin to yours!'

'But what about your fertiliser conference?'

'Ah, you know what? After last night's chat, I couldn't very well leave you to deal with all this on your own. Plus, to be perfectly honest with you, fertiliser isn't really my favourite topic.'

'So you're coming to Erzurum?'

'If it's not a dreadful imposition, I'll even accompany you to Ararat.'

It might have been the hangover but Harris suddenly felt overcome. Tears pricked his eyes. It was too much.

'Ararat,' he blubbed. 'You'd do that for me?'

Fisher grinned and slapped on the shoulder.

'Don't let it get to your head, Harris. Seriously, anything beats fertiliser!'

AFTER THE FLOOD

Chapter Twelve

Beneath the Siebel's smooth silver wings was a landscape of dark browns and brilliant greens, of ramshackle towns with domed mosques and outlying farmsteads. The past hour alone had shown them sumptuous rolling hills, lakes and wide, unexplored forests. Anatolia offered broader horizons than Drabble had ever imagined.

He was sandwiched between the window and Celik, his hands still bound tightly at the wrists. Siviloglu and the girl were on the other side of the narrow aisle and he had not heard them speak over the incessant din of the twin engines. Drabble had willed himself to remain still and to ignore his nagging instinct to fight or at least put up some resistance. There was no escape from an aeroplane in flight, nor the cage that Siviloglu had him trapped in. The only positive perspective was that so long as he was alive and useful to Siviloglu, then Charlotte ought to remain safe and alive too.

Drabble exhaled. In any event, contemplating the alternative was too difficult. He had to trust that, in this if nothing else, Siviloglu would be true to his word.

Drabble closed his eyes and bowed his head. But Charlotte and the life inside her were not the only concerns. What was the moral cost of in helping General Siviloglu to find the Ark, the fabled ship of Noah? Not that it was in the least bit likely, of course.

But what were his man's plans for it? And could Drabble allow himself to be responsible, or at least partly responsible, for bringing the Ark into this man's possession, not knowing what iniquity he could achieve with it? Drabble sighed wearily and stared up at the ceiling.

He stretched out his arms, pressing his wrists together to reduce the pressure from the rope. Charlotte was alive. That much he had to believe. And before this was over, he would find her and they would be together again. They would be together again. He lowered his arms and balled his hands into fists. Of that he was certain. He looked over at Siviloglu, and knew also that he would be held to account.

A change in the note of the engines brought him from his thoughts.

They were starting to descend. Drabble experienced that unerring feeling of the world falling forwards, followed by a slight buzzing in his ears, as the pressure eased. They had been up for a couple of hours, which would easily put them another four or five hundred miles or so deeper into Anatolia. From his geography he knew that Turkey didn't go on that far, so they had to be close to Ararat.

The plane began to descend more steeply. The engines grew louder and in the gap between the swaying curtains Drabble saw the world go from a blue to greeny brown in the pilots' window. They levelled off abruptly and bright blue sky returned – and that's when he saw it. Mount Ararat. From this elevation it was an enormous white, near symmetrical pyramid, streaked and veined with rock and ice. And it filled the horizon.

The mountain was still transparently a volcano underneath all that snow and Drabble knew immediately that it would feel dreadfully exposed on its higher flanks. The snowline ran deep and gave way to a dark brown landscape, one that Drabble knew would also be anything but hospitable. Oh, to have his old mountaineering friend Hubertus at his side…

General Siviloglu leaned forward in his seat and called over.

'You know what we call Mount Ararat?' He paused and smiled. '*Agri Dagi*. It means the Mountain of Pain.' He started to laugh. 'Who says the Turks don't have a sense of humour?'

Movement caught Drabble's attention through the cockpit window. He saw the airstrip – a dark brown smear –

AFTER THE FLOOD

approaching fast; a building, several lorries and fire engine in sight. The pilot pulled back on the stick, while the other wound down the landing gear. Drabble felt his stomach push through the seat.

Moments later there was the snatch of the tyres on the gravel runway and the plane decelerated smartly, before taxiing over towards a low structure, even more agricultural-looking than the last. They came to a halt next to a waiting car and several tan-painted military lorries.

Celik popped the oval door of the Siebel open and shoved out the ladder. On the ground outside men in military fatigues began to assemble in neat columns. Drabble saw they were armed with rifles. One of them sprang up the steps – his boots ringing on the metal rungs – and appeared at the open door. He turned to Siviloglu and smartly removed his field cap, revealing blond hair cropped short. He wore no military insignia.

'General!' barked the man, his German accent indisputable. He saluted, extending his arm straight into the air and clicked his heels together. 'Heil Hitler!'

The heat was building outside on the arid scrub that sprang up around the rusty rails visible from the window of the carriage and the sun beat down on the platforms at Ankara Station. Inside was pleasantly cool; there was after all a great deal of varnished hardwood between the interior and the sunblasted outdoors. Harris heard a quiet knock at the door of his compartment. He turned towards the narrow door and frowned. A bead of sweat trickled down his side, but not because of the heat. He knew the knock did not belong to Fisher, nor, he suspected, was it that of the elderly railwayman. It was too speculative.

He stood up.

'Enter!'

The door opened and an undoubtedly Turkish face appeared in the gap. It was neatly moustached, with a military care and belonged to a lean face of perhaps forty, atop a trim torso enclosed within a smart dark single-breasted suit of Western cut. The man offered a courteous bow.

'My name is Yurttas, Sir Percival. If you'll forgive the interruption,' he smiled, 'I have come here to save your life.'

'Really?'

Harris chuckled nervously and said the first thing that came into his head. 'Cigarette?'

The Turk declined the offer with a shake of the head.

'Well,' Harris lit up, 'I shouldn't put yourself out for me, not if I were you.'

The Turk glanced over his shoulder.

'May I come in?'

Harris swept his bag from the bench seat and offered it up.

'By all means, but please be brief as it's imperative I catch the eleven-o-five to Erzurum. Also I'm positively gasping for a cup of tea.'

The Turk closed the door behind him and remained standing.

'It will only take a few minutes of your time, Sir Percival, but it is a matter of life and death.'

'I do with you'd stop saying that.'

The man nodded solicitously, as if accepting the point. He said, 'You are travelling to Ararat to find the Ark? Correct?' Harris's frown confirmed that this was true, or mostly. 'May I ask, what is your interest in the Ark, Sir Percival? Is it fortunate you seek or fame, or are you actuated by religious devotion?'

'Religious devotion?' bleated Harris. 'Christ alive, I'm C of E. We don't do devotion. We do church, and that's an entirely different kettle of fish altogether. What on earth are you blithering on about?'

AFTER THE FLOOD

Yurttas laid his hand across his breast. 'Do not dishonour me with feeble attempts to deny it, Harris *Bey*.' The cove spoke with utmost respect, like a penniless curate in a Jane Austen novel, which rather offset the suspicion in Harris's mind, though not entirely. Harris pecked at his cigarette.

'How on earth do you know about this?'

'It is my duty to know such things, Harris *Bey*. The Ark must not be found,' the Turk continued. 'Its precise location has been preserved, undisturbed for more than ten thousand years, since the day that Nüh and his family disembarked with the rest of the animal kingdom.' Yurttas let this settle. 'I have been sent here, with others I should add, to ensure that it remains safe.'

'Safe!' gasped Harris. 'Goodness me. And how, pray, do you expect me to be of any service in this matter?'

'Rest assured you are not required to undertake any acts of heroism yourself Sir Percival –'

'That's a relief!' Harris stifled a callous laugh.

'You would be of assistance to our cause merely by passing us information to help us in our duty to prevent anybody else – and especially unwanted foreign actors – from finding the holy ship of Nüh.'

'I see.' Harris stubbed out his cigarette and reached for his pipe. This was fast developing into a distinctly cigarette-and-pipe problem.

'You are travelling with an American, correct? A newspaper reporter named Fisher?'

'That's right. Of the *New York Times*.'

'And what is your intention?'

'Nothing more than to find my friend Drabble and help him dig himself out of the soup as best as one can.'

There was a pause, presumably as the Turk made his best of Harris's reply. Idiom was always the best way to keep these clever, polyglot Johnny foreigners on their toes. Harris was about to restate his response in less idiomatic terms when Yurttas spoke, his voice rising.

'You swear that you have no interest in the Ark yourself?'

Harris hesitated. How could he swear on something when events were apt to alter one's outlook? For instance, if the Ark really existed, and they actually found it, then it would be the biggest news story of the century. Well it would. And of his career. He'd be a mug to miss out on that. Plus, the discovery would come with riches. Think about it: he'd probably even earn enough off it to buy a proper castle somewhere, something with a moat perhaps, and with actual water still in it. And then who knew? A chalet at Val Thorens and fancy pad in the Cote D'Azur? He could then turn his hand to writing that…

'Sir Percival. Swear you have no intent on the Ark for your own gain!'

Yurttas stared intently at him, the whites of his eyes showing in an alarming fashion. The vision of an ivy-clad castle surrounded by a broad moat with swans faded from Harris's mind.

'Swear it!' repeated Yurttas.

'I do – *really*,' hissed Harris, suddenly afraid. 'I do,' he repeated, in a voice so quiet he hoped God wouldn't hear.

Yurttas nodded sternly.

'And your friend, Ernest Drabble? Does he have any ambitions on it?'

Harris sucked on his pipe.

'You've got nothing to worry about there, old *bey*. He's here on his ruddy honeymoon. The only thing he has designs on is about five foot seven with fair hair and has an unfathomable mutual interest in the Lord Protector.'

Yurttas frowned. Harris cleared his throat.

'No. He doesn't. He wants his wife – and his life – back. And yes of course, he's academically interested in its discovery – who wouldn't be? But he's no personal ambition

AFTER THE FLOOD

to go down in history as the man who found Noah's Ark. God forbid.' Harris broke into a chuckle, 'Sorry…'

Slowly, a smile stretched out beneath the Turk's sceptical face.

'*Chok iyi*,' he pronounced at last. 'Very good.'

Yurttas stretched out his hand – which Harris took – and he gave a handshake firmer than the alabaster pillars in the Hagia Sophia.

'In which case, Sir Percival. I and my associates will be pleased to help you.' Harris flexed his hand discreetly behind his back.

'One final question, then, Sir Percival. Have you ever heard of the Order of the Green Fez?'

'No. But it sounds like they go in for topping regalia!'

Yurttas shook his head, like a man was dismissing the offer of the soup of the day.

'It is a clandestine paramilitary Turkish nationalist organisation, *Effendi*, one committed to the reconstitution and resuscitation of the Ottoman Empire. It is the bastard offspring, if you excuse the expression, of the Committee of Union and Progress.'

'Sounds like rum crowd,' opined Harris. Otherwise known as the Young Turks, the Committee of Union and Progress were the military hardliners who had seized power in 1913 after Turkey had finally lost its European empire – Bulgaria, Albania and sundry other bits of the Balkans that no one had ever heard of. They had then led Turkey into the First World War on the wrong side, and everyone knew how that went for them.

Yurttas continued, 'The Order of the Green Fez is committed to reviving the Ottoman Empire and explicitly wants to recover the empire's lost territory in Europe and elsewhere, if they can. They want to dispense with parliament in Ankara and restore the monarchy – as well as the Caliphate. They know that finding the Ark will give them the prestige to lay claim to power, once President Atatürk is gone.'

'Gone?' asked Harris. 'Where's he planning on going?'

'The president is dying, Sir Percival. It is not widely known, just how unwell he is, but, most surely, he is dying. He suffers from advanced cirrhosis of the liver.'

'Hell's bells! So the poor sod's yellower than a battalion of Italian reservists?' Harris crossed himself, 'There but for the grace of God go I…' Yurttas, he realised, was still staring at him in that strangely intense way that he had. 'All right then, Mr Yurttas, so poor old Atatürk is on his last legs, and you've got the Order of the Green Pheasant pursuing the Ark. What on earth do you want me to do about it?'

The Turk discreetly drew his long coat open, revealing an automatic pistol in a shoulder holster at his side.

'I propose that I travel to Mount Ararat with you and Mr Fisher, and together we will see if we can endeavour to halt this madness before it's too late.'

Harris swallowed. He knew nothing of Yurttas, about his true sympathies or whom he worked for, except that he came loaded with an absurdly far-fetched story and a semi-automatic pistol. But the fact was it was too late to ask. Or was it?

'Before I accept, you need to tell me who you are, and who you're working for.'

Yurttas nodded.

'*Effendi*, I will explain everything in due course, but for now I think we must alight and board our train for Erzurum.'

AFTER THE FLOOD

Chapter Thirteen

In barely more than a day and night Charlotte had gone from being in the bliss of her honeymoon – notwithstanding Harris's presence – to being snatched and removed from those she loved, and made a prisoner. Curiously, after tears and anger, she had grown quickly accustomed to incarceration. At first, when they had taken her, she had been intensely afraid – not a pleasant feeling, nor one she was ever likely to forget. The realisation of the loss of her autonomy as she was physically lifted and bundled into a car had hit her like fist to the stomach, and left her feeling actually cold with a lingering acridity and heavy head as though she'd spent the evening sitting to close to a smoking fire. But that visceral, pulse-racing horror had passed, leaving in its place, a damaged, deflated vacuum. By the time she had reached that stage, she had arrived by motorcar – her head covered by a thick cloth, in some ways the single most terrifying part – and marched into her present abode and been brought to room in which she was still confined. A man, her jailor, brought her food at intervals, and the food was good. There was a water closet and a marble lined bathroom; from a plumbing perspective it was bordering on the palatial, especially when compared to weekends in the country in draughty houses where running hot water could not be taken for granted. If she had not been a prisoner, she might well have enjoyed it.

But that was a far cry away. Charlotte was exhausted and lay motionless on the large bed in her prison.

The principal source of vexation – and it was a deeply vexing experience, let it not be understated – was the not knowing what was happening to her: and the not knowing *why* she was here. The not knowing why someone had picked her out of all the millions – and the not knowing about Ernest, of course. The poor love would be frantic with worry about her. And what of him? If she had been targeted, might he also be in danger? She took a deep breath and stilled herself. There was no use crying about any of it. As it was, the last thing she remembered was meeting an elderly Turkish gentleman in the churchyard who led her through a doorway in the wall…

Since then Charlotte had dried her eyes too much and now, enough was enough. It was best not to think about Ernest or what she ought to be doing, if she wasn't locked in the bedroom of what was evidently a house of considerable proportions. More than that she did not know. The only slight clue came from a familiar whiff of salt in the air that she chanced upon from time to time. She realised it carried the smell of seaweed that one finds at the seaside. So she decided she must be on the Bosphorus somewhere, hopefully not too far away from Ernest.

The smell was all she had, however, since she did not have a view of any sort from her room because of wooden shutters which had been fastened shut. And there was no way that she was able to open then from within. The slats did permit some light, however, so hers was a twilight incarceration. She found that she could in fact see something from the bedroom if she peered with care. She could see fragments of the driveway of the house – a slither of a gravelled expanse in which there was the gleam of the bodywork of a car in the stark Turkish sun. Every now and then a figure walked through her narrow field of vision offering a snapshot of a pacing pair of trousers or of a man's bald head. Among those she had seen more than once were the pinstriped brown trousers of one man – he of the bald head, too, whom she reckoned to be some sort of driver. The sad truth was, these fragments told her little about her predicament, though they

AFTER THE FLOOD

did help pass the time. Nevertheless, she filed the snapshots away – it was all information – and kept up her vigil. After all, the snapshots belonged to people who knowingly or not were instrumental to her kidnap or accomplices to it. Which was not unimportant.

With what felt like great effort she left the bed and resumed her watch. It helped to stave off darker questions in her mind. And that's when she saw him.

At first it was the aged brown full brogue and the lower portion of a sagging, linen trouser leg of an Englishman in the Tropics, that caught her attention. It takes a certain conceit, a certain complacency about one's position in the world to dress quite so badly, she realised. Like dropping your 'Hs' when you know better.

She decided that if the trouser-wearer wasn't an Englishman then he was undoubtedly as expatriate of some sort – an Australian or New Zealander perhaps. She had started to concoct a backstory for her louche colonial when she saw something that she recognised beyond doubt, the crumpled crown of a Panama hat that had seen better days. Few come quite as battered as that.

The hairs stood up on the back of her neck. She recognised the hat. But it couldn't be. She moved to one side to return her gaze to the scuffed brogues, then to the trouser legs that had long since parted company with their creases and sagged around their skinny wearer like a Bedouin's robes. If only she could see his face. The figure was talking to the bald man in the brown pinstripe. Just then he turned – Charlotte snatched over a chair and climbed up. From higher up she could see the man's chin and lower jaw, revealed by the tilt of the brim of the hat; the thin beard confirmed her suspicion, and then he looked up at her giving her a clear face-on view. She gasped. Andrew Streat. She already knew it from the hat, but seeing it was so much more shocking that simply knowing.

The fiend!

Charlotte jumped down from the chair, her heart racing. There had been nothing right about that man – Harris was correct about that, and she had felt it too immediately, not that she had mentioned this to Ernest, mind. But there had been something untrustworthy about him. Charlotte's right hand dropped protectively to her navel. Well, well, well, now she had something on her captors. Her spirits rose – a flush of elation, in spite of her circumstances. Then it started to unwind... and she started to feel dizzy. She had to warn Ernest. He needed to know, because, after all, Streat would be among the first people that Ernest would turn to and rely upon.

Her hand formed a fist. If Andrew Streat touched a hair on Ernest's head she would pursue the man to the ends of the earth to punish him. But first she needed to escape from her confinement. And that was an objective still wanting a solution. For now.

Drabble was bundled into the back of a canvas-topped lorry with about two dozen soldiers. His hands were bound fast at the wrists. It struck him that this was probably surplus to requirements – overkill was the word that came to him, for the restraint of one unarmed professor of history.

The engine revved and they set off at pace, jerking him sideways into the man next to him. Another soldier shoved him sharply back in his place and gave him a curt bark.

A second military lorry quickly fell into line behind them, followed by another. They drove from the airfield, dust flying up from the tyres, and sped through the outskirts of a town. Around them gravelly, grubby terrain was peppered with poor, irregular huts and shacks, interspersed with sandy

AFTER THE FLOOD

coloured dogs, spartan goats and gaunt chickens. The town disappeared from view and soon they began to climb, the rest of the little convoy coming into view as they snaked around the switchbacks. Rocks and boulders began to protrude through the sharp-leafed foliage at the sides of the road.

Like the solider who spoken to Siviloglu on the Siebel, these men were German, though their uniforms carried no insignia. They said little because of the effort required to be heard over the din of the grinding engines and road noise. They would not know that he could speak the language nor be likely to expect him to, given the monoglot reputation of the British. Drabble did not advertise the fact.

The lorry struck a pothole throwing its occupants forward. Amid the cursing, Drabble was yanked back to his place as the lorry righted itself. The swearing continued – along with ripe comments about the state of Turkish roads – before a bark from the NCO silenced them. The soldiers lowered their eyes hastily, showing no defiance. As well they might: the sergeant was a particularly nasty-looking piece of work.

The lorry laboured on, leaving a palpable cloud of dark exhaust fumes from its tailpipe.

Drabble shut his eyes and tried to think.

What were the Germans doing here? Hoping to claim some of the credit for finding Noah's Ark, if Siviloglu's absurd plan came to fruition? Was that Berlin's interest in this? Would finding the Ark underpin Hitler's claim to have God on his side when war came or corroborate his assertion that he was leading a chosen people? Would this prefigure some gross Nazi effort to recast Noah as an early Aryan saviour of mankind?

It didn't bear thinking about. And it meant that regardless of his own personal safety, he could not possibly help them locate the Ark. Absolutely not.

Drabble stared up above the head of the German soldier opposite at the flapping dark green canvas. There was no question about it. He could neither aid the attempt to find the Ark nor offer his endorsement of it, which was presumably what Siviloglu really wanted of him. Neither, however, could he refuse to help or escape, not if he ever wanted to see Charlotte alive again. There was one other option, though; if he died during the act of seeking the Ark – in a fall, perhaps – before the artefact were discovered or before he could endorse it, but having appeared to his captors to have been a willing accomplice, then they might release her.

They might.

Drabble turned to the parched-looking valley below, his mouth dry. It wasn't much to hope for. On the other hand, he could not help the Nazis weaponise the Ark for their own purposes.

He leaned his head into this hands. There was one other option, of course. Stay the course and do – secretly – whatever was in his power to prevent Siviloglu and his German helpers from finding the Ark. After all, the chances of discovering it were absurdly slim in the first place. Then again, if Trotsky's dossier did lead to a large wooden structure of some sort, one of undoubted antiquity, then you could undoubtedly claim it was the Ark, whether you believed it or not.

In which case, why was he here? Drabble raised up his head and saw a deep valley falling away behind them. There would be a solution. But right now he was damned if he knew what it was.

After the best part of an hour examining the bookshelves that lined the sitting room, Charlotte gave up. There was nothing for her to read. Despite scanning the spines of about a thousand volumes, and making liberal use of the library

AFTER THE FLOOD

ladder – to no avail, there was nothing there in English or indeed in a language that she could read. She returned to the large bed and lay down, contemplating her dismal position. She was tired, again. It was after midday and the sun was bright and hot against the shutters of the windows and the heat drifting in through the slits making the room balmy, verging on stultifying. Even the ruddy air in her lungs felt warm. If she wasn't careful she would drift off...

Lunch would be in shortly. That would do something to break up the monotony, though not the solitude or the despair. Perhaps a nap afterwards was desirable. If nothing else it would speed the day along, taking her either closer to her release or...

It was best not to consider the alternative prospects. Her hand went to her navel, especially given the existence of 'it'. She yawned. Actually, despite the heat, despite her fear, she found herself looking forwards to lunch. Was this how prisoners got through the day? By slicing it up into four or five segments interspersed by mealtimes. She yawned loudly. At this rate she would be asleep before lunch got here.

And that would not do. She should not wish her life away. She propped herself up on one elbow, piling up the plump cushions and pillows behind her to raise her up. That was better. She sighed and surveyed her prison; books and books, an empty wooden dresser, a settee and matching armchairs and an adjoining bathroom and bedroom. All elegantly done out, and the books themselves handsome but entirely illegible as far as she was concerned. If only she read Arabic script or Persian – or whatever it was. Above the chest of drawers was a landscape in oils showing columns of prettily-dressed Ottoman soldiers carrying out some ceremonial on a parade ground. The men wore brightly hued uniforms and turbans and were armed with muskets and lances, adorned by colourful pennants. Judging by the headgear and the arms she dated it to the early eighteen hundreds, back when the Ottoman Empire still had some vim.

Charlotte's mind drifted to Napoleon, who helped set the rot in, of course, and his famous remark – 'If the world was only one country, Istanbul would be its capital' – before drifting through time to more prosaic matters. Yes, she was famished. Lunch could not come fast enough. One of things she had noticed about pregnancy was that she was hungrier, much hungrier than seemed credible, and mercifully the gruesome sickness had passed. And now she was eating a like a ruddy horse, just as her mother had promised she would. Charlotte rested her hand on her stomach, feeling a new sense of comfort from the posture. It was a boy.

She hadn't told Ernest, but she was positive.

A boy… What would they call him? She sighed and stared dreamily into the space, imagining this little life out of her and real all of a sudden. Would they call him Ernest? No. It was a lovely name but that wasn't *him*. Charlotte smiled a soft smile and caressed her stomach. Oh yes, he was a boy…

A sharp knock at the door roused her. Her eyes blinked open and she found herself looking up at the high ceiling. And look at that. Right there, framed by a narrow line on four sides, she saw a hatch. At first glance it was essentially invisible, lost in the deep crimson of the elaborately decorated ceiling, but there it was. Undeniably. A hatch. The knock was repeated and she snatched her gaze away from the ceiling as the door opened and in came the masked gaoler pushing a trolly with her food.

Don't look at it, she told herself. Don't look at it.

Don't look at it.

The thickset gaoler left the trolly close to the door, said nothing and departed immediately, banging the door shut after him.

AFTER THE FLOOD

Suddenly Charlotte didn't feel hungry. Her eyes darted to the hatch and she allowed herself a small smile. Here, at last, was something she could work towards. She lifted the largest of the silver domes on the trolley and was hit by a heady savoury smell from a moussaka-type concoction. A smaller domed dish contained a peculiar looking white pudding that did not fill her with confidence. She replaced the lids, still displaced from her appetite.

The question was, how to reach the loft-space, and then how not to advertise one's route of escape. She glanced around the room.

And then she had it. The library ladder. It was easily tall enough to get her to the hatch and then, *possibly*, she might be able to draw it up after her, hiding her exit. Not that it would take them long to realise that it was the only available option... But it was better than nothing. That said, lifting the ladder up after her would take some doing. Never mind. She could be try. Charlotte snatched up the knife and fork and took the largest domed dish over to the table. She was most certainly not hungry anymore, she was too excited for that. But that did not matter. Lunch came first. Energy was all.

Chapter Fourteen

Harris looked through the compartment window as the Erzurum train built up speed, leaving an intersecting multitude of tracks and sprawling platforms behind. He was finally leaving Ankara Station and beginning to feel his confidence returning.

He was not, to be precise, *hugely* confident, but – you know – he was on the way. With every minute that the so-called Erzurum Express chuffed its way eastwards he was a mile closer to Ernest and, presumably, to helping him out of whatever bind he was in. And that was enormously satisfying. How he would find him and what he would do when he did? They were questions that would need answers in due course. But, importantly, Harris was not alone in his endeavour. He had the help not just of Fisher, but now also this mysterious Yurttas fellow, who was also armed. So if they encountered any funny business that would be just the ticket. Moreover, he claimed to be the representative of a larger body of men intent on protecting the Ark, the existence of which – however fanciful – was clearly part and parcel of this entire brouhaha.

And when push came to shove, as far as Harris was concerned, it was jolly well a case of the more the merrier.

Accepted, Harris had no real idea yet *who* Yurttas was, but if he was an informer or agent acting on behalf of the other side then he had already had an opportunity to thwart them, so on that basis – for now at least – Harris resolved to trust him. So long as that pistol of his was pointed at the odious Green Fez Johnnies, it was all tickety-boo by him.

Harris checked his watch. It was time. He locked his cabin door behind him and set off to find the bar, where he had agreed to meet Fisher and Yurttas for a pre-prandial libation.

AFTER THE FLOOD

He found the American waiting for him already, having availed himself of a rye whiskey. On seeing him, Fisher ordered himself a second and asked for a glass of Crémant for Harris.

Harris plumped down into the leather seat.

'This ruddy heat is getting a bit much. I've been to India, so I know something of the heat, but how do these people cope? Look at it.' From the window the landscape was already turning to brown. 'It's only May. I ought to have brought my ultra-light safari suit.'

The waiter set down their drinks and Harris fell upon his Crémant like a drowning man reaching for a life-jacket.

'Good God,' he moaned, as the first mouthful sluiced inwards like a breach below the waterline on a tanker.

'I know –' Fisher chuckled. 'Welcome back Sir Percival. Next stop Erzurum – well, last stop, that's the end of the line.'

'Cheers!'

They clinked glasses.

Fisher lowered his voice.

'Is our new friend, Mr Yurttas, joining us?'

'Yes,' Harris grinned, and pulled out his pocket watch, flipping it open. 'Dare say he'll be here any minute. Doesn't strike me as the tardy sort.'

'Good. In a gambit like this, allies are essential and allies with local knowledge are worth their weight in gold.'

Harris set a match to his pipe and as the first rich cloud of tobacco ballooned from it, the door to the carriage opened. They both glanced over expectantly: a fat Turkish businessman in a pale grey suit wove his way unsteadily between the booths.

'Where did you say he was from, again?'

'I didn't,' Harris took another bob at his fizz. 'He hasn't told me. I suspect he's with a department of the Turkish government. Dare say we'll find out.' The carriage door creaked open – Harris looked up – and a European man of middle age entered, removing a pith helmet. He looked German, Harris decided, before restoring his attention to Fisher.

When they finished their drinks and still there was no sign of the mysterious Yurttas, Harris decided to take matters into his own hands. Lunch was calling. 'I'll go and chivvy him along,' he announced, as he parked his pipe and got up. 'Feel free to order me another.'

Moments later he knocked on the varnished door of Yurttas's compartment. There was no reply. Harris sighed, and contemplated returning to the bar. He knocked again, louder than before. No answer. For God's sake. He knocked again and as he did so, brushed the door handle with his hip. It moved surprisingly easily and the door swung open.

Harris, never backwards in going forwards, stepped in and called out.

'What ho! Mr Yurttas?'

The cabin was in darkness, the shutters fully down. A fly darted about, buzzing in the gloom. Yurttas, he saw, was kneeling, facing the bench seat, looking rather as if he were in church. Was he lacing a shoe? It might have been a trick of the light but Harris thought something glistened on the back of his head.

He cleared his throat.

'Mr Yurttas?'

The Turk did not move. Harris glanced over his shoulder, rather as he might
if were about to pocket an ashtray from the table of a smart restaurant (he'd
never done that, of course), and took a step closer, his voice falling.

'I say, Mr Y-Yurttas... are you, er, *incommoded*?'

AFTER THE FLOOD

He swallowed. The fellow was not moving. Not a jiffy. Moreover, there was definitely some dubious-looking moistening on the back of the head – and it wasn't hair pomade, that was for certain. Come to think it, he could see it was staining the back of Yurttas's jacket, leaving it darker than the surrounding material.

'Y-Yurttas… ?'

Still nothing. Harris reached forward and dabbed the stained area of the jacket, then stepped back into the light in the corridor; his fingertips were stained red.

Harris gasped. Blood!

'Yurttas?'

Harris stepped back, taking it all in. Yurttas wasn't moving – or any sound. Blood was seeping abundantly from his head… slowly Harris arrived at a troubling conclusion, with all the pace of a branch line train slowly drifting into its sidings...

Great Scott! He stared heavenwards. Yurttas was dead! And given the posture of his body was in it was not credible to conclude that he had fallen. No, the only rational conclusion was that the poor blighter had been biffed on the back of his head with something that had also cracked open his skull.

Harris retreated – and then cursed as he noticed he had just walked a pair of bloody footprints into the corridor. He swore under his breath as he inspected the red-stained sols of Tickler's. *Ruined!*

Then he ticked himself off. *Hardly the point, old man* – and returned to the scene. Blood, of course, is what you got with head wounds. They went off like geysers. Always did. Something he'd learned on the rugger pitch. Which also confirmed – drawing on Harris's limited pathological range – that the head injury was probably the killing blow.

Harris stepped back into the cabin, spotting a broad pool of blood on the floor running under the bench seat. His mind filled with overlapping questions, but one thought found its way to the top: Yurttas, plainly, had been murdered; yes, *murdered* in cold blood. *Quite so,* interrupted a separate gruff voice originating in Harris's mind, presumably emanating from the cerebellum – the moiling engine room occupied by greasy, light-avoiding Morlocks of subconsciousness. Consider the facts, said another voice, here was the cove sent to help Harris help Drabble in respect of this Ararat business – part and parcel of the same business that had led to Charlotte's kidnap. It surely meant that it was perfectly rational to conclude that the very same people had discovered Yurttas's intention to stymie their plans and therefore moved instead to stymie him first. They had presumably known that he was armed and so surprised him.

Implausible as it might seem, this must surely be the case.

Which was all highly disappointing, realised Harris, whose unbidden thoughts continued…

Get the gun, grunted the Morlocks. Arm yourself. *You might be next*. Christ alive, thought Harris. So I might. He stole a glance over his shoulder. What if the wise old trolls in the cerebellum are right? He stepped closer to Yurttas, aware that his suede Tickler's were slipping back into the blood. He reached out a shaking hand and patted Yurttas's side – erratically at first like a man putting out flames, flinching at the touch of the torso. In the outside jacket pockets? No. Check the flanks under the outstretched arms. Yes. There, under his left arm, a dense metal object.

It was excruciating. Harris held his breath, for fear of smelling what he was touching. The fabric was moist and tacky from blood and still warm; he swallowed, half-recoiling, his face squeezed shut like someone having the soles of his feet stroked by a feather. Harris took another

AFTER THE FLOOD

deep breath, then gritted his teeth and tensed himself for one more effort. He bent forward and peeled the jacket open, feeling in the darkness between Yurttas's chest and the bench seat. At first nothing quite made sense, then Harris's fingers found the bulbous metal shape of the handle of the automatic pistol and he began pulling at it, eventually – yanking it from the holster. He staggered back, panting with the horror and effort.

Christ alive. His head was spinning. He shut his eyes, clasping the pistol to his chest like an infant with a teddy bear.

There was step in the corridor behind him; he turned...

An unshaven guard stood before him – frowning hard at him, accusingly. His eyes narrowed on Harris's chest. Harris looked down, seeing his bloodied hands for the first time, and then the bloodstained gun and red smear across the front of his best cream, mid-weight linen–wool Fowler & Larman tropics suit.

The railwayman reached for this whistle...

Charlotte ate enough lunch for two. Those were the rules. And after she'd eaten too much, she paused for half an hour and waited for the trolley to be fetched away. She did not rest entirely, of course – she gathered up a few essential items – a couple of pieces of fruit and so on – in a pillowcase to keep for later.

That done, Charlotte set about escape.

It was not to be a conventional escape, in that it would initially take her
further into the depths of the prison she was escaping from – and therefore, technically, further from an exit on the ground floor. However, she was confident it would lead *somewhere*, and that somewhere was better simply remaining *here*. For a start she would be in control of her destiny, at least briefly,

and there was no need to worry about any reprisals for her attempt if it failed, because – after all – she had not got clue about their ultimate intentions as they stood for her anyway.

In other words she had everything to lose, whichever way you looked at it. And that meant doing nothing was no better than doing something.

Charlotte took down a framed picture from the wall and wedged it under the door. It might slow down someone seeking to enter. By the time she had finished it was well jammed in. Satisfied, Charlotte now lifted the library ladder from its runner – to her relief it came away easily, but it was terribly heavy. She walked it across the floor towards the ceiling hatch, swivelling it from foot to foot. With disappointment she realised it was well short of the height needed to reach the hatch but if it she could lean against something it would almost certainly get her close enough.

What she didn't want to do, if possible, was the leave evidence of her escape route behind. Her idealised scheme was for her vanishing act to prompt a generalised search, buying her time and opportunity to slip away. She swallowed, her hand going to her chest. Heartburn was not a pleasant aspect of pregnancy, nor one that people tended to discuss, if they discussed pregnancy at all, which they did not. Charlotte brought herself to order and focused on the ceiling.

She lifted the ladder off the floor and pressed it against the ceiling hatch: it lifted – her heart filled and she forgot her heartburn – and she pushed it back and off to the side. Perfect.

She lowered the ladder and caught its metal hooks onto the edge of the hatch: it caught satisfactorily, and letting go, the ladder now dangled happily from the framed hole in the ceiling. The only point now was how the ladder would respond to her weight – though she knew it would kick out beneath her and be nigh on impossible to climb. The other challenge was whether the hatch would take their combined weight, though the probability was that it would. But how to keep the ladder upright while she climbed it?

Charlotte surveyed the room, her eye glancing upon the chaise long with the damask cushions and the lamps, the French Empire-era desk and the other exotica of her refined prison. She removed the brass reading lamp from the desk, unplugged it from an electric socket several yards distant and placed it on the floor beneath the foot of the ladder. She then dragged over a tall, jade-coloured ceramic dragon, one of a pair that guarded the squat green ceramic stove in the corner of the room. It was heavy and required all her strength, but she got it beneath the hatch, recovered her breath and then wedged the ladder so that it rested on the broad bridge of the dragon's nose. Bingo. She pressed down on the ladder and was satisfied that the combination would hold. Finally, she looped the desk lamp's cable around the neck of the dragon and tied it off.

There.

She gathered up the pillowcase containing the fruit and the desk lamp, and grasped the ladder. With a deep step, she hauled herself up. The dragon wobbled as she got all her weight on the first rung, but she righted it by leaning left and got to the second rung.

On the fourth rung there was a knock at the door.

Charlotte didn't miss a beat.

There was another knock as she hit the fifth rung and a bang on the door – as the person outside turned the key in the lock. But now her head was inside the darkness of the loft. There came a shout, muffled but angry. Charlotte slipped inside the loft, nimbly drawing up the ladder. Then, with effort, she pulled up the dragon, the flex stretching, hand over hand.

There was a loud bang and a tearing crash as the door splintered...

Charlotte silently slipped the wooden hatch into place and lay on her back motionless, except for the thunderous beating of her heart. Below she heard footsteps roam around the floor – and voices beginning to raise in alarm. How long would it take for someone to notice that the loft hatch existed? How long would it take before the absence of the library ladder was noticed? All unknowable. She daren't move – an audible groan of the ceiling joists might expose her position immediately.

There was another loud shout right under her – she froze. Then the voices melted away. Perhaps they were searching the room.

Charlotte lay in the darkness, blinking, waiting. Waiting to be found. She exhaled. The sound of her breathing crowded out the noises from below and she checked herself: the heavy footsteps faded and the exchange of voices fell away. Was that two of them leaving?

She lay for a minute or more, in the pitch dark, not knowing whether she could move without alerting someone below to her presence. There was no sound from below. They must have gone. For now. They might yet remember the library ladder.

They might yet.

Time would tell.

Charlotte rolled onto her side; the beams beneath her whispering and she raised herself, placing her weight carefully on her knees and hands. The hatch was at her feet and the broad wooden joists ran left and right. If she went straight ahead she ought to leave the bounds of the room soon; then she would need to find another hatch to get out. What would have been useful was a torch, or failing that, matches or a lighter. She had none of these since they had

AFTER THE FLOOD

taken her handbag. So, the darkness would have to do. Charlotte edged forwards and smiled. The uncertainty was undeniable, but action was absolutely preferable to inaction. Rightly or wrongly, for the first time in two nights Charlotte at least now felt like a human being – one in control of her destiny, and that was hugely gratifying. Her left hand went to her stomach and she pressed gently against the little life. I'll get you safe, she said. I'll get you safe.

Harris had but a moment to decide what to do before the railwayman blew his whistle and alerted the world and his dog to the bloodied remains of Yurttas and the fact that he, Harris, was covered the cove's blood, too.

He raised Yurttas's pistol and pointed it meaningfully at the guard's face, the blunt sights at the end of the barrel just inches from his mouth. The whistle fell from his lips – bouncing silently on its cord – and his hands bobbed into the air.

Harris grinned.

'*Tres bien, Monsieur l'Inspecteur –*' He wasn't sure why he had begun addressing the Turkish railwayman in French but it seemed no less inappropriate than English, since he probably didn't speak that either. What now? '*Donnez moi votre cravat,*' Harris snarled, in his best theatrical villain. He was thinking Robert Donat in *The 39 Steps*.

'*Maintenant! Vite!*'

Harris plucked at the man's tie and he got the message, hastily removing it and handing it over.

Harris snatched it away. '*Bien!*' He shoved the fellow round, and seizing the man's wrists, tied them roughly together behind his back. Then he snatched out his silk handkerchief and pressed it into the railwayman's mouth. He shoved him into Yurttas's cabin.

'*Assiez toi!*' he snarled. 'Sit!' he hissed. The man's eyebrows raised; he was none the wiser, and Harris pushed him unceremoniously backwards and he collapsed into a seat. Harris bent down – put the gun to one side – and then started unravelling Yurttas's tie. He was going to have to bind the fellow down, otherwise he would alert the world to Harris's presence and that was no good either.

It was harder to extricate the bloodied tie from the dead man than Harris had anticipated; not that he had hitherto given the topic much consideration. Quickly, his hands were slimy with the fellow's blood and the knot was becoming intractable.

He growled, in retrospect unceremoniously, and pressed his foot against the man's sternum as he pulled on the tie – 'Christ!' he hissed, releasing the implacable garment. Yurttas's lifeless form slumped to the blood-soaked floor. Defeated, Harris slid off his own tie – pausing only because it was one of his favourites. But this was no time for sartorial sentimentality.

A moment later the guard's arm was attached to brass handhold on the wall. He wasn't going anywhere.

'*Dormez bien!*' declared Harris, with a jaunty salute.

He removed his blood-stained jacket and exited the cabin, hurrying for his own compartment. Harris wasn't the always the sharpest, but this time he knew he had to get himself as far away from this mess as possible.

AFTER THE FLOOD

Chapter Fifteen

General Siviloglu's convoy drove for several hours before stopping. Drabble wasn't quite sure how long, because his watch had long stopped. They were now high up, though still within Ararat's treeline, and probably approaching the performance limit of the vehicles given the steep gradients. Drabble's lorry pulled up next to the others in front of a small compound comprising several dozen tents, many large enough for small units of men. As the drone of the engines died and the fumes dissipated, the soldiers spilled out from the lorries, stretching and blinking at the glare of the late afternoon.

Drabble looked out over the broad landscape below of low rolling hills, dotted by cowed trees and hamlets with broken down roofs and the occasional minaret poking up from a mosque. Sheep and goats specked the fields but this was not a rural landscape as he knew it, though one likely unchanged since the coming of the Ottomans eight hundred years before. Underfoot the grass was sparse and hardy and uphill he could see a black, volcanic rock starting to predominate, soon overtaking the brown scrub in shades. The view above that was then lost in cloud – wisps which swathed the upper reaches of Ararat, concealing its peak, which was up there somewhere.

Orders barked in German – accompanied by cheery 'Heil Hitlers' and 'Sieg Heils' – abounded, as did the martial stomping of feet and Teutonic snapping of heels. An officer led Drabble to a tent at the heart of the canvas conurbation – a large, round circular job, like a miniaturised bigtop, guarded by a uniformed sentry. Drabble guessed that like the language spoken by those wearing it, it was German, even if it was denuded of military and national emblems. The sentry came smartly to attention – heels, rifle, the whole lot.

Drabble was pushed inside, finding a surprisingly airy space dominated by a substantial desk – although it could have doubled as a dining table – covered in papers and photographs. Various campaign chairs were dotted about. Boards had been erected showing maps of Asia Minor, Anatolia and the Ararat region. General Siviloglu, looking tired and drawn, was opening a new file. They were alone. The man looked up from his papers, the oddly coloured eyes fixed on Drabble. He gave a calculating smile.

'Whisky, Professor? I have Glenmorangie.'

Drabble realised that inside two seconds he could have his hands around Siviloglu's throat – and be throttling him to death, if only tried. But it wasn't that easy and not simply because any unusual noise would predictably alert the sentry. Not was not, alas, in Drabble's make-up to kill a man in cold blood, even a man as apparently deserving of it at Siviloglu. He would almost certainly be signing Charlotte's death warrant, too. Drabble's eye fell on the bottle of whisky.

'Go on then… although I didn't realise we had something to celebrate.'

Siviloglu offered a reproving look and drew out two cut-glass tumblers from a wooden case. 'As a matter of fact, Professor, I've just been reviewing some very compelling information, information which I think you'll be interested in. Take a look –' He inclined his head towards the desk where under the glare of an Anglepoise lamp were scattered a half dozen or so photographs – enlargements, a section of a map, as well as various papers, the writing in Cyrillic. Drabble approached the cache of documents without enthusiasm, his gaze falling on the photograph closest. It was blurred and showed a grainy white landscape flecked with

AFTER THE FLOOD

black and dark grey shapes. But there, among the indistinct, he immediately saw the pointed outline of the bow of a ship.

The hairs stood on the back of his neck.

'So you can see it –' Siviloglu's eyes glistened as he presented Drabble with a glass of whisky and proffered a small china jug of water. 'Astonishing, eh?' the general added smugly. 'And at 4,000 metres!' The Turk grinned happily, and it was ever so slightly nauseating. Drabble looked down at his whisky, having second thoughts. Perhaps he could throttle him after all.

'What you are looking at are aerial photographs of the north-eastern portion of Ararat a little beneath the summit, taken by a Tsarist air force photographer in 1916.' As he spoke Siviloglu pointed. 'The larger grey area is a mountain lake, the black rectangular shape is what you think it is. Here you can see photographs of what appears to be the interior of the structure which the detachment of Russian engineers found six weeks later.' There were photographs of large rectangular rooms – quite regular and clearly man-made. 'See the compartments? Yes? … too exciting for words, isn't it, Professor? And to think this secret has lain hidden under the floorboards of the presidential suite at the Pera Palace Hotel all these years!' He drew over a large scale map. 'And here we have marked what we hope is the precise location of the, er, structure.' He raised his glass. 'Impressed, Professor?'

'I am.'

'*Sherife!*'

Drabble nodded slowly, his eye returning to the grainy aerial photograph that had first caught his attention. It was a daunting prospect. The chances of all this not being some elaborate hoax were now vanishingly small. He reached for one of the accompanying pieces of foolscap, the text all in Cyrillic letters.

'And this is all from the hotel?'

'Correct. Contents of the file that Trotsky repressed for decades and then concealed at the Pera Palace.'

Whether or not you bought into the Biblical interpretation and specifics of a divine inspiration behind the Flood story, or even the fact of the simple existence of a man called Jesus some two thousand years ago, the extent of this documentary evidence was hard to argue with. In the case of the flood it was impossible to offer some credence to the text of Genesis – itself likely written thousands of years before the birth of Christ. Vague as it was, you could not deny that the flood story might well relate to an actual historic catastrophe, a significant, deluge or inundation, one likely took place during what we would call the Stone Age. Drabble had not made a study of it, but was aware of the coincidence of the flood in Genesis and the flood detailed in the Epic of Gilgamesh – albeit with Noah replaced by a fellow called Utnapshtia and the ship square rather than rectangular. That the Babylonian myth could have been written down fifteen to twenty centuries before the birth of Christ told you something about how old the story was. It had been rattling around mankind millennia. So, regardless of whether or not there was a greater being – Drabble was personally sceptical on that matter – the fact was that, once upon a time, the chances were that there was indeed a mighty flood and at least a few people somehow saw it coming or were lucky enough to have pre-empted it, and survived it by their own ingenuity, and by taking some animals with them. After that, since everyone else was presumably dead, it was only natural that those survivors would crow about it. After all, wouldn't you?

And now, thousands of years later, one of their distant descendants was perhaps staring down at twenty-year-old photographs of these hastily snapped shots of the self-same

AFTER THE FLOOD

ship. Drabble took a sip of whisky and shook his head disbelievingly. There was a chance, of course, that this was a forgery: the Russians loved forgeries, after all. Might this be Stalin's idea of a joke, one left precisely where it might be found? Drabble looked down again at the shot that showed what most resembled the bow of the ship. Could that really be the Ark?

There was undisputedly a large object there, unless it was shadows thrown by cliffs, of course, or a cloud perhaps. Might it be some large mountain hut, half sunk in a glacier? He looked over at Siviloglu; his zealous expression brooked no doubt. Drabble looked back the pictures, the words of the Book of Genesis coming to him. They had been ingrained since childhood thanks to decades of institutional religious repetition:

'And God said unto Noah … Make thee an Ark of gopher wood; rooms shalt thou make in the ark, and shalt pitch it within and without with pitch… The length of the ark shall be three hundred cubits, the breadth of it fifty cubits, and the height of it thirty cubits.

Quite what a cubit was, nobody knew of course. And then it went on.

'A window shalt thou make to the ark, and in a cubit shalt thou finish it above; and the door of the ark shalt thou set in the side thereof; with lower, second, and third stories shalt thou make it…'

Nor was gopher wood now known to humanity though many had presumably guessed. Drabble set down his glass and gestured at the aerial picture, 'How big is this area?'

'The photograph covers an area approximately one kilometre square, meaning parts of the black object we can see are perhaps fifty to sixty metres in length.'

Siviloglu arrived at Drabble's side.

'I assume you know, Professor, that the Flood story also features in the Koran, albeit with some variation in the duration of the deluge? It also gives the Ark a different landing position, three hundred miles away to the south on Mount Judi.'

Drabble nodded, 'The ship of Nüh. The Babylonians also had their story, too.'

'Quite right.'

Drabble nodded, as a further extract of the King James' Bible breezed into his mind:

'And of every living thing of all flesh, two of every sort shalt thou bring into the Ark... they shall be male and female. Of fowls after their kind, and of cattle after their kind, of every creeping thing of the earth after his kind, two of every sort shall come unto thee, to keep them alive.'

Still gazing at the photograph, he shook his head. It could not be possible. But … but … Drabble was beginning to despise the sound of his own thoughts. He drank down his whisky and wincing at its undiluted strength. The only way to know for sure what these pictures showed would be to see the site for himself. But it beggared belief. The Ark… Noah… how ridiculous!

'How far up did you say these photographs taken?'

'Not far from the summit – about 4,500 metres.'

Drabble sucked his teeth.

'Higher than Mont Blanc.' He looked over at Siviloglu. 'If this really is the Ark then that would mean that everything in the world – with the exception of the peaks of about dozen mountains that exceed 5,000 metres – were flooded when this happened.'

Siviloglu smiled, satisfied. 'Well Professor. You know the expression. The camera does not lie.'

It doesn't always tell the truth, either. Drabble pushed his glass towards Siviloglu for a top-up.

AFTER THE FLOOD

Ararat was high, high in Alpine terms, if not in comparison to the Himalayas or the Atlas mountains. But with mountains height wasn't the whole story: finding and excavating a lake at that height would take some doing, especially at this time of year. It ought to be easy enough to get to the spot on the map indicated by the Tsarist engineers, though. But finding this object under several metres of snow up there … that was another kettle of fish altogether.

Siviloglu topped up their glasses, and raised his, '*Sherife* –'

Drabble lofted his silently.

'Here's to finding the Ark!' declared the Turk.

Drabble hesitated.

What was he doing? There was no way in God's green earth that he would be responsible for handing the Ark to a man like this, particularly one supported by Nazi Germany.

Not a chance. If you gave the Ark to Adolf Hitler he wouldn't know what to do with it. He'd probably burn it.

Yet as exciting and momentous as such a potential discovery was – and it really was – it was also inconceivable. Whatever his and Charlotte's needs – not to mention the needs of their unborn child – they were but small beer in comparison to the global context of this discovery. And that was a crushing realisation. If you believed that war in Europe with Germany and Italy was essentially inevitable, then handing the 'other side' such a powerful, totemic symbol as Noah's Ark – was unthinkable.

And therefore if this shadowy image really were the Ark; the actual Ark, built by a man called Noah or Nüh and filled by his sons, plus all the animals on the Earth, then it had to be saved from these people. Or denied to them. Or destroyed to prevent them from possessing it and subverting it.

'Tell me, General, why do you want it so badly?'

'Isn't the answer self-evident?'

'Perhaps, but I'm curious. What do you plan to do with it?'

Siviloglu reviewed him coldly. 'All I'll say, Professor, is that this artefact will support our wider objectives.'

'And what might they be?'

He chuckled, before deciding how to answer. His expression changed, 'There are forces at work in Turkey which you, as a visitor, would be not cognisant of, Professor. Suffice it to say that it would do Turkey no harm to locate this artefact on its own soil. No harm at all.'

'And what of Herr Hitler. Presumably it would do him no harm, either?'

Siviloglu shook his head. He was not going to answer.

'If you won't answer that, perhaps you will answer this. Surely there are plenty of Turkish or German academics who could help you find this thing voluntarily, or could be strong-armed more easily? His eyes were drawn to the heap of papers on the desk. 'Why me?'

Siviloglu grinned.

'Come, come, Professor, you do yourself a disservice.' He saw that Drabble was still unconvinced. 'Do you really think that the world would listen to a Turkish academic if stood up to announce the discovery of the Ark *in Turkey*? Whereas if it's Professor Drabble, the internationally known Alpinist and celebrated historian, says so, that's another story. You are a uniquely qualified and widely respected historian from a globally pre-eminent academic institution, Professor. With your help we will get a fair hearing.'

'But it's not my period, not even my subject…'

'Don't quibble, Professor,' a victorious smile crept across Siviloglu's face. 'And what's more this discovery will make *you* a global celebrity. It will be like finding the tomb of Tutankhamun and Babylon all at once. But the Ark is worth more than all the pyramids in the world. Once we've finished you will be worth twenty Howard Carters.'

AFTER THE FLOOD

And the rest. The Ark was the significant artefact in the creation myths of entire Judeo-Christian Abrahamic world and, as such, was arguably a find of greater historical importance than a piece, even, of the True Cross.

And that made it tantalising. Drabble could not deny that. But knowing that sickened him, too. He half turned away, suddenly ashamed of himself, and thinking of Charlotte – as well as and the unit of German soldiers marching about outside.

'How on earth did you even know I was in Istanbul?'

Siviloglu met his gaze, 'That, Professor, is not a question which I will dignify with an answer…' His eyes glistened. 'But when we locate the Ark, you'll just have to be pleased that I did.'

Chapter Sixteen

Harris was out of breath when he found Fisher in the bar. His hands were shaking badly, too, though not from the usual *delirium tremens*. The pistol in his breast pocket had felt enormous and incredibly heavy, like it was going to bump into everything passing thing so he had concealed it in the cabin and done his best to clean Yurttas's blood from his hands – a harder thing to achieve than you might think. Harris had also had to change his jacket, which was plainly ruined. After a moment's hesitation he had disposed of it out of the window, watching the ruinously expensive piece of Savile Row tailoring billow and fill with air before taking off and landing in a distant farmer's field.

The cost, however, was the least of it, sighed Harris, who determined to be feel sanguine about it.

Arriving at the bar, he wove his way through the fixed seats and tables to Fisher and clapped the American on shoulder.

'Fish!'

'Harris.'

Fisher removed his cheroot, 'I got you a sidecar. Fancied you'd want to go up a gear from the Crémant.'

The pre-emptive gesture almost brought a tear to Harris's eye and reinforced the trust that he had come to have in Fisher. Granted the fellow was an American, so was likely to be out for himself, but he had shown himself to be decent – broadly conveying a degree of sensitivity to the trials of a fellow man and so forth – and moreover he was a journalist. And that counted a lot with Harris. Journalists were men and women of integrity, after all, even if they told the occasional porky.

'What's our Turkish friend having?' asked Fisher breezily, before registering Harris's expression.

AFTER THE FLOOD

'What is it?'

Harris leaned in.

'Yurttas is dead. *Murdered.*' He glanced over his shoulder and then announced, 'I've got his gun.'

Harris took a swerve at his sidecar before registering Fisher's look of horror. 'It's a ruddy disaster,' he hissed before giving a rapid precis of the preceding fifteen minutes.

'Have a smoke –' Fisher handed over a cheroot and pushed his lighter towards Harris's glass. 'And then give me all that again at a quarter of the speed… spare me no detail.'

By the time Harris had finished the story again, a second sidecar had disappeared and a third was in the works. Meanwhile the express train had chugged through another ten miles of Anatolian landscape, inching them closer on the great map towards their destination. There was a pause as Fisher digested the information.

'OK. So who was this guy, again?'

'Yurttas?' Harris finished the cheroot and took out his pipe. This was definitely a moment for maximum tobacco. 'A species of crank, I think you'd call him.' He edged forward in his seat and leaned in. 'Self-confessed member of a clandestine group tasked with protecting the secrecy of Noah's Ark and its location for eternity and being prepared to do whatever it takes so to do.' He shrugged. 'It doesn't sound like much of a gig, but then what do I know? He said there were more of them out there and it strikes me that they might be a bit peeved when they discover that their mate is now pushing up the daisies. Moreover, it strikes me that we now have the added problem of *who* killed him to consider – and whether or not we're next on the list.'

Fisher stared bleakly down at his drink.

'I hadn't thought of that.'

'Nor had I, I confess till a few moments ago.' Harris lit his pipe, drawing comfort from its tidy familiarity as well as the nicotine. The reverie, however, was short-lived, as a pitter-patter sensation began in the basement of his stomach. An unpleasant notion was dawning upon him…

They were out of their depth. Utterly, incredibly, Captain Nemo-ly out of their ruddy depths. So far out of their depths that they were over their necks in it.

Bugger. He stifled a belch and gazed down at the surface of his drink. *Bugger*. Harris looked over at Fisher sought refuge from his despair in forcing a smile, but it broke halfway through and he lunged for his drink. Refreshed, he came up for air.

'Time for another,' he croaked determinedly, waving his empty glass.

He met Fisher's waiting gaze; there was something striking about it – the American almost appeared to be staring through him. It was altogether most disconcerting and Harris restrained the impulse to glance over his shoulder.

'Don't worry, Harris.' Fisher gave a flat smile. 'Everything is going to be OK. You'll see.'

'If you say so, old man.'

They chinked glasses.

'We'll be in Erzurum in four hours – we'll just need to keep our heads down. Then it's a drive to Ararat. That's a day. Then we'll get up the mountain and be able to get to the bottom of whatever's going on.'

Harris looked at the slim, prematurely ageing, liver-spotted face before him; at his neat teeth and thinning hair. And somehow, in it, he found himself diving into a well of reassurance. He grinned, and his heart swelled like a rugger ball with an extra press of the pump for luck.

'By Bingo, you're right.' He grinned, his spirits rising. 'And, who knows, there might even be word from Streat waiting for us in Erzurum, too?' Harris was rallying heartily

AFTER THE FLOOD

now. 'Yes, Streat might have good news for them about Ernest and Charlotte; it might all have blown over…'

Perhaps, thought Charlotte, this was how Catholic recusants and heavily robed monsignors had felt, all those centuries ago, hiding out in the clandestine recesses of Tudor manors and remote castle-houses in stuffy priest holes, not knowing when or if they would ever be found or indeed released. Her priest hole, at least, was commodious in the extreme – not a mezzanine crevice stashed between storeys or rooms. She did not quite know how long she had been in the darkness of the attic, half an hour – perhaps longer? – and her thoughts had started to drift, from fear and the need to remain perfectly still to avoid detection to early modern England.

It might have only been fifteen minutes, truth be told. But it was warm, rather warm in fact, the afternoon sun effectively making the attic into an oven. As it was bound to. She ticked herself off for not bringing water. That was an oversight – her first and probably not her last – and it might prove to be enough to undo her entire good work. Still the good news was that despite first impressions there was in fact some light in the attic: her eyes had adjusted to it and she could now see countless tiny shards of light piercing in between the roof tiles, offering some depth and form to what had at first been a black void.

Charlotte had a plan, so it was time to put it into action. To delay further would be unwise. Gingerly, she inched forward feeling with her hand for the next joist and following on with the opposite knee till she had successfully advanced a pace, all effected as silently as she could. The joists had made no sound audible to her, meaning there was a sporting chance that the same could be said below.

Well, maybe.

Charlotte continued in this way and after a span of perhaps five yards, she began to stretch her reach down to the left and right to feel for a hatch, one that might lead to a room outside of her enclosure.

But then, all too soon, she arrived at a blockage. It rose through the loft-space like a wall and Charlotte followed it up with her fingers, until she could reach no further. She then went left and right, before realising what it was – a chimney breast, its narrow, herringbone brick arrangement foreign and pleasing. Clinging to this brick titan she slowly circumnavigated it by stepping cautiously from joist to joist, as lightly as possible, before crouching down and resuming her prior course.

She continued her slow progress for perhaps another five minutes before finding herself at the eves, where the roof met the floor. Evidently, she realised, this was a building of some considerable proportions. In accordance with her plan, she shuffled sideways by about five feet to her right and then swivelled around to face the other direction. She now advanced, her hands feeling out in search for a hatch and escape, as her thoughts returned to her thirst. She really ought to have drunk something before leaving the room – or else brought water with her. Still, you lived and learned. If you were lucky.

Charlotte met no chimney on this route and was fairly confident that she would soon passing over the top of her old rooms. Reaching the far end, she went sideways and then about-turned and began the other way, moving as quietly as she could and checking an arm's length either side for evidence of a hatch. There had to be another up here soon. *There had to be.*

Beads of sweat were now dripping from her face. It occurred to her that soon the absence of drinking water might become critical. She pushed this consideration to the back of

AFTER THE FLOOD

her mind and hurried on. Find the hatch, she told herself. Find a way out. Find water.

In the worst-case scenario, so long as she followed her plan she would be able to retrace her steps and even in the darkness find her way back to the hatch through which she had entered the space.

The horrifying notion that she might never find her way out of the loft only began to enter on her mind after she reached the far end of the next run and still found no evidence of another hatch. Then her hand slipped from the edge of the joist and she fell – gasping in horror – with all her weight on the top of the ceiling below. The ceiling held, but it must have made a hell of a thump, and she scrambled for the joist, her heart thumping. That's when it all became too much for her; the imprisonment, kidnapping – it was all too absurd and awful and gargantuan to conceive. And what in God's name was she doing, ferreting about in the dark? It was all too much, *too, too* unimaginable, too vexing, too horrific, too ridiculous. Charlotte's hand went to her mouth, and she bit down on her knuckles, silencing herself as she felt a stab of anguish, anxiety and the fear. She emitted a low moan and her face contorted painfully and stretched as she took long, elephantine breaths and as tears cut through her eyes and ran unshepherded down her face. Sob quietly, she told herself, if you must. Charlotte rocked back onto her knees and her other hand went to her stomach where she held Little Ernest. Be quiet, woman, be quiet. Stop being weak.

Her tears plodded onto the dry joist. Had the recusants and heavily robed monsignors also shed tears of fear in their dark, oppressive priest holes?

Charlotte caught her breath.

There were still Catholics in England. The recusants and monsignors had lived, some of them at least. They had escaped their captivity. And so must she. Charlotte wiped away her tears and steeled herself.

The only thing she could do was go on. Even if she couldn't pull herself together she must continue. And so she did, soon completing her sideways manoeuvre and then carefully rotated her axis of advance, before advancing once again, joist by joist. She felt her confidence returning and smiled out into the darkness. She was going to get through this. *They* were going to get through this horrid episode together.

Suddenly she stopped. Was it her imagination or could she feel a warm breeze playing on her face?

Yes, there was a faint breeze. Charlotte continued on her path, not quite sure which direction the breeze came from; one moment it seemed to be on her right cheek, then the next on her left. She wasn't ready yet to break free from the mental pattern she had set herself to follow it yet but it gave her hope...

Just then there was a noise. A scratching sound, close and loud. Charlotte's heart skipped a beat. A hatch was being shifted. She knew it. She turned and looked back – just as a blinding shaft of light filled the attic.

There was no time to lose.

She got to her feet and scampered, leaping from joist to joist, not looking back. Charlotte knew that the cry would come at any moment, as surely as she could see her shadow on the floor before her. Her hand cradled Little Ernest and more tears stabbed at her eyes, trying to get out… but there was no time for that. She had to get out.

And there it was.

There it was.

Charlotte had the hatch open in a second. She was panting. Daylight lit her face, her eyes squinting as she lowered herself onto her backside, feet dangling through the gap. She leaned forward, grasped the frame of the hatch and slid

AFTER THE FLOOD

forward, her grip helping to break her fall. She landed hard on corridor floor, her left ankle turning, but kept moving. Through a window she registered a view over lawns, shrubberies and ornamental cypress trees. Beyond was water, lots of it. Limping now, she followed a narrow corridor along a scruffy green linoleum floor, presumably deemed adequate for the needs of servants. She realised that she was breathing hard; that there was a pressure in her chest, like heartburn which filled it and pushed it out in every direction. There was a staircase. She took it, oblivious to the pain in her ankle, trotting down the steps rapidly, forgetting herself, almost like a child playing.

But this was not game.

Her feet moving quickly, she coasted the handrail, ready to seize it, her other hand sheltering Little Ernest. She had to get out. *They* had to get out. And they were ruddy well going to.

The stairs led down and down. She did not stop at intervening storeys but pressed on till the linoleum became red tiles on what must be the ground floor. Then she slowed herself, her ears pricked up as the smell of a kitchen – woodsmoke, fat and spices – found her nostrils.

There were voices. Turkish chatter; aimless, nothing alarming. She was at the foot of the stairs now and could see the doorway from which the conversation – and the odours – were emanating. And directly ahead was the main event: a glazed door leading to the gardens and those lawns and the water. She looked up and down – the coast was clear – and stepped onto the tiles reaching the door within seconds. It opened and her feet were crossing the lush lawn and breaking into a sprint. She did not know where she was running to, but the pressure in her chest was gone and she took in mouthfuls of the saline sea air. Gravel crunched underfoot and she found the row of ornamental cypress trees and beds of tall tulips and spiky shrubbery. The crunch of the stone gave way to another soft lawn and there – *there* was the sea, beyond a strand of sand, bonnie and blue. In that second, Charlotte stood, hands on knees, panting at the scene before her. In the far distance there was land, a shoreline grey and insignificant, perhaps an inch high at most on the horizon.

Good God, she thought. Five miles away if it was a day. And then it hit her. This wasn't the Bosphorus. She looked left and the shoreline was greyer, fainter and lower. Looking right, was not much better. Then she saw a white passenger ferry, black smoke billowing from its yellow and white funnels, passing between her and the far shore.

This was not the Bosphorus. It was the sea. She was on an island. Turning, Charlotte reached out her hand, feeling suddenly nauseous, as if to balance herself, her legs unsteady. *This wasn't the Bosphorus.* It couldn't be... too blue, too wide, too much like a sea ... But which one? She staggered and turned.

Under the shade of a Turkish pine tree she saw an elderly gentleman, his white beard tumbling down over his chest. The erect figure wore an artist's smock and an abundant fez, and stood at an easel, paintbrush in hand. He frowned at her through circular, wire spectacles. What are you doing here? was the expression on the commanding face. Charlotte met the imperious gaze and he looked away, affronted at her presence.

The insistent crunch of footsteps on the gravel behind her caused her to turn. Multiple figures approached from all around. At the vanguard was a stocky, bearded man – pale-looking, in a white short-sleeved tunic with two rows of white, cotton buttons down the front, like a dubious osteopath in a basement flat in North Kensington. He was plainly her gaoler, now without his mask and he looked like the sort of man who was no stranger to casual sadism. He

AFTER THE FLOOD

stopped just short of her, slightly out of breath, his watery, pink-rimmed eyes regarding her balefully. His fatty skin was whitish and his teeth were visible between his thin lips. His large hands were flexing into fists. For the first time since arriving at the house Charlotte was afraid. She raised her hand in fear and took a step back…

Chapter Seventeen

The heavy canvas flap of Siviloglu's tent lifted and a figure lumbered into view, accompanied by a chilling gust of wind. The newcomer wore a circular cloth cap and a thick leather sheepskin-lined leather waistcoat that was belted, restraining a paunch, from which a curved silver-handled dagger glistened in the gas-light. A revolver hung in a holster. Tall sheepskin-lined boots completed the look of a man who in another time, in another continent, would have resembled a trapper – or perhaps a brigand in the pages of Jules Verne. A thick beard stood out from a robust face, one which eyed Drabble with grave distaste.

General Siviloglu looked over from his maps.

'Ah, Sahin, this is Professor Drabble ... Professor, this is our guide – Ibrahim Sahin knows Ararat better than any man alive.'

'Or dead,' stated the trapper without removing his hostile gaze from Drabble. There was a pause as he waited to register any change in Drabble's expression – which remained impassive. Then the guide approached the desk and took out a crumpled packet of cigarettes. A lighter in his hand rasped and a cloud of baleful, bluish grey smoke wafted across the space between them. He addressed Drabble.

'You'll find Ararat rather different from the North Face, *Ingilizce*.' He cleared this throat, bringing up some phlegm. 'She's higher – for a start, considerably, and she's alive, not like the dead Swiss limestone of the Eiger.'

Drabble snorted.

'I'm not sure I like the sound of that.'

Sahin grunted humourlessly. Cigarette in mouth, he tossed his cap onto a chair and approached the cabinet, taking out a glass and snatching up the bottle. He uncorked it with his

AFTER THE FLOOD

teeth and poured himself a surgical measure – that is, something adequate for cleaning a scalpel – and swilled some in his mouth before swallowing.

'There's not much to like, *Ingilizce*. I am sure you won't *like* the sulphur which seeps through the rock — it stinks and it can make a weak man sick. Even if you can bear it, it slows you down, clawing at you like sucking mud on the soles of your boots.' He took another half-inch off his whisky. 'The sheer altitude will make you sick too, if you're not accustomed to it, which no one is because few mountains in the world are as high as Ararat. Then there's the static electricity; it builds up between the rock and the atmosphere and then it explodes in rages on the barren face – there's nowhere to hide from it and your ice axe and crampons sing tunes because of it.' He let out a baritone cackle. 'This time of year there is the melt. In the melting season you face the constant danger of avalanches – great towering waves of snow, ice and rock that come careering down the mountain. I've seen a boulder the size of a house go by me like an express train – *like an express train*!' Another half-inch of whisky vanished and he tossed his chin arrogantly at Drabble. 'Oh, yes. Ararat is more than a match for your White Spider, *Ingilizce*.'

Drabble held the guide's contemptuous gaze. It wasn't *his* White Spider, as well Sahin knew. And it never would be. Once was quite enough for that. Just then, Drabble felt his body tense and he braced himself. He knew what was coming… suddenly the dim gaslight, the guide, the tent – all of it – vanished in a deafening black deluge of rock and ice. Nothing else could permeate the senses but he held on. When the noise and blackness lifted Drabble found the guide's gaze waiting for him, a curious smirk in the corner of his mouth.

Whatever this man presumed to know of Drabble's experience two years before on the North Face of the Eiger, there was nothing he could say or imply that was worse than the actual experience of it. Just shy of four thousand metres if you were an Alpinist (or just over thirteen thousand feet if you were a British geographer), it was a vertical Hades where the sun did not shine and never had. Nowhere in the world was there a lump of limestone quite so formidable – or justifiably terrifying. And it was here, during a violent ice fall, that his climbing companion Hubertus lost his footing. Drabble was unable to break his fall and before he knew it, Hubertus was gone and Drabble was dragged with him. Drabble fell a hundred and twenty-eight yards down a near vertical slope, saved by a snag in the rope. Drabble felt pangs of nausea rising up from his stomach and forced himself to smile benignly at the guide.

'Mr Sahin, I salute your bravery – and evident accomplishment. Tell me, where do you stand –' He hesitated, not quite believing the word he was about to utter, 'on the Ark?' Drabble glanced over at Siviloglu. 'Is it really there, as the General here believes?'

The guide held his gaze, a shimmer of something unpleasant arriving in his expression. Then he blinked.

'I was a boy, no more than ten. I was with my father in high summer overlooking the Ahora Gorge on the north-eastern side of the mountain. The view was amazing, I remember and we were descending from the summit. And all of a sudden we came across a ship in a well in rock. It was not quite like any ship you have ever seen, *Ingilizce*, but it was a ship without doubt. It stuck out from the ice and snow… here,' he went to the desk and took a piece of paper and a pencil and began sketching what he remembered seeing. 'What I saw had been exposed by the summer melt, as surely as you are standing before me, *Ingilizce*. So be under no illusions, it's there.' He chuckled and tossed the sketch towards Drabble: it showed a rectangular, blunt-

AFTER THE FLOOD

looking structure, with a couple of stick men next to it dwarfed by it, presumably Sahin and his father.

The hairs went up on the back of Drabble's neck.

'I take it you've not seen it since?'

Sahin threw down the pencil.

'On the way back my father was full of excitement about what this discovery would mean for us. He was already dreaming of going to Constantinople to meet the Sultan and riches that would inevitably follow. I was a child, I had little sense of the magnitude of it all.' He shifted the weight on his feet and when he resumed his voice had dropped. 'The summer melt was well advanced but as the sun went down so the temperature fell and the ground became icy and deadly.' He swallowed. 'My father slipped and before he could react, he slid – straight into a crevasse. His body was never found. As I always tell people, this is a very greedy mountain.' The guide took several deep breaths, his head almost bowed. 'I cried out for him for hours till it was dark – I was but a boy – and I was cold and my tears were freezing to my cheeks. Then something happened that I will never forget. I met a goatherd. He was old and he told me he was lost, but he led me down the mountain and took me to my mother.'

And then this boy had grown up, made the mountain his life, his career. Given what happened you might wonder that he hadn't run away to sea. Or perhaps ... perhaps, after all these years, he was still looking for his father. Sahin took a tilt of his whisky, his large eyes looking down mournfully at his drawing. The bombast that he had arrived with had now vanished. He cleared this throat.

'To answer your question, *Ingilizce*. I have looked for the Ark many times but I have never seen it again. I have been to the very spot – or what I thought was the spot, but never seen anything like what I saw then. But I know what I saw. I know what my father saw. We definitely saw it.'

And presumably everyone had doubted him ever since.

Drabble looked down at his sketch. This, at least, explained why *he* was here, why he was prepared to collaborate with Siviloglu and the Germans and not to – presumably – be too curious about what they would do with it all once they found it. That's if he had any scruples, of course. But if you had seen the Ark once, you would want to see it again, especially if your father had ended up giving his life for it. Discovery would not only be making good on his father's endeavour it would also silence all those critics who had questioned and derided him ever since. What interested Drabble was why he'd failed to locate it since, but mountains could be very perplexing.

Then he experienced a strange premonition, and a realisation struck. Assuming Sahin was in his early forties – he looked all of that but also, curiously, less – then he and his father would have made their discovery in around 1909 or 1910. By coincidence Drabble knew that 1911 was notorious for the heatwave that struck Britain, but it also affected the United States and the Continent, leaving the landscape parched and thirsty. Presumably the long hot summer took no prisoners in this corner of the world too. It might be. And perhaps it had simply hadn't been hot enough for long enough since to melt enough snow and ice enough this structure to expose it once again?

'Out of interest, was your sighting of the wooden structure in the same approximate location as that of the Tsarist pilot and engineers in 1917?'

Siviloglu cut in.

'It most certainly was, Professor. And that is why we are going to find it this time, whether we need to dig for it or use dynamite.'

AFTER THE FLOOD

'How far it is it?'

'From here?' Sahin planted a finger on the map. 'Two days. Minimum. Our camp is at two thousand five hundred metres. The peak is five thousand, one hundred and sixty-five metres.' The scale told Drabble that they were perhaps just three miles distance from the peak as the crow flies – but they would need to ascend a mile and half in that distance, too. Sahin continued: 'We then have to circle the peak to reach the far side of the mountain and the saddle above the Ahora Gorge. And that is where the ship of Noah can be found, *Inshallah.*' The trapper lit another cigarette and grimaced, showing his teeth.

'Good –' Siviloglu addressed Sahin, 'Fetch Major Hauptman. We leave at dawn.'

Chapter Eighteen

The goaler led Charlotte back to her room and closed the door behind her. As it was bolted she saw that the ceiling hatch had been nailed brutally into place – with angular timbers and unnecessarily long nails which had been struck poorly so that their heads were bent over into the woodwork. It was a surely metaphor of what would happen to her if she attempted an escape again and it spoke louder than any words that the silent osteopath had failed to utter.

Charlotte surveyed her prison and quietly retreated to the sofa; it was striped in reds, oranges and golds, Ottoman colours, she supposed, and hard, excepting its silky tasselled cushions. She lay down and curled herself into a ball. What on earth had she been thinking?

In all honesty, what had she been thinking?

That she could escape? Yes. But how could she? If she had been where she thought she might be – in one of those imposing houses overlooking the Bosphorus, then she could perfectly reasonably have anticipated escaping the compound, once out of the house. Then she might have flagged down at passing taxi or stopped a stranger, or simply fled on foot. That was a reasonable plan.

But she was on an island. And she had something precious inside of her that she could not afford to drown or have broken or taken from her by a traumatic incident. Imagine if she had fallen from the hatch? *Imagine it*. Imagine what would have happened if they had decided to physically punish her for her attempted escape? While they had not, she had seen the anger in the gaoler's face. And she had seen then that anything was possible. They had not hurt her this time but she may not be so lucky next time, supposing there

AFTER THE FLOOD

were a next time. And in the meanwhile, they had plenty of opportunity to do whatever they liked with her.

Charlotte shut her eyes and prayed. Unfortunately she knew her history. There was not special dispensation for women, pregnant women included, in the annals of history. They went to the sword just as frequently as either men or children. Charlotte took a long, deep breath and tried to settle herself. This wasn't a moment to dwell on history. It was a time for assessing the known facts. How long had she been here? Two, no, three days. Had her captors actually harmed her or overtly threatened it? No. Not yet. Had they fed her and looked after her? Indeed they had. If they had wanted to kill her or hurt her, could they have done it? Yes. They had had ample opportunity.

So what was going on? *No idea.* All she could hazard was that it was likely to do with Ernest since it had something to do with Andrew Streat – who, don't forget, was there when this all began on Sunday at the church. Andrew Streat, she remembered, had also sent Ernest a postcard in January congratulating them on their engagement and planting the seed of the idea of their honeymooning in Istanbul. 'Come and visit,' he had written in his rather alarmingly erratic handwriting. Well, then. Now Charlotte knew why, or at least *more* of the why. A shadow passed over her mind, darkening her thoughts: Ernest was in danger. How selfish she had been: all this time she had been fixated on her own and Little Ernest's safety, but it was Ernest who must be in real danger. Moreover, he would be worrying about her. If only she hadn't gone off to explore the churchyard with that old man on Sunday morning! This was all her fault…

She rocked back and forth, soothing herself, her eyes closed and her arms wrapped around her middle. Soon her long fingers retracted as she rocked to form tight fists. Streat was going to answer for this. She was going to get out of this prison. She was going to get away from the vile osteopath and his poorly suppressed intentions of violence. She was not going to leave it in the hands of others to decide whether she lived or died – or whether her child lived or died. *She was going to escape.* And what's more, she had seen a small sailing boat on that jetty, and she would jolly well find a way to get to that boat and sail it away. So help me God, she vowed. So help me God.

AFTER THE FLOOD

Chapter Nineteen

Harris was mostly drunk by the time the train arrived at Erzurum. He had had at least six, maybe seven, drinks with Fisher, potentially eight, which meant they were well on their way – eight drinks being the internationally recognised yardstick for conclusive inebriation – and he knew he was squiffy. What's more, night was falling and as their bags were deposited on the platform next to them and as Harris handed over a fistful of coins of unknown value to the assembled porters, he was increasingly aware of the chill in the air and the lack of vertical resilience in the old pins. He steadied himself against his trunk, shut one eye and looked back through the station towards the stationary train they had just alighted from.

Somewhere inside it was poor old Yurttas, probably still kneeling in a pool of his own blood with the poor guard that Harris had tied up in there hours before. Half-cut or not, they needed to get as far away from the station as they could – and fast. He stifled a belch, and moved towards the exit.

'We need a car, sharpish, don't we?' he managed to say.

'That we do my friend...' At this Fisher stepped out into the path of an unfamiliar-looking saloon, its headlights peeping through a thick layer of dirt. The American leaned in to the driver and there was verbal exchange largely drowned out by the drone of the engine. Seconds later the spindly driver was energetically loading their luggage onto rack at the rear of the vehicle and roping it down. Harris climbed inside after Fisher.

'This chap know where we're going?' asked Harris as the car pulled away.

'Yup.'

'And where's that then?'

'First stop Dogubayazit. It'll take us about six or seven hours, I'd guess.'

'Christ alive! seven hours? Is there no end to Anatolia?'

Fisher chuckled as the car jolted and bounced along the road. Harris muttered under his breath: well that meant only one thing; he would have to finish what they started on the train and get properly blitzed. He fished out his hipflask, presciently replenished at the bar, and jammed it to his lips. The car was still jolting about like a frog attached to a battery but he managed not to spill too much. He passed the flask to Fisher and sat back, the whisky now flooding into his body and giving him the fortitude he needed to confront the grim reality of hours trapped of this jarring hell.

'By God I hope the roads improve or this is will be the longest eight hours of my life.'

Fisher laughed and handed back the flask.

'Get some sleep. The driver reckons we could be in Dogubayazit by just gone midnight if we're lucky.'

'Lucky? I'll be lucky if I don't need a spinal surgery after this.'

Harris did sleep. A little. It was cold when he awoke and the sky was inky black with no hint of light left in it. They were in the middle of nowhere, the grimy headlights of the car boring an inadequate tunnel of light before them; the cantankerous syncopations of the straining engine giving him a headache – or perhaps it was a hangover, he reluctantly conceded – and he was savagely thirsty. He was also aware of a gnawing feeling at the pit of his stomach, hunger presumably. Fisher was sleeping soundly – exhibiting that irritating habit some people possess of being to slumber under whatever conditions life throws at them. Harris glared at him and realised that they had not eaten since breakfast. Which explained the gnawing rodents in his stomach. He

AFTER THE FLOOD

cursed as the car pitched into another deep pothole, sending a spasm of pain shooting up his right side and back. *Ruddy hell!* At this rate he'd be a cripple by the time they reached where-ever it was they were going. What was it again? *Doya? Doggy-something-or-other-zit?* He gave up and tugged out his hipflask. Empty. Could you ruddy well believe it?

Fortunately Harris always travelled with a spare. One for each side, one for each kidney, because you never wanted to run aground. He smiled. The backup flask, sadly, was smaller, but it contained something even more special, a taste of distilled Albion – more precisely, four wonderful fluid ounces comprising three parts of his mother's sloe gin and one part Russian vodka. This would get him to their destination.

And it did. When Harris next awoke they were in a drowsy-looking town and there was a life-affirming silence in the place of the indignant drone of the engine. He stretched, adjusted his neck and looked about, seeing Fisher and the driver standing beside the car, smoking and talking…

Harris lit up a Craven A and Fisher came straight over, looking annoyingly fresh.

'Good news. The driver's going to take us right up the mountain – well, as far as the road goes.'

Harris managed to croak, 'Topping stuff.'

'It's about twenty miles, so if we set off first light we should get to wherever the road meets the path by mid-morning. He says there are several main paths up to the summit but this is the most popular one for those ascending from the Turkish side of the border. I can't imagine that Drabble is further ahead of us.'

'Touch wood.'

'Yep. The driver's gonna see what he can rustle up for us. I just gave him fifty bucks so I hope we see him again.' He chuckled darkly and tossed his cigarette out of the window. Harris nodded and began searching in his pockets for the reserve hipflask.

'I tell you what else we haven't discussed,' announced Harris, the hipflask emerging from the back of the seat. 'But what in the dickens are we going to do when we actually find Drabble – do you think? I mean to say, it's presumed he's been kidnapped, so we will have to contend with whoever's got him.'

Harris took a deep drag on the remains of the Craven A, which illuminated the hint of a frown on Fisher's face.

'You've still got Yurttas's gun, right?'

'Yah.' Harris paused – words failing him. In his time he'd shot plenty of pheasants, a few rabbits and even a tiger, although not very well. But he wasn't experienced in the art of shooting people. In fact, as far as he was concerned, actual persons were a completely different category of game altogether, even Frenchmen. Fisher broke in before he could begin to expatiate on the topic.

'I get it Harris, but if it comes to it – if it's them or us – then, mark my words, I'm sure you'll be able to pull the trigger.'

Harris smiled doubtfully.

'I dare say you're right, old bean.' But Harris knew that heroics were what other people did, not him. 'Let's hope it doesn't come to that, eh?'

'Well –' Fisher lit another cigarette, a metallic snap killing the flame of his lighter. 'It'll probably depends on how many we're up against.' Harris hadn't considered that. 'The best we can do is arrive without being seen, suss it out, and then try and break up the party. I just hope, between us and Drabble, we'll be able to spook the ship, so to speak, and stop this madness before it gets out of hand.'

Harris nodded sombrely.

AFTER THE FLOOD

'More out of hand, you mean.'

It was madness. He was meant to be on honeymoon, for Christ's sake. They would need provisions, he realised. Food, heat, water. Blankets, too. Mountains were cold places. They'd need those funny metal over-shoes that mountaineers – except Drabble of course – put on their boots to walk on snow. He felt the weight of Yurttas's revolver in his jacket pocket. At most it would have six bullets in it. That was a fine start but hardly enough to shoot their way out of the OK Corral, if that's what was required. Harris put the flask to his lips and took some heavyweight refreshment on board.

As the offered the flask to Fisher – and the American uncharacteristically declined it – a question formed in his mind.

'I say, what about you Fish, have you ever shot a man?'

Fisher shook his head his voice becoming small.

'No.'

'Do you think you could?'

Fisher half chuckled. 'If someone was pointing a gun at me, I'd have no difficulty whatsoever.'

Harris's chest tightened, like he was holding his breath, except he wasn't. He exhaled, hoping to release the pressure, but it didn't go. He realised that he was exhausted, physically weak. It was like he had the flu or something. Perhaps it was the feisty little sloe gin and vodka? Perhaps he was drunk, not tired? Perhaps… then something else occurred to him, something Fisher had just said as though he knew it.

'I say, Fish, what is this madness? Is there someone, really, trying to find ruddy Noah's Ark?'

The American chuckled.

'It beats me, Harris. I suppose we will find out soon enough.'

A glimmer of a smile appeared on Harris's wet drunk mouth.

'Why are you here, Fish?'

'How do you mean?'

'Well, why are you actually here, putting yourself in danger like this... for a deuced stranger like...'

Whatever Fisher said, Harris didn't hear it. He had gone to sleep before even reaching his own question mark.

AFTER THE FLOOD

Chapter Twenty

Drabble was awake. He lay, staring into the darkness of his tent. Wind snatched at the canvas, whipping it back and forth and piercing the tent in its extremities, sending cold draughts over his face. He had been dreaming that he was back on the Eiger. Mostly this came at him in fragments – his climbing companion Hubertus's sunburned face, grinning through the smoke of a German cigarette, or it was steam clouding from the mess tin during the mundane act of brewing up, on a ledge by a drop of several thousand metres, or the rushing, coarse sensation of the icy wind on your face, like sandpaper glancing at your cheeks. These would be interspersed with snapshots of the mountain looming above; the dark rock, the foreshortened White Spider – that mass of ice, a field at ninety degrees. Then there was the moment when it all went wrong.

In life it had happened in the blink of an eye: a sudden darkness like a total eclipse, a tumult of ice and rock. Hubertus snatched from the face. Then Drabble, falling, after being swept from the rock like a crumb might be brushed from a table.

And then he keeps falling, as the gear securing them to the rock fails, leaving him fully a hundred and twenty-eight feet below where he started, suspended thousands of feet from a single rope, bruised and battered and somehow alive. That had taken as long as it might take you to sneeze. At the end of it, Hubertus was dead and what now began for Drabble was an eight hour wait before he was rescued. But, of course, for most of that time, he had no idea if he would be rescued or not. (The delay, it turned out, was largely down to the fact that Harris had fallen asleep after a heavy lunch so was neglecting his task of watching the climbing team through a telescope from the hotel bar in Grindelwald.)

But the nightmares didn't dwell on the not knowing if or when he would be rescued, nor the waiting. The nightmares lived in the moment of horror, making a split second of life last the duration of the sleep, so that when Drabble awoke, his heart was palpitating, and he found himself drenched in sweat and in the grip of intense terror.

Drabble looked up at the twitching canvas above. It made the same sound as their bivouacs on the Eiger, he realised. He swallowed, his heart rate settling. His hair was wet, he knew – it felt cold.

There was nothing he could have done to have saved Hubertus's life. Nothing, except for talking him out of doing the stupid climb in the first place, which wouldn't have worked. Not with Hubertus. He would have gone up with someone else instead if Drabble had refused.

Drabble lay blinking in the darkness. The ruddy fool. He sighed wearily, feeling himself more at ease in the wakeful present. Unfortunately he really needed to go back to sleep, though that was the last thing he wanted. The fact was that on Ararat, the North Face of the Eiger was too close for comfort.

An hour later the camp was up. The sun was rising somewhere behind the mass of the mountain and the world they inhabited on its great western slope was one of half-light and shadows. It was cold and breath steamed at the mouths of the men and the donkeys. The peak was concealed by a wreath of cloud and Drabble knew that that alone would not make for easy or enjoyable climbing once they got that far, even if it was technically no more difficult as walking up Scafell Pike on a January morning. Yet Ararat was highly

AFTER THE FLOOD

exposed and he hadn't forgotten Sahin's warnings from the evening before.

They breakfasted at six and broke camp through the dawn to be ready to leave when the last of the tents that were coming with them were lashed onto the backs of the donkeys. In front of the animal section was the detachment of thirty German soldiers – Bavarian engineers was what Drabble had gleaned – formed up in three columns with their NCO. The soldiers now wore white mountain fatigues with peaked field caps and carried backpacks affixed with ice axes and crampons. Rifles were slung over their shoulders. Even denuded of their military insignia there was no doubting them. They looked about as Turkish as Marble Arch in the rain.

Drabble had been issued with an ice axe and crampons and clothing more suitable to the task. He was placed at the vanguard with a group that included Siviloglu, his female companion, the guide Sahin, Major Hauptman and Celik, the heavy-handed henchman, who unlike the others – presumably because no such clothing fitted him – was wearing the grey lounge suit which he had on before, covered by a vast woollen poncho, with the addition of leather gloves and a thick furry hat. Celik's job, plainly, was to prevent Drabble from absconding or doing anything untoward with his ice axe, not that either option was in his mind. Nonetheless the man did not take his savage eyes off Drabble.

As the last of the packs was secured, Siviloglu nodded to Sahin, who discarded his cigarette.

'Right,' he announced. He raised his voice, 'Let's go.'

The column set off, following a route that led them over grassy scrub and into the underbelly of a misty, low cloud. It didn't take long for the sheep and goats on the steep hillsides and the scattered, gnarled trees to give way to snow and rock and scree. Sliding stones fell away from their feet, sapping their strength with each stride. Progress was accordingly slow – it was always going to be: with the soldiers, as well as donkeys and all the kit that this number required After an hour or so they had gone a mile or so, and climbed perhaps four to five hundred metres. Not that you would notice.

Most of the time the focus was on one's feet and the immediate terrain. If you looked up, when the cloud broke, the view was stunning. From up here the landscape of Anatolia stretched out before you, offering a vast vista of Lilliputian towns, rivers, villages, farms and fields, hills and forests. In the south Drabble had spied the grey streak of Lake Van, and closer to home, the broad smoky smudge of Dogubayazit, which he knew was the biggest town in the region. That was some twenty miles away, a couple of hours' drive, and his best way out of this mess, if or when the opportunity for escape came.

But not yet, not until he knew that Charlotte was safe. Drabble looked back and saw Celik a dozen or so paces behind, as he had been all morning. So be it. At some point Siviloglu's Biblical wild-goose chase would be over – and he would be released or escape. Or not, as the case may be. His one, *his only*, outstanding source of hope was Harris. If Harris could get together with Andrew Streat, then it was just possible that between them they could make a difference – make a noise, get some help… find Charlotte, get the authorities into gear. You never knew. Sometimes Harris could be surprisingly effective, most usually when he saw a news story in it, admittedly. But if Noah's Ark wasn't a big news story he didn't know what was. The question was, would anyone notice his message hastily scrawled on the bathroom wall?

After the delay of a flat tyre it was approaching noon before

AFTER THE FLOOD

Harris and Fisher arrived at the foot of the mountain, the spot where the road finally gave up the ghost and became a track. Here they found their guides waiting. Harris paid off the driver and their luggage was unloaded and packed onto several mangy donkeys. There was a great deal of loud chatter going on – some of it, Harris noted, in rather a querulous and barking tone – and then and various bits of extra outer clothing were then handed around – hats, gloves, overcoats, far more clothing than seemed strictly necessary.

'We have at least one night on Ararat during our climb, *Effendi*,' explained the guide submissively, when he saw Harris frowning at the fur-lined hat that he had been handed. Harris's head thumped in agony and he desperately needed water – not an overcoat, and in any event it was still rather clement. He shook his head at the man with the coat, waving him off irritably and strode towards Fisher hissing.

'Christ alive…'

He shook his head. It was going to be all right. It really was. They *would* find Drabble and they would *somehow* rescue him, if still strictly necessary. Harris, after all, had the mad monk's revolver, or whatever he was. Just then he swore as he watched his bag fall from the side of the donkey, after being incompetently attached. There was a cry from the guide and shouts from his partner. O Lord, thought Harris. These people… I can't cope. He turned away and looked back down towards the road. If these people weren't competent to do a clove hitch they couldn't be trusted to take them up a ruddy mountain. He turned back to confront the landmass before them, most of it lost in a gloomy grey fug. Christ alive. He glanced back and his eye fell on Fisher – now remonstrating with the guides, one of whom was berating another – and Harris once again doubted the whole set-up.

What's in it for you, pal?

What's in it for you, Fisher? You don't traverse Turkey for nothing. Well, I wouldn't. Presumably he was doing it for the story: the faintest chance that the Ark or something else newsworthy might be at the heart of all this nonsense. Now there was nothing wrong with obeying that impulse. *But… but…* Harris bit his lip. He sensed that this was not the case, or not entirely. He couldn't be sure, of course. He had no basis for his suspicion, but… He felt the mass of Yurttas's revolver in his jacket pocket. If it came to it, he would use it, even on Fisher if had to. Mind you, he suspected that he'd be more likely to be hit with it, than actually to pull the trigger and hit someone else.

Fisher turned from arguing with the donkeymen, and met Harris's lingering gaze.

'Everything OK?'

'Rather.' Harris forced his best jovial smile. 'Raring to go, what?'

The American frowned and nodded.

'Don't worry, Harris. We'll lick these clowns into shape, you'll see.'

Harris hoped so. For now he had doubts about the whole situation. And doubts were apt to make him drink, and even he knew that he did quite enough of that already. Fisher returned to the guides, now fussing around the bags and the beasts of burden, and all seemingly arguing with one another. Fisher started shouting.

'Lunch? No, no, *no!* We need to go.' He gesticulated towards the higher ground. 'The MOUNTAIN. There's not a moment to lose!'

It did no good. The guides began undoing their bundles and jabbering at one another. They produced loaves of bread… Harris rolled his eyes. Christ alive. There was nothing to be done. He perched on a boulder and took out his pipe. They would have to wait. But now he thought about it – as the

AFTER THE FLOOD

guide who had first spoken to him began to set out the foodstuffs – he remembered that he was rather peckish: ruddy starving in fact, and one absolutely needed sustenance before one took on such a thing as a mountain. It was just common sense, what?

General Siviloglu had ordered a halt while rations were distributed. After half an hour they then pressed on, in order to take full advantage of the daylight. They climbed for several more hours before stopping for the night in the late afternoon, it being an hour's work to set up camp, something not best done in the half-light. And then there were preparations for the evening meal, the lighting of fires and so on.

Drabble was summoned to Siviloglu's tent for dinner – a robust mutton stew that would win no plaudits for its culinary finesse but was welcome after the physical exertions of the day. Drabble had Celik on his left and Sahin on his right.

The flap of the tent was brought back and one of the German soldiers entered and spoke into Hauptman's ear. The major frowned as he nodded, and after a brief exchange dismissed the soldier with a curt nod.

'That's the scouting party back,' he announced to Siviloglu across the table. 'One of the men is missing.'

Siviloglu looked up from his meal with mild interest.

'What's happened?'

The German officer raised his eyebrows. 'He must have wandered off and fallen – it's the only explanation.'

Siviloglu considered this.

'Might he have found his way back down?'

Hauptman looked doubtful but the reply came from Sahin.

'That would be foolish, General.' He tore a piece of bread between his fingers. 'There are crevasses everywhere. I've warned the men about this. It's vital to stay on the path. Major, remind your men.'

The German officer glowered over at Sahin. He did not, evidently, appreciate receiving a lecture from the Turkish guide.

'I am confident that my men know what a crevasse looks like, Sahin. They would not be that careless…'

The guide bridled at that – his whole frame tensing angrily – but he held his tongue. Drabble looked speculatively at Hauptman. It would be one thing taking orders from Siviloglu, at least he was a general, a decorated Great War veteran and a senior politician, but such condescension from a smelly Anatolian peasant – as he would see it – like Sahin was quite another. In fact it was precisely the sort of thing that would stick in a Nazi's craw.

Siviloglu's voice cut through the silence.

'Major, you must remind your men to be careful, as Sahin has said. Now,' he pushed away his plate and took up his wine glass, 'I think we should have some entertainment.'

He looked over significantly at his female companion, who dutifully bowed her head and then rose, wordlessly from the table. The stewards cleared the meal things away, replacing them with a tray of cigars, cigarettes and snuff, and ashtrays, along with a selection of liqueurs in cut-glass decanters all produced as if in gentlemen's club in St James's and not halfway up a mountain in deepest Anatolia. The stove in the corner was primed with fresh logs and the tent was soon filled with heat, smoke and chatter. The entrance flap went back and several men came in clutching small instruments and sat cross-legged at the floor; that's when Drabble realised what was about to happen. The tent flap was drawn back again, permitting another gust of cold air to probe the heat, and the girl returned, this time swathed from head to

AFTER THE FLOOD

foot in a hooded cloak. An expectant hush fell across the party.

The cloak dropped from her shoulders and she kicked away her shoes, leaving her standing before the party in what might politely be described as her underclothes. The bare parts of her body were adorned with necklaces and bangles including a golden string of coins and decorative stones suspended around her waist from her hips.

A small gem was lodged in her navel. In the lamplight her milky-coloured skin was velveteen. Drabble saw that for all of his presumed fantasies about racial superiority, Major Hauptman's hungry gaze was fixed on the woman's generous breasts, which were compressed within a skimpy flesh-coloured brassiere.

The music began, offering a whiney, light beat and providing pulsating syncopation. The girl extended her lithe arms to her sides, her wrists flicking in time to the music, as her hips began to sway. Her hands began to spin circles above her head and then the pace of the music quickened, and her hips started to circle as she circled the table, dwelling before each of the men in turn, meeting their eyes momentarily, before moving along. Reaching Sahin, the girl greeted his broad U-shaped grin with a smirk before turning away before him, and then, slowly drawing away the silken cloth wrapped around her waist. She stretched her hands into the air and began to vibrate her torso, the music reaching a new pinnacle. The men fell silent, until Sahin exploded with laughter – and the table followed.

The girl span around, landing in front of Drabble, collecting his eyes, her shoulders thrown back and her navel shaking invitingly. The coins and stones caught the lamplight and rattled with sensual possibility. Drabble's gaze ran down the shimmering contours of her body, locating the small thong, and followed the muscular contours of her thighs to her knees, shins, feet and toes, where he decided to keep his gaze.

The woman moved on and the dance continued until she arrived at last at Siviloglu, where she stopped and the music once again began to intensify – but not all at once. As before she spun around, before facing Siviloglu, her feet splayed and her knees close to his. Her gyrating hips began to form an ellipse, thrusting towards him as her nimble hands worked above her head. The coins and stones suspended from her hips whipped and flew, glinting in the light; in the background the whine of music became louder and intensified. She crabbed towards Siviloglu – her knees now touching his, her pelvis plunging in a diving circle just inches from him.

Siviloglu sat impassively, his unblinking stroking her body. At length he withdrew his cigar, his small mouth fixed, terse, flat, and efficient-looking, as if he were inspecting a military inventory. Then, the corner of his mouth briefly flickered, like a bad poker player bluffing over a royal flush, and Drabble saw Siviloglu snatch away a tear. The girl saw it and tossed her chin and the hint of a smile arrived at her mouth. Stepping backwards, she flung out her arms, her chest heaving as she regained her breath.

With the exception of Siviloglu, the table broke into rapturous applause, as the cloak was replaced and the girl stepped out into the night.

Siviloglu dabbed his eye with his napkin and rose from the table.

'We leave at dawn.'

There was a shout and Drabble was awake. It was not morning. He heard another shout and could not tell if it was German or Turkish. Then another. Drabble snatched up his boots and overcoat and emerged just as a figure sprinted past

AFTER THE FLOOD

him in the darkness – Hauptman, he was sure of it. Then a shout cut through the clamour. 'Halt!'

A high-calibre rifle shot boomed through the air – it will have been heard for miles around. The muzzle flash showed several figures fleeing in the far distance. Turning the corner of the kitchen tent, a group of Germans was being issued with lanterns; then Drabble saw immediately the cause of the alarm – the donkeys had vanished. All of them. The Turkish donkey chap stood there bawling his eyes out and gesticulating out into the darkness, sobbing. A pair of breathless soldiers came running into the camp.

The thieves were gone, they reported – and so were the donkeys. They looked like hill farmers, the men said, and had lost them in the dark. Then the first soldier turned to the second, who glanced over his shoulder, as if looking for something.

'What is it?' demanded Hauptman.

'Ganshof,' replied the soldier. 'Where's Ganshof?'

The third man who went out after the donkey thieves was found three hours later after an extensive search of the area. A leather strap – evidently from German military issue webbing – was found near the top of a broad crevasse about sixty yards from the camp. It was deduced from the footsteps in the snow that had fallen in, and eventually his body was spotted at deep in the snow below.

'As I said,' sighed Sahin to Drabble. 'Ararat is a greedy mountain. The Germans need to stop running around in the dark.' His tone suggested his warnings had so far gone unheeded.

The loss of the beasts of burden seemed to be a more significant blow than the loss of the poor Ganshof and occasioned a change of plan. Essential pieces of kit were now distributed among the men – either in backpacks or on litters carried between soldiers. The otherwise unemployed donkeymen were now pressed into helping to carry the gear that their charges had formerly borne, while Celik had a massive cooking pot on his back.

A dozen Germans, meanwhile, were tasked with staying behind to guard what remained of the camp – which included Siviloglu's grand tent and all its paraphernalia, including desk and dining table. Among the various items left behind were also the girl, whether this was for her own safety or some other reason, Drabble did not know. They would be spared more belly dances for the duration of this expedition, however.

The reduced column made slow progress, having lost nearly half the day and ascended through low lying cloud, which was cold. The snow was not thick underfoot, a blessing, but it was icy and compacted, so it was not difficult to slip over or lose one's footing. The air was heavy with damp. As expected, the temperature was falling too – by several degrees Fahrenheit for every hundred yards or so that they climbed. As a result their bodies were now working harder than before, and not just because they were carrying their kit.

While the ground was not steep – not compared to what Drabble was used to in the Alps – the constant gradient was arduous and, together with the cold, the lunch stop was welcome when it came. The soldiers threw down their packs gratefully and broke out their rations. Small fires were lit for hot drinks.

Drabble sat by a fire with Siviloglu, Celik, Sahin and Hauptman – along with the other German officers while stewards served them lunch. It was not a cheerful party, and for several minutes Siviloglu stared gloomily into the fog.

AFTER THE FLOOD

'We are not moving quickly enough,' he pronounced to Sahin. 'We need to get to the Ark location today. Is that possible?'

Sahin made a blowing motion with his lips communicating doubt. Hauptman cut in.

'If you order us to get there today, General, then it is possible.'

The guide's eyes flashed angrily.

'Have you forgotten about the crevasses already? We cannot continue after dark. We can barely see as it is for the cloud.'

'Exactly – ' Siviloglu pounced on this comment. 'So the darkness changes it little. We have lanterns. We will use torches. If everyone keeps to the path we will be able to continue, no?'

Sahin hesitated. It was clear that he did not want to go against Siviloglu, but he was far from willing. That was plain. The guide took out his hipflask and contemplated it before meeting Siviloglu's gaze.

'As you wish, General.'

A smile arrived at Hauptman's face and Sahin took a swig. He snatched up a piece of schnitzel from the platter and heaved himself to his feet.

'If you want to traverse the summit before the end of the day, General, then we'll need to get moving. Hauptman, give me two good men. I'll go ahead now and start to scout our route. I'll send one of them back to fetch you in half an hour. General, I advise you give the order to move as soon as possible.'

He shouldered his pack and plodded away. Hauptman received a nod from Siviloglu and immediately rose and started barking instructions. A pair of soldiers, still chewing, grabbed their packs and charged after the guide who was fast disappearing from view.

When Hauptman returned, Siviloglu got to his feet. 'It's imperative that we get started on our search of the location tomorrow.'

'Yes General!'

Siviloglu tossed the remainder of his coffee into the fire.

'Come on,' he said. 'Let's go!'

It did not take long for Harris to remember that he was no mountaineer or, indeed, fell-walker. On the contrary, the repetitive and strenuous aspects of hill-walking held little attraction for him. The views were magnificent, but as well as being tiring and cold – and not conducive to drinking – it was all just a bit boring. Now, polo or shooting, or cricket, was more his thing. A few exciting minutes and then it was all over and you could head to the bar for a top-up.

He groaned as the cloud swathing the highest elevations of the mountain shifted, showing an unknown and expected mass which had so far not revealed itself. Christ alive, whenever he looked at it, the top ruddy well never got any closer.

He sighed, looking ahead to Fisher's back, and reflected on how he was beginning to despise the sight of it. Why was he always at the back? His legs weren't shorter than Fishers, or were they? No, no…

And where was Ernest? Surely, they should have found him by now? Surely? If he was really up here, wouldn't it have been blindingly obvious? Wouldn't there have been footprints or signs of another party? And what were they going to do when they found them? Whatever Fisher's swagger, it would not be straightforward, and it would likely be dangerous.

He paused and got his breath back. And Christ alive, he was tired. Positively done for. His legs were like lead. Wet lead at that. Lead that had been soaked in a peaty bog for ten

AFTER THE FLOOD

years before being smothered in glue and then sprinkled with lead dust.

He ambled on and glared at Fisher and the guides. It would be nice to stop for a pipe or a cigarette. But it was probably too soon to stop again. Looming ahead of him, was a bigger question, something that had been nagging at him for some time: what would they have for supper? He couldn't imagine anything especially palatable emerging from the bedraggled party of local donkey-drivers and guides; maybe some tough old goat, if he was lucky. His eye fell on the grubby-looking packs heaped up on the backs of the rearmost donkey; oh, that it was filled with jars of caviar, and methuselahs of Krug!

Hah! He growled. It was just too bad. This was no way to travel. Where was the wagon train? Where was the legion of native bearers? Surely, they should be *riding* the ruddy donkeys and the guides be carrying the baggage? After all, these fellows were suited to the conditions, the altitude. They were acclimatised, weren't they? And if they weren't, they weren't doing their ruddy jobs properly. Harris cursed. Twenty years ago he'd have been carried up in a sedan chair like a god. He swore under this breath and called out.

'Hey – Fisher!' The American paused and turned.

'How long have we been going for since lunch?'

Fisher made an ostentatious show of checking his wristwatch.

'About forty-five minutes, Harris.'

Harris scowled. 'Really? It can't be.'

Fisher rolled his eyes. 'Come on–' Harris nodded reluctantly and pressed on, raising his hand in defeat. The things he did for Ernest…

Chapter Twenty-one

The cloud that had enveloped Siviloglu's party for the whole day was finally dissipating and by the time dusk fell a great glacier had emerged out of the gloom. It had a subliminal brilliance to it that made it stand out from the grubby snow lying all around, a luminous quality – giving a sense, almost of power and magnificence, that it was a living thing in its own right. Which, supposed Drabble, on a certain level, it was. This was the glacier that covered the top of the mountain and over which they would have to pass on their way to the top of the Ahora Gorge. They were probably now half a mile from the summit and were they to walk on, regardless, in a straight line, they could be there within the hour or so. But by then it would be pitch black and well below freezing and men that had been walking for most of the day would be exhausted. In truth, if it were up to Drabble they would have stopped thirty minutes ago.

The vanguard halted and Drabble, followed by Celik, caught up with Sahin who was at the front with Siviloglu. They broke off their discussions when he arrived.

'We move on,' determined Siviloglu. He called out: 'Hauptman!'

The guide turned his toes to the incline.

It would be dark sooner than they thought. They ought to be looking for somewhere to camp for the night, presumably was Sahin's position. The temperature had been falling all day as they climbed, but it would fall far more steeply as the sun disappeared. Not just that but many of the men had been carrying the additional kit on top of the rigours of the ascent; what's more, if Drabble knew anything, then it was that people who were tired tended to have more accidents – and glaciers were by definition places where accidents could happen. There was ice – lots of it, and crevasses, of course –

socking great fissures in the ice that could gobble up men like Sahin's father or the poor Ganshof. The trouble was that in the seeping darkness, these holes in the ground tended to look very much like the ground itself.

The only salvation lay in following the man in front, religiously sticking to the same path, and hoping that he had not been the last to tread on a piece of weakening ice that your own footprint would be the first to go through.

The snow grew deeper and heavy as their shins kicked through it. The cold bit in deeper so that your knuckles felt through the gloves and your face began to feel sore and like it wasn't quite your own. Mercifully the gradient was no steeper but it was more arduous. After twenty more minutes Sahin came to another stop and pointedly lit a lantern, showing everyone whose eyes were adjusting to the gloom just how dark it had become. Bathed in yellow light he now lowered the lantern to show a broad crevasse crossing their path. The cavity glistened ominously, hungrily, like a mouth in the ground. It was an open question which way was better to go around it – and without being able to see it the only safe way was simply to walk it, to follow the mouth of the abyss until one could safely skirt it.

Sahin turned abruptly from the crevasse towards Siviloglu and Hauptman, who were bunched up behind. Drabble kept a few yards further back.

'We stop here for the night. It's too dangerous to continue. We must rest.'

The General nodded, deciding not to overrule the guide, and Hauptman began organising his men. Within minutes tents were going up and fires were being lit.

Up head lights shimmered in the misty gloom. Night was falling fast, shading the last of the sky's blue to black. Several hundred yards further along the path, they saw the warm glow of lanterns and a large fire with shadowy figures moving around it. Harris could distinctly hear something else, too. He lifted his ear in concentration, not quite believing what he could hear.

Merriment. Not just that, ruddy singing. In German. He and Fisher exchanged worried glances and scampered after their guides and the baggage.

Fisher hissed at the guides.

'*Durmak! Geri, geri!*'

He made large shooing gestures at the guides who slowly stopped and then quickly began to retreat. Fisher, satisfied that the guides were moving in the right direction, turned to Harris, 'Now let's get a closer look.'

Keeping low they approached the encampment, pausing every now and then to take stock and ensure they had not been observed. They could see several men in military fatigues gathered around a campfire. They were drinking and smoking, and judging by their volume and the way one of them was lurching about, they had clearly taken on board a fair amount already. Harris spoke in a whisper.

'They're definitely Krauts.'

Fisher was looking at them through a pair of binoculars.

'And they're drunk. I don't speak German but I can spot slurred speech in any language.'

'They're positively roasted,' observed Harris enviously.

Fisher nodded. 'Could this be Drabble's party?'

'Well, I can't *see* Drabble…'

'I count five – no, six men at most. There are an awful lot of tents, though. More than half a dozen men need.' His tone was doubtful. Whatever it was,

Harris was inclined to agree with him.

'They look like they're in uniform – that's johnny's got a greatcoat on and those hats are distinctly military.'

Fisher lowered the binoculars. 'Yes, but I don't see any military badges.'

'It's dark.'

AFTER THE FLOOD

'Yep. But they aren't wearing any.'

'They're definitely squareheads, though.'

'Categorically. I can see a swastika and German eagle on one of the tents which is a big give-away.'

'Certainly is.' Harris was suddenly feeling rather blindsided. 'So, what do we think a bunch of drunk German soldiers are doing up Ararat?'

'Apart from having a party?' Fisher lowered his binoculars. 'Search me, but I'm sure they're up to no good.'

'Do you think they're involved?'

'What? In this Drabble business?' He shrugged. 'I struggle to see how it's a coincidence, but who knows?'

'Well, we can't see Drabble, but who's to say he's not in a prisoner in one of the tents? What do you want to do? Assume it's a coincidence and go around them?'

Fisher shook his head. 'I don't fancy that in the dark. We leave the path in darkness at our peril, I say.'

'But we can't very well stay here and light a fire, because they'll see us and then, if they are involved, we've had it.'

Fisher cleared his throat.

'I think the only option is to wait for them to pass out and then get by them at a safe distance. In the morning we move off at first light – at which point they'll all still be too drunk and hung over to be a threat. Chances are they'll still be asleep.'

Harris nodded. 'Judging by the singing we shouldn't have to wait too long for them.'

They had to endure two more hours of German singing and a flatulent extravaganza of competitive burping during which time Harris smoked twelve cigarettes. Eventually the last of the Germans finally yielded to the inevitable and fell silent during the middle of a ballad of some sort. They decided to give it five minutes before approaching – by which point the sound of snoring began to emanate from the camp.

'Thank the Lord,' sighed Harris, as the singing finally abated. 'This must have been what it was like on the Western Front. It wasn't the Jerry howitzers that made the poor Tommies go potty – it was the singing.'

They advanced towards the camp; two fires burned low in the midst of the encampment, providing some illumination of the target. They kept close to the line of the path.

Aside from the noise of at least two identifiable patterns of intense, booze-soaked snoring the only sound was the wind rattling cans or canvas or the creak of straining guy ropes. They passed through a rather eerie, darkened tent village, one that was seemingly abandoned. Here and there were dotted disordered packs of kit or stacks of boxes – some of them left open, giving the place the semblance of a basecamp of sorts. Harris noticed more swastikas stamped on things. There was no doubting the nationality of this lot.

Even the empty bottles of beer littering the place were German pilsner. They were now past the middle of the camp and had not been detected. At this rate they should able to make it pass successfully.

Suddenly a long woman's cry split the air, followed by a snarl – drunken, guttural and loaded with anger.

Harris stopped and turned.

There came another shout, something inaudible, and then another roar, one that was more akin to a growl.

Harris broke from the convoy and dashed towards the midst of the tented compound. He heard another growl close by – so close that he could almost smell the German pilsner on its breath. His roved from tent to tent – and his eye caught a light. That moment he heard the sound of tearing fabric and knew exactly where it came from. Before he had time to think, he charged into the tent and roared…

'HALT!'

The assailant before him froze … for a split second. He then spun round, confronting Harris, and stood up to reveal

AFTER THE FLOOD

his full height. The crown of his bald head was almost pressed into the ceiling of the tent. Beyond, Harris glimpsed a slight figure huddled on the bed and then looked up at the man now towering over him. Just his bulging jaw muscles looked like they could snap a swan's wing, while his abnormally developed torso was covered in a mosaic of violent-looking tattoos. Swastikas, swooping eagles and pickelhaubes formed an obscene human fresco. And then Harris noticed that the chap's flies were undone. The man was muttering angrily at him in indecipherable German – clearly he was very drunk, but evidently still in possession of enough coordination to put his glorious temperament into action. He lurched towards Harris.

Harris's first impulse was to flee – but then he remembered Yurttas's revolver.

'Halt!' he barked, pulling the gun free from his coat pocket. The Kraut wasn't convinced and lunged, sending his enormous hands arcing forward to seize Harris and presumably snap his spine like a twig under a boot.

Harris stepped back. The Johnny was drunk, thank God, but nonetheless Harris's courage was evaporating faster than a pink gin in the Hindu Kush. He lifted the gun up and said in his loudest, meanest voice:

'Halt!'

It came out like a whimper. And now he could see the whites of the Jerry's bloodshot eyes and the anger and fury in them. Harris knew he had to act. He had to shoot. There was possibly a split second before he was about to be strangled to death or beaten to it. *Christ, do something!* Harris's cerebellum caught up with reality just as the giant was on him.

Harris held out the gun and pulled the trigger, a reflex rather than a decision. The noise was ear-splitting and the flash of the muzzle was blinding in the confines of the tent. There was a high-pitched cry and as the smoke dissipated, leaving behind a cloud of sulphur and cordite, the beast from black forest lay slumped on the floor before him, blood seeping from his exorbitant shaven cranium.

Standing over him on the end of the bed was a girl. Grasped in her hand a small bronze bust of Hitler, bloodied on its face. But Harris wasn't interested in the bust, so to speak. Because it wasn't just any girl, it was *the girl* – the girl from the night to remember forever on Havyar Sokak. Yasmin. And she was standing right there on the side of this perishing mountain, *and* she was every bit as beautiful as the creature who had haunted his dreams since Sunday. It couldn't be. But it was.

They locked eyes. Harris broke into a broad smile, birdsong erupting in his ears. He rushed forward to embrace her – and stumbled straight over the felled Kraut. Collapsing on top of Yasmin, she cried out in pain.

She was bleeding.

'My God!' Harris pulled back, his eyes finding the source of the blood – her upper arm. 'You're hurt!'

'Yes Harreez. You shot me!'

It wasn't so much an accusation as a simple statement of exasperation.

'Oh, God… I'm sorry, *I'm so sorry.*'

Harris was on the brink of tears, but that wouldn't do. He pulled out his handkerchief and pressed it to the wound. She flinched, but was brave, gritting her teeth as he bandaged her arm.

'There,' he said, shooting her a winning smile (he was rather proud of his medical endeavours), and meeting her gaze. 'How will I ever make it up to you?'

Yasmin arched an eyebrow and her broad, delicious mouth widened invitingly. Harris broke into a salty chuckle.

'I don't believe it…'

They started to kiss and rolled onto to the bed, the girl moaning and pulling urgently at her clothing…

AFTER THE FLOOD

Harris heard footsteps approach but didn't stop. It was Fisher.

'Harris!' he hissed.

Harris didn't respond. The world could go to pot. The girl was now moaning his name.

'*Harreez!*'

'HARRIS!'

Harris felt someone grabbing at his foot and kicked out savagely. He shouted and turned to see Fisher at the end of the bed, a German submachine gun slung over his shoulder. He had also acquired some useful-looking army-issue sheepskin mittens and a hat.

'Put your pecker away, Harris. Stay focused. You've done your heroics – now let's get out of here before the rest of these squarehead bozos wake up. Bring the girl if you want to. *Come on*!'

Fisher strutted from the tent and Harris returned his attention to the Yasmin. *Stay focused.* Good point. Yasmin had pulled the blanket over her, and lay smiling at him. She started to draw back the covers…

'Stop –' He raised his hand like a policeman on Piccadilly. 'Tell me… what are you doing here, half-way up Mount Ararat – not to mention with a bunch of drunk Kraut soldiers?'

But, of course, he knew the answer, or at least part of it – namely that it had something to do with the snap-happy, dodgy-eyed cove he had seen her with outside her flat.

Yasmin held his gaze and then, with an irritated grunt, threw aside the bedcovers. 'Come Hareez, your friend is right... we must leave before *this* –' She glared down at the smitten German soldier – 'vakes up.'

The girl pinched up a vest and pulled it down over her breasts.

'B-but are you going to tell me why you're up here or not? What's going on?'

She set about sliding her hips into a pair of slacks.

'I say,' said Harris, not appreciating being ignored.

She placed a finger on his lips. 'All in good time, Hareez. Now –' She handed him Hitler. 'Keep an eye on this moron and don't be afraid to use the Fuhrer if you have. I'll get my things.'

She finished dressing and pressed a few personal items in a small, bag while Harris kept guard, Hitler in one hand, Yurttas's revolver in the other.

Moments later they found the rest of Harris's group waiting for them at the far end of the camp. Moving fast, they continued, the stars now shining brilliantly in the gaps between the clouds. Harris and Yasmin followed behind Fisher and the guides with their donkeys. Like Fisher, both Harris and Yasmin had acquired thick winter gloves and fur-hats from the German camp and beneath the thick fur lining Harris's mind swirled with questions. Not the least of these was what on earth, quite, was going on. But first, he needed to know if she had seen Drabble.

The question was met with a cautious nod. Then Yasmin threw her chin in the direction of the peak.

'They are one day ahead at most.'

Harris contained his excitement, 'And where are they going?'

'Close to the summit. The Ahora Gorge. Your guides will know it. It's the place where Mehmet think the Ark is.'

Harris halted, as his brain unravelling her statement.

'Hang on. So, the Johnny with the funny coloured eyes that I saw you with, really thinks he's going to find Noah's Ark?'

The girl broke into a rich laugh and walked on.

'What?'

'You don't know?' She shook her head either with despair or disapproval, he couldn't be sure. 'Come on, Hareez.' She reached for his hand and pulled him along. 'Let me tell you a story…'

AFTER THE FLOOD

They continued for another hour before stopping for the night. As Harris and Yasmin retired to a tent together, he realised that, despite the circumstances, he was happy, undeniably so. Perhaps the happiest he had ever been. But how could he be otherwise? Yasmin was a marvel. In fact, his mind wondered, could she be the one?

Yes, she might be about as English as a croque monsieur. Yes, she didn't come with a moated castle and several thousand prime foxhunting acres in somewhere like Leicestershire? But no one was perfect.

Fact was she was a green-eyed goddess with a figure like a Pacific Island fertility statue. Moreover, she made love like no woman he ever encountered before. But all that seemed to pale when he simply considered, *her*. Harris caught his breath, and looked over. Could this be love? *No, no, no… it was probably altitude sickness, or a species of delirium brought on by physical exhaustion.*

Anyway, Harrises didn't do love, they did matrimonial alliances and lepidoptery. If you saw a butterfly you staked it to a board and framed it – you certainly didn't let the ruddy thing flutter around your tummy.

But the butterflies were undeniable now. Absolutely tumbling they were. Harris turned in his bedclothes and saw the girl, eyes wide, looking at him. She met his gaze. Goodness me. It was altogether the most distracting sensation he had felt in his life. Could this be love?

She smiled at him.

'What is it, Hareez?'

Chapter Twenty-two

A distance away, further up the mountain, Drabble was awoken by the sound of bearish, exultant voices. Cheering it was. Something had happened. Drabble pulled on his boots and overclothes and headed out.

Around the main fire, now died down low, was a ring of soldiers – and at their centre was a young Turkish man, on his knees and under restraint. He was probably no more than twenty, maybe twenty-five and dressed like Sahin in a rough leather jerkin and woollen layers, evidently a variety of regional dress. His cloth cap had been pulled off to reveal a mop of black curly hair. His arms were now pinned back by a brace of the Bavarian engineers, while a third stood examining the blade of a silver dagger. The skinny-looking sergeant was busy stripping down a short-magazine rifle of some description. So the Turk – or whatever he was – had been armed.

Major Hauptman was present, too, but it was his second in command, a young captain named Bloch, who was questioning the prisoner. This was what Drabble had ascertained when Siviloglu arrived, dressed like most in a combination of nightclothes, militaria and mountaineering gear.

The Germans came to attention – and Drabble spotted the prisoner clock Siviloglu and the violently repellent look on his face. Captain Bloch spoke first.

'This man was found prowling around our perimeter, General. He says he was out hunting.'

Siviloglu smiled at that.

'Did he say *what* he was hunting?'

'No, General.'

'Has he confirmed his name or anything else?'

AFTER THE FLOOD

The captain shook his head.

'Well, I'll say this, he is a very well-armed hunter.' Siviloglu reached for the man's rifle and inspected it in the light. 'A French carbine — not a something I would have thought was much use on rabbits – and not something one would pick up at the bazaar in Dogubayazit either.' He handed the rifle back to the sergeant, thunder written across his face. The lightning came soon enough.

Siviloglu addressed the prisoner in Turkish, the note of his voice savage. After the faintest of pauses the prisoner spat his reply – fire with fire, it looked. You didn't need to understand a word of Turkish to know that the man had no intention of cooperating.

Siviloglu nodded, as if reaching the same conclusion and turned towards the fire. Drabble's view was blocked, but he heard a low cheer rise up and when Siviloglu stepped into view, he held out a burning ember from the fire, its glowing tip illuminating the face of the kneeling prisoner. Drabble had seen enough.

'No!'

He shoved his way forward and slammed his fist onto Siviloglu's wrist, sending the flaming ember flying. The general turned to him, disbelief, affront and fury in his eyes. Unseen hands hauled Drabble back and held him fast.

Siviloglu stalked back to the fire and drew out another burning ember – broader, larger and redder than the first. He swept this close to Drabble's face and held it close – the heat coming off it was intense and the woodsmoke clogged his nostrils. 'Do not think that you are untouchable, Professor,' he hissed. 'Do not forget that we have your wife in our care.'

He turned on the balls of his feet to confront the prisoner, whom he again addressed in Turkish. The words were meaningless to Drabble but he could see a question being put – and the tip of the burning stick being pushed close to the prisoner's cheek. The man grimaced – doubtlessly feeling the heat on his skin as Drabble had done – and said nothing. Siviloglu growled out another question at him: still silence.

The general shook his head and issued a growling bark. The soldiers restraining the prisoner braced him, holding his head back by his hair. Siviloglu turned the ember over in the fire and then advanced on the prisoner with the burning rod.

Tssssthssthssss....

The prisoner jerked as a combination of steam and smoke escaped from his lean face. His eyes were shut and no cry emerged from his gritted, contorted mouth. Immediately the stench of burning flesh filled the air.

And then it was over. Siviloglu removed the burning stick and repeated his question to the prisoner. The man's head was now bowed, he was breathing hard, a livid red welt scarred his left cheek. He was muttering under his breath – a prayer or a curse, Drabble could not tell which, shaking his head. Siviloglu turned towards the fire and reached down...

Drabble's temper flared.

'Siviloglu – this is madness. This man is clearly not going to talk. What are you going to do? Kill him?'

The general glared at Drabble, his narrowed eyes cold and full of hatred. The small bank-manager's head was now transformed into something entirely different, something demonic. And Drabble now saw what was going to happen. Bile rose up in his throat and he surged forward but there was no escaping the grip of the soldiers who restrained him.

Siviloglu pulled on a pair of leather gloves and with two hands slowly drew out a metal poker from the fire. Raising it to prisoner, its tip cast a red, penetrating glow on the fearful face. The general bent forward and addressed the man in a low, controlled voice – and then waited, the tip of poker hovering over the man's cheek.

AFTER THE FLOOD

The prisoner clenched his jaw and shook his head. Siviloglu nodded, a vicious cast to his lips.

With the poker poised, the Turk glanced over at Drabble from the corners of his eyes, finding – and briefly – holding his gaze. Sickness swept through Drabble, there was murder in Siviloglu's eyes.

The general grunted with effort and jammed the poker into the prisoner's eye. Blood spat out, followed by the crunch of bone as Siviloglu hammered the end of poker deep into the man's brain. Blood jetted from the prisoner's head and his lifeless body fell forward, taking the poker with it. Siviloglu tore off his bloodied gloves and tossed them into the fire.

'Hauptman! Dispose of this vermin and send out a patrol to see if there are any more rats out there. Double the guard.'

'*Jawohl*, General!'

As the major began issuing orders and men scampered back and forth, Siviloglu turned to Drabble. 'You see Professor, any obstacles in our path will be ruthlessly eliminated.'

'You just killed a man in cold blood, Siviloglu.'

'And what of it, Professor?' growled Siviloglu. 'Compared to our objective – finding the Ark – that Kurd's life is meaningless. *Was* meaningless. You would do well to remember that.' Drabble wondered how he could ever forget it. 'Anyway –' The general's eyes glistened triumphantly in the yellow light from the fire. 'Haven't you always wanted to see what happens when you spear a man in the eyeball with a red-hot poker?'

Drabble looked away. On the far side of the fire, Sahin was watching. The flames caught an expression of disgust on his bearded face, utter disgust.

Chapter Twenty-three

By six in the morning the men at Siviloglu's camp were clustered around fires eating porridge. The patrol sent out after the interrogation of the prisoner had evidently found no one else to bring back and torture. Drabble, under Celik's close watch, sat on a bench at a narrow table eating his breakfast, watching the stewards seeing to their tasks and the men pack away the tents.

Sahin joined Drabble at the bench, his distinctive smell of body odour, stale tobacco and whisky announcing him. They ate in silence for a moment before Drabble heard the man's gruff, heavily accented voice, low in his ear.

'You will know that I have no liking for your people, *Ingilizce*.'

Drabble lifted his eyebrows in ironical surprise – but resisted the temptation to make eye contact with his interlocuter. Instead he stared ahead at a German private sitting opposite him and waited for Sahin to continue. The words came soon enough from the corner of his mouth.

'You people have brought nothing but misery to mine. You know that? You English promised us a homeland in 1920 – and then you stole it from us in 1923.' Drabble looked and saw pain in Sahin's expression.

'You're a Kurd?'

The guide nodded.

'My countrymen have a lot to answer for.'

'Pah!' The guide took a spoonful of porridge. 'You weren't the only ones. No one wanted the Kurds to get their own homeland.' He brushed the air aside with his hand. 'It is past. What I wanted to say is that what you did earlier was brave. And right.'

'It didn't do much good.'

AFTER THE FLOOD

'True. But at least you tried. In life that is the better half the battle.'

Drabble scraped at this bowl.

'I don't suppose you have any idea who the poor devil was?'

Sahin shook his head, 'He will not have been acting alone, so we can expect more.'

'More?'

Sahin nodded in affirmation as he spooned the last of his breakfast from his bowl. 'That's right, *Ingilizce*.' He got up from the bench and they exchanged a parting glance, a thin smile on the weather-bitten face. 'So, watch your back.'

Harris and his party were already on the move. They had left before dawn, and breakfasted on a gritty slices of flatbread smeared with sweet walnut jam as they travelled. Not only could they not risk the possibility of revenge-crazed, hungover German soldiers coming for them – especially after finding their pal with the Hitler-shaped impression on his scalp – but they were also, don't forget, on race to catch up with Drabble and a crazy Turk who was hell-bent on finding the Ark. So every minute counted.

The trouble was that walking was bloody monotonous. Even in a good cause. Short walks, to the pub, for instance, were fine, although driving was strictly preferable. But walking up Ararat was worse, much worse, than anything Harris had attempted before because of the gradient, which while not steep as such, was unremitting. And the bloody thing just kept on going forever. That's right, he thought bitterly, Ararat went on forever.

But the wind had died down a bit. And the stony ground was giving way to snow, a sign of progress. They must be near the top now.

Thirty yards went by and he could see further into the distance. Christ alive. Up it went, as far as the ruddy eye could see. And he knew enough about hill walking to know that whenever you could see the top, it never was, and that there was always another peak lurking behind it to rob you of all hope.

He sighed and reached out to take Yasmin's hand. She smiled, and smiled back.

'You wanted to know about the man you saw me with outside my apartment?'

Harris gave her hand an encouraging squeeze.

'His name is General Mehmet Siviloglu –' She looked down at her feet. 'He is a warrior, a politician.'

'What does he want with the Ark?'

'He thinks he can find it and become a national hero – then use it to become prime minister and restore the monarchy.'

So just what Yurttas had told him.

'And why are the Germans involved?'

'Because Hitler wants to find Noah's Ark.'

'Hitler?' Harris stopped in his tracks and stood blinking in disbelief. 'Just a second.' His eye fell on Fisher, the donkeys and the guides plodding on ahead. 'What in the name of God does that haemorrhoidal berk want with Noah's Ark?'

The girl shrugged and pulled at his hand to keep going.

'Well it can't be good,' sighed Harris, as he moved off. Adolf Hitler, Leon Trotsky, Noah's ruddy Ark... even allowing for Ernest's recent escapades this beano took the biscuit.

Hitherto the Bavarian soldiers had worn their rifles in slings over their
shoulders. Now, following the events of the night before, those that weren't burdened by baggage, progressed with their weapons at the ready. They were on high alert.

AFTER THE FLOOD

The pyramidical summit of Ararat now loomed over them, tantalisingly close. Rising some six hundred metres above, the great summit was a beastly, Moby Dick white and ridged to the point deeply like the pinched mouth of a deeply committed smoker. As their destination lay on the far side of the mountain, in a plateau above the Ahora Gorge, there was no need to reach the peak, so they were skirting around it instead. This saved them a steep ascent and the best part of a half-day's detour, too. More's the pity, thought Drabble, as he gazed up at the summit, close enough almost to touch it. The climb would have sorted the men from the boys.

Even down here the wind whipped around the face of the mountain, blowing up clouds of stinging, biting ice.

Drabble shielded his eyes, feeling the weight of altitude in a dull headache that had persisted since they set off that morning. Altitude sickness was an old and unwelcome acquaintance. It made you feel rotten, less than yourself, like the way a bad cold does. In extreme it could be more debilitating than that, but mostly it just brought you down. It certainly didn't make you feel very heroic – far from it. If anything, it caused you close in on yourself, to simply get your head down and not do much else. It was the moment for endurance, if you had it. Bad luck if you didn't.

As well as a grinding headache, altitude sickness manifested itself in a mild sense of dizziness and a nausea which dented Drabble's appetite for lunch, slowing his progress. But he was not alone. Their footsteps had become noticeably more sluggish the higher they got, all contributing to the sensible decision to avoid the summit and those hardest yards, especially when all they would do is sap their strength for the principal objective.

And it was cold. The higher up they were, of course, the colder it got, and as the chill intensified you had to be sure that it didn't get hold of you. Certainly not when you were a quarter dumb from altitude sickness.

In the distance, seemingly level them, Drabble saw the stunted pinnacle of Lesser Ararat poking through the cloud, like a small island in a white sea of fog. In point of fact it was still enormous as mountains go – standing three thousand six hundred metres or nearly twelve thousand feet. Enormous, but just not as enormous as Ararat herself. Below them somewhere beneath the cloud on their right would be the top of the Ahora Gorge, which ran in easterly direction for more than five miles and, Sahin told him, was a mile deep.

Up ahead he could see Sahin leading them down a deep descending ridge as the landscape fell away steeply to their right. This would presumably lead down to the top of the gorge or the plateau before it. Descending ought do wonders for altitude sickness – every hundred metres should help, but there wasn't, sadly, a directly linear relationship between height and recovery. From up here the landscape below looked featureless, a white and grey mass, but that disguised the steep changes in topography. Drabble focused on following in the snow-packed path of the man in front. It was now just a question of waiting for the altitude sickness to lift.

They were now higher up than he had been on the North Face of the Eiger, they were higher even than the summit of Mont Blanc — peaks that felt so much more exposed, so much more inhospitable, so much closer to the stars. Yet because Ararat rose like a monolith from the vast eastern Anatolian plateau it was unlike anything in the Alps. From up here the world was grey, rambling and showing only hints of human habitation as far as the bending horizon. What was certain, however, was that if ten thousand years ago there really had been a great deluge then you could not miss the fact that Ararat was a gigantic natural lifeboat, regardless of whether it could float or not. If there had been a great flood,

AFTER THE FLOOD

then at five thousand metres you would have kept your feet drier here than anywhere else. Drabble looked back, seeing the higher ground rising up surprisingly steeply behind them. His head was beginning to clear.

Up at the front, leading the winding snake of men, strode Siviloglu with a cleft stick for support. He was followed by Sahin and Hauptman, his frame taller, leaner.

That morning's hike had given Drabble plenty of time to reflect upon Siviloglu's nocturnal act of brutality – not least the sadistic pleasure that he had clearly taken in it. There was no trusting a man who placed such a small value on life. Plainly, if Drabble didn't do what was asked of him, Siviloglu would have no hesitation in killing him – and then Charlotte would follow. The trouble – as well Drabble knew – was that even if he *did* do exactly what Siviloglu asked of him, then the Turk would still have no hesitation in killing him. And then Charlotte too.

Fortunately, as every historian knew, there was no such thing as inevitability. Drabble consoled himself with this thought and then with another: an opportunity would arise, it would. And doubtlessly the mountain would help before long.

What, for instance, would happen if a crevasse claimed Siviloglu's life? That, surely, was not inconceivable nor beyond the wit of man to accomplish, too, if it came to it? Drabble now knew that he could be the agent of that change, if necessary. And he was sure there would almost certainly be others, not least friends of the dead man, who would want to take that step too. The question was *who*, and whether or not they would intervene before it was too late?

Beyond the long train of men and provisions, Drabble saw Sahin and Siviloglu stop and the soldiers begin to gather around them. That meant lunch. Good. A rest would be welcome – even if the prospect of food wasn't. Though – you never knew – the altitude sickness might start to shift.

Then as Drabble caught up with the growing knot of men, he saw it. And he realised that they were there: the Ahora Gorge suddenly emerged through the thinning cloud, as if a vast curtain had just been withdrawn. So there it was, a vast gaping void stretching out below them as far as the eye could see beneath the ceiling of mist. It was breathtaking and dizzying. The terrain fell away leaving a drop thousands of feet in depth. It was magnificent.

And this meant that they were here, the very place where Sahin claimed to have seen the Ark when he was a boy and where the Russian pilot and Tsarist engineers believed they had found it too. Notwithstanding the power of suggestion and the powerful potential for self-deception in the human mind, the possibility remained that something might just actually be here, albeit likely under five to ten metres of compacted winter snow. Whether or not that something was Noah's Ark or something else remained to be seen. Surely, however, they would find out in the coming days. And that was an altogether terrifying and exhilarating prospect.

AFTER THE FLOOD

Chapter Twenty-four

Two memories continued to haunt Charlotte after her return to the chintzy, book-lined gulag on the top floor. The first was the sight she had registered of an unattended little sailing boat on the jetty, perhaps a mere hundred and fifty yards from where she stood. It remained a benign portent of liberty and just knowing it was there continued to give her hope. And that was not to be sniffed at: the sensation of the existence of hope left her feeling warmer, stronger, more resolute and somehow more whole and herself. The second memory was the image that persisted in her mind of Andrew Streat, foreshortened by perspective and his in battered panama hat, looking up at her room from the gravelled drive. What he was doing there was not a subject she could possibly discover from the confinement of the room – moreover it was too mind-boggling to contemplate – but the fact was that she, in one respect, now had the upper hand. The knowledge of his involvement gave her a sense of agency, setting back the dehumanising misery of her imprisonment. The question was, could further advantage be made of it?

What would happen, for instance, if Charlotte summoned him? The very act would shatter any delusions he entertained of anonymity in the venture. Would he come – or would she be ignored? Would she get to say, with either drama or tears, or both: '*J'accuse!*'? And what would be the outcome of her revealing this knowledge and in making such an accusation? Her hand went to her navel as her mind registered the inherent danger. There was another possibility: if Streat knew that she knew he was involved then that might seal her fate, in order for him to ensure that secrecy was maintained once whatever it was that had prompted her kidnap was concluded. Therefore, perhaps feigning ignorance was the safest course? After all, their decision to blindfold on her way there and the fact that her gaoler had been wearing a mask all indicated that they wanted to preserve their anonymity. That could only mean that she was to be released at some point. Otherwise why bother?

Did that mean that her escape attempt had left her in greater danger, now that she had seen the face of her gaoler? Charlotte pushed away this darkest thought. *No, no*. They would surely have done away with her already, if that was the case. Yes, that was incontrovertible. But so was the unquantifiable hazard in her initiative. It could, potentially, alter their assessment at a future date, thereby putting her – and Little Ernest – in greater danger. Yes it could.

She sighed and held her head in her hands. But doing nothing is never an option. Not when one has so much time on one's hands. She raised her head. On the credit side of the balance sheet, if Streat were to come, then she could at least talk to him and whatever he said would improve her stock of information immeasurably over what she knew at the moment, which was close to zero. And that was the case even if he deliberately attempted to mislead her, because deception often was revealing in itself. Life had taught her that more often than not lies pointed towards the truth. You had only to look in the wrong direction. Yes, she decided, I'll ask to see Mr Streat, and we'll see what comes of it. She lay back on the sofa, cradling her stomach and imagining the small blue boat with its red sails filled and her at the tiller. Yes, that would do very nicely. Somehow she would reach the boat and then she would be reunited with Ernest. She would.

The Bavarian cooks started dousing the fires and packing up even as lunch was being served. Quickly the snake of fifty or so men and provisions started to descend through the snow

AFTER THE FLOOD

towards the open mouth of the Ahora Gorge, Sahin leading the way. As before, dotted evenly among the procession, were soldiers with weapons at the ready, keeping look-out. Siviloglu was taking no chances. Meanwhile, Celik was also keeping an eye on him.

They were up to their knees in snow and the compacted ice was hard underfoot. The seasonal melt one might expect in May had hardly begun at this height, and as a result finding anything up here would be doubly hard, if not nigh on impossible. Sahin's pessimism on the first night had not been misplaced.

After twenty minutes' descending towards the lip of the vast chasm, the front of the column stopped as Siviloglu and Sahin consulted various maps. The soldiers were disciplined, keeping silent as their leaders considered their position. Several men set down their packs and rested; a couple lit cigarettes. About a dozen stood sentry. Drabble looked down at the gorge – the ground fell away alarmingly, and was then lost from sight until very much further in the distance by which point it was several thousand feet below their position. Drabble didn't fancy descending into that.

The maps were promptly folded away and the soldiers got wearily to their feet, shouldering their packs. Sahin led them in northerly direction, putting the head of the gorge on their right. They proceeded slowly for a mile before stopping in the midst of a broad slope beneath the smaller peak of Kopgel, which stood above them on their left. The gorge opened up several hundred metres on the right. Sahin, Siviloglu and Hauptman stopped and consulted their maps once more.

They must be close.

Drabble checked his wristwatch. He was aware that the fuzziness muddying his brain for the last twelve hours was clearing, something to be grateful for. It was now after four o'clock. The leaders folded away their maps. Hauptman broke from them, and the lithe German sergeant called the soldiers to gather round. So this was it. They had arrived.

It was rather a rum thing but Harris was sure he had a hangover coming on.

It was despite the fact that altogether inexplicably he'd hardly touched a drop all day. He'd had a dram after breakfast, true, to rinse down his coffee and get the old constitution going, and then there had been the snifter of the local gut-rot that the guides had produced. But aside from those two brief tastes and another of the last of the Talisker, he hadn't touched a drop. Mind you, they'd hiked for hours through the ruddy snow, to the point that their toes were ice cubes.

Now he was thawing out in front of the fire, his boots were steaming like the denizens of the Granville's Turkish bath, and his ruddy bonce was throbbing like anything. And he could barely touch his supper either. Right off his tuck, he was. Dash it all, it was beyond him. Besides him, the girl was ravenously devouring a bowlful of goat stew, the sight of which was making him feel queasy. In fact, now he thought about it, he was downright bilious. He stifled a belch and looked away from his untouched plate. What was happening to him?

Wine was the answer, of course. If one had overdone it then a quarter of a pint of Château Margaux will always set you right. And if that didn't fix you then a hefty beaker of Gevrey-Chambertin, Napoleon's favourite tipple don't forget, would put you back on track. That's what sustained the Corsican on the retreat from Moscow and kept him going on Elba. Harris's stomach was turning and he excused himself – the savoury tang of the food was peculiarly distasteful. Standing up, he stretched out his back and looked

AFTER THE FLOOD

out over the broad, sloping landscape, his hands planted on his hips. Goodness something was not quite right.

He turned to the American.

'Fish, I don't know what's up but I feel dashed queer –'

The American chuckled.

'Got a headache?'

'I'll say, a right ruddy thumper.'

'How's your stomach?'

'Not quite itself, truth be told.'

'Altitude sickness. Drink some water. Get some rest, and you'll be fine.'

'Easy for you to say.'

'Everyone's got it Harris. It goes with the territory.'

Harris looked across at the girl, her cheeks swelling with food. *Well she didn't*. In that moment, he felt himself softening. Goodness... even eating Yasmin was stunning. Harris found his first smile of the day. Suddenly altitude sickness didn't seem such a problem. Well...

Night had fallen on Ararat. Sentries stood in pairs at burning braziers around the perimeter of the German encampment. Various others were dotted about, deployed in dark corners — all on the look-out for whom, they did not know.

It made sense, not that it was obvious to Drabble how much good a few pairs of cold Bavarians warming themselves by open fires would be against a concerted covert attack under the cover of darkness. But who would be attacking them and why? Sahin, he sensed, had some notion of trouble, but Drabble's chances of getting an opportunity to quiz him about this were low.

Over dinner, it struck Drabble that Sahin was on edge, though nothing was said. Rather, the guide was taciturn, even more so than usual, and appeared, Drabble wondered, to be a man burdened. Perhaps it was the realisation of just what Siviloglu would do to him if he failed to find what they were seeking? Perhaps it was also the prospect of recovering the very steps he had taken with his father all those years before? That would surely be weighing upon him. Perhaps it was the prospect of finding what he had spent his life looking for...

'We will begin surveying the territory around the camp tomorrow morning,' declared Siviloglu, nodding towards Hauptman, who was joined by Captain Bloch, his eager junior. The general looked over at Drabble, drawing him into the discussion. 'Let us hope that the Russians were right.' He allowed himself a satisfied smile. 'Sahin, I don't doubt you.'

The guide nodded, but said nothing. Siviloglu raised his metal beaker of wine and the party followed suit.

'Good. We are all set, gentlemen. In the morning, we will begin our historic search.' He beamed expansively and raised his beaker. 'Here's to our mission – for the greater glory of His Imperial Majesty, Sultan Adbulmejid II, and,' – he nodded meaningfully towards the Hauptman, Bloch and the others – 'and the Führer! Tomorrow, gentlemen, we search for the ship of Noah!'

The dinner trolley arrived a later than usual. Charlotte had been passing the time looking at the books – all in a Persian or Arabic script – imagining what they were about, and quietly going out of her mind with impatience.

Because she had resolved on her course of action.

There came the usual knock at the door and she quickly stood before the door, waiting as it was unbolted. It swept open and she took a step back. The pasty osteopath looked at her dubiously, his eyes twinkling pugnaciously at her. He probably thought she was looking at him a little too imperiously. Well, she no longer cared. Don't misunderstand her: Charlotte was determined not to throw caution to the wind – she had already done that with her pitiful escape attempt. But she would not let them get the wind up her. Oh, no she would not. As the man settled the trolley in its usual spot, she addressed him.

'Do you speak English?'

There was enough of a hesitation about him to give her the answer she was looking for.

'Good. I want to speak to Mr Andrew Streat,' she declared. 'Bring him to me. Bring him here.'

The cruel slab of the man's face did not register the command, but the mackerel eyes peeping out from it narrowed at her. He withdrew without comment and the door closed after him.

Chapter Twenty-five

Under brilliant blue skies, the luscious light gave crystal clear visibility for miles. Several hundreds of yards below them down the long inexorable slope lay the Ahora Gorge, leading to nothing but daylight. The peak of Ararat towered above but distant, perhaps a thousand metres or so away, looking starkly white and plausibly like a child's simple drawing of a volcano. Looking south, Drabble could see the small coned pinnacle of Lesser Ararat blocking out the broad horizon.

The Bavarian engineers broke up into parties carrying pickaxes, poles and bags of kit, and began the survey of the mountainside, from the limit of the gorge rising up to where the landscape began to climb steeply to Kopgel, the small peak just several hundred metres above them. The Germans staked out sections methodically into rectangles with long black tape. By mid-morning the whole immediate area was gridded and the soldiers had started digging trenches in the sections. Dotted here and there were bored-looking sentries, stamping their feet to keep warm. Siviloglu took Drabble out to show him the works, Celik following at discreet distance.

'The men have been ordered to dig down through the snow until they find bedrock. If the snow proves too deep, we have dynamite to expedite the process.' Just nearby a party of engineers toiled with axes and shovels, a heap of snow emerging from the section. Already, the head of the lead man was at ground level, so they weren't hanging about. Siviloglu gave a satisfied smile and lit a brown cigar.

'These Germans work hard,' he said, tossing the flaming match aside. 'The New Turkey will benefit from their energies as well as their efficiency.'

AFTER THE FLOOD

'Is that a New Turkey in which you are to be the Grand Vizier?'

The slight man turned sharply to Drabble, cocking an eyebrow.

'It will be for this Imperial Majesty to call upon whomsoever he sees fit, but if I am called, I will serve my Sultan and country. You can be sure of that.'

The last sultan had been given the boot in the early 1920s by Atatürk, then basking in his victory over the Greeks – who had been supported by us no less – in what the Turks described as the war of independence. Atatürk was the sort of energetic individual who was born to be president, but would chafe as anything less. Siviloglu, clearly, was cut from a different cloth.

Drabble nodded towards the Germans in the trench.

'So that's what this is about?'

Siviloglu reviewed him but made no immediate reply. Drabble waited, leaving a void for Siviloglu to fill, but it didn't come.

'Why does the Ark mean so much to you?'

Siviloglu's narrow mouth offered a conceited smirk.

'By finding the Ark here in Turkey – by Turks finding the Ark here in Turkey – we will show the world that we are every bit as good as the Europeans, better in fact – as the Ark is the arguably ultimate human artefact, one that is prized by the Christian, Jewish and Islamic faiths, all constituents of the Ottoman Empire and of modern Turkey. More than this the Ark goes back into the dawn of known time through Babylonian tradition. And we will have it, and because it's ours it will not be carted off to a museum in some damp European capital. Instead it will seal our human authority and by finding it in the name of His Imperial Majesty it will reinforce the Sultan's claim to the crown and as Caliph, he will in turn reinforce the New Turkey's position in any coming general conflagration.'

Siviloglu cleared his throat, took a puff at his cigar, and began to stroll away. *The coming general conflagration.* Drabble sucked his teeth and called after him.

'Why would you throw your lot in again with the Germans? You saw how it ended last time? You lost.'

'We didn't lose. It was the Austrians who lost.'

'Come off it. Turkey capitulated with Allenby knocking on the door of Anatolia and the Army of the Orient just twenty miles from Constantinople.'

'It won't be the same next time.'

This comment came with a steely force that rather took Drabble by surprise.

'And what's so wrong with 'peace at home, peace in the world', isn't that Atatürk's phrase?

Siviloglu scoffed.

'Atatürk is a fool. A brave fool, in his day, but a fool nonetheless.'

'He's a fool who knows better to keep out of a fight that's not his.'

'Who says it's not ours?'

'And the caliphate?'

'Once the people of Islam are united under the Caliph there is nothing we will not be able to achieve – from Bengal to Casablanca, we could still turn the map green.'

It was Drabble's turn to scoff.

'Yet last time India stayed loyal. Hundreds of thousands of Indians fought for Allies.'

Siviloglu turned on his heels.

'They died too. But times have changed, Professor. Britain's grip on India has diminished greatly over the past two decades. Also, India's Muslim community has a far stronger political voice now. And don't forget that the Soviet

AFTER THE FLOOD

Union also contains many tens of millions who count themselves as followers of Allah. Stalin is no friend of theirs, as well you know, and they chafe under his cruel yoke. You are an historian, Professor, so you must know better than I, that history never repeats itself. It's the people that do that.'

'Yes, and in particular their mistakes.' A realisation came to him and he added bitterly: 'You're stuck in the past, General. You'll be wanting to march on Vienna next.'

Siviloglu looked over, half a smile on his lips.

'We can but dream, Professor.'

Drabble gasped, 'You're not just delusional, Siviloglu you're crazy. The Nazis won't let you anywhere near Vienna.'

'But they will share the Balkans with us, Professor. And that is a start.'

'And does your would-be sultan agree with this ambitious territorial expansionism?'

Siviloglu inhaled as if having to explain something simple to a child.

'He will gratefully accept his position and responsibilities as a constitutional monarch, Professor. As well you know. After all, it's perfectly normal for monarchies that have become republics to readopt their monarchy. How long did Britain's republic last?'

'Eleven years, give or take.'

'There you have it. Ours will have lasted eighteen.'

'We'll see.'

'I'm not surprised that you doubt me, Professor. But it won't be long before Atatürk will be no more, and then we shall – '

A shout rang through the air. It was not a shout of fear or a warning, but of jubilation. Cheering followed. Drabble realised it was Sahin's voice – raised in celebration. The guide sprinted towards them from the far side of a rocky bastion. As he got closer Drabble saw tears in his eyes, his arms outstretched.

'General! Professor! Come. Come! We have it!'

High above the German position above the Ahora Gorge, Harris, Fisher, Yasmin and the guides were watching. Fisher had his binoculars out. They could see the carefully staked-out ground and men beavering away, swinging axes, digging straight trenches and shifting impressive quantities of snow in huge piles. Harris took a deep drag of his cigarette and sighed.

'Whenever this ruddy war comes, we're going to have our work cut out. These Johnnies are jolly industrious.'

Fisher wasn't listening. He was far too interested in the scene below. Harris looked over at the German encampment with renewed interest – just in time to see a man running around, waving his arms about. He craned his neck, squinting down at the melee. Several small white figures were converging on a local guide, it appeared. He glanced over at Fisher.

'What are they hollering about?'

'They think they've found something,' said Fisher. He lowered his binoculars, but continued to stare ahead as if he'd seen a ghost.

'Holy fuck.'

'What?' Harris snatched for the binoculars, taking them. 'Don't joke, old man.' He found the bearded face of the guide that he had seen running about – the smile, the cheeks glistening with tears; he saw him embracing various men and then they all started pouring after him, back in the direction from which he had just run. Harris lowered the binoculars.

'It's simply all too bonkers. Preposterous. Christ – you know what? They think they've found it.'

AFTER THE FLOOD

The sound of cheering was clearly audible. They watched in silence as most the tiny white-clad figures before them started charging after the large chap in furs. He vanished around a bastion of rock and out of sight.

Harris broke into a cheer, 'I can see Drabble!' He giggled excitedly. 'He's running after the rest of them. Look!'

Harris handed the binoculars back to Fisher and sparked up a cigarette.

'Now what do we do?'

Fisher glanced over.

'We wait for nightfall.'

'And then what?'

'That's the bit I haven't figured out yet.'

Harris nodded with understanding.

'We need to get Drabble out of here.'

'We also need to stop this mad Turk and the Nazis from getting their hands on the Ark, assuming that's what they think they've found.'

That was all unavoidably necessary. He put the cigarette to his lips and inhaled the lion's share of it in one go. 'I can only foresee one problem,' he croaked. 'We are two journalists, one young woman, profession unconfirmed, and a pair of donkeymen. What chance do we have in stopping fifty armed Krauts and at least one demented Turk from keeping hold of something they've come an awful long way to get?'

Fisher lit up. 'I counted twenty Krauts.'

'You get my point.'

Fisher nodded. 'Let's stay out of sight, get some supper and then wait and see.'

Wait and see. Harris sighed. How much of life seemed to depend on those three words. Unfortunately, as ever, he could think of nothing better.

Drabble pushed his way through the bundle of Bavarians, their voices raised in excitement. The lithe non-commissioned officer bellowed and silence fell, and then Hauptman's baritone cut through the air.

Drabble reached the front, where a six-foot-wide swath had been cut into the snow, deepening to perhaps fifteen feet beneath the surface level. Down there, Sahin and Siviloglu were kneeling on all fours, inspecting something in the ground. Hauptman stood behind them, watching intently.

Sahin's voice was rich in excitement.

'There's definitely something here…' He reached up with his hand. 'Pass me a rod.'

A pole was handed to his waiting fingers and Sahin slotted it into an unseen hole in the ground. The pole disappeared from view and he pressed his face to the ground. Siviloglu was up.

'Hauptman, clear this ground. Five metres either side to begin with. Jump to it!'

As Hauptman's men scrambled to fetch their tools, Drabble slid down the snowy ramp and got in next to Sahin.

The man's face glowed with pleasure.

'Take a look, *Ingilizce*,' Sahin shifted aside and Drabble bent down to the small hole in the ice. Peering into the darkness, he could see nothing, but there was a void of some sort, because somehow there was a draught.

Sahin beamed.

'We've found it, Professor. I swear that this is the ship of Nüh!'

The engineers were upon them now, calling back and forth, new work areas delineated and digging began. Siviloglu stood above the pit, his eyes twinkling.

'Hurry. There's an hour at most before darkness, we mustn't waste a second.'

The door to Charlotte's rooms was unlocked with customary vigour – and then there was a knock. It was too early for supper and as she got to her feet and pushed the creases from the front of her dress, Andrew Streat, appeared. He nodded to the osteopath who withdrew, and the door was closed behind him. Streat wore a benign expression of sympathy on his face and he extended a hand to shake hers.

'Charlotte...'

Charlotte kept her hands clasped rigidly together in front of her. 'I rather think we're beyond Christian names now, don't you, Mr Streat?' Her tone was bitter and he withdrew his proffered hand. 'It's Dr Drabble, if you must call me anything.'

Streat nodded and looked over towards the window, turning his crumpled Panama hat in his fingers. He swallowed, disappointment and contrition written across his fair, boyish face. Charlotte scoffed. Honestly, what did the man expect? For her to embrace him?

'I am jolly sorry that you and Ernest got mixed up in all this,' he said. 'It's hard to explain it all really.'

Charlotte would have laughed if laughter was not now beyond her. Being kidnapped and imprisoned will do that to you. She cleared her throat.

'I suggest you try and explain what this is about. That's if you ever wish to redeem something of yourself.'

A curious expression flitted across his face, almost as if he had heard a joke, and she realised to her dismay that it was surprise: presumably redemption was the last thing that had ever crossed his devious mind. Streat laid down his hat and with it any pretension to having the normal range of human feeling. He gestured towards the sofa – 'Sit,' he commanded – and then he sat down in the armchair opposite, waiting for her to comply.

'You don't know this about me. No one does, not really.' He paused, and chose his path into the knot of his tale. 'I suppose it's not strictly relevant but I'll say it anyway.' He waited for Charlotte to acknowledge him with her gaze and announced, 'We breed late in my family. My great-grandfather was the second son of a Shropshire yeomanry farmer who went into the cloth trade and came east in 1774 to find his fortune. He didn't find money but he found his calling – the Ottoman Empire, not yet the sick man of Europe but certainly a shapeless, merciless bag of populations and creeds, one that ran from Algiers in the west to Belgrade in the north, to Baghdad in the east; a kingdom of the four seas – spanning the Mediterranean, the Caspian, the Black and Red. And all quietly ruled over from the Sublime Porte in Constantinople until a conspiracy of fools unravelled it two decades ago in the pursuit of self-interest and black gold.'

He smiled ruefully, 'The second son from Shropshire fell in love with a Greek girl from Smyrna, now Izmir thanks to Mustafa Kemal's revolutionary zeal, and he never looked back. His son, that's my grandfather, then grew the family business and was wealthy enough not just to establish himself in some style in what was then the first Greek city of the empire, but to return to Britain and marry up, gaining title and status both here and at home. My father went into Ottoman imperial service, rising to become a vizier under Abdulmejid I in what we now call the Tanzimat period. His services were rewarded with estates in Trabzon on the Black Sea. He enjoyed a life and status that his grandfather could scarcely have dreamed of.'

'And then what?' demanded Charlotte. 'All that came crashing to an abrupt end when the empire collapsed and the Turks binned the sultan?'

'The first of November 1922, to be precise.'

'You have my sympathy. But what, pray, does any of this have to do with Ernest and me?' She shook her head, fighting back the tears.

AFTER THE FLOOD

Streat's grey eyes returned to her. 'Ernest is potentially extremely valuable to our cause in what is a most pivotal moment. That is the extent of your bad fortune.'

'Oh, let's hope so.'

He swallowed. 'I am truly sorry,' he said.

'No you're not. We're only here because of you, since it was you who wrote to Ernest suggesting we come here in the first place. That's why we honeymooned in Istanbul.'

Streat gave an unfortunate smile. 'I'm afraid that Ernest's help is essential. I willingly appreciate that you are both innocents in the crossfire. All I can say is that I sincerely hope that the inconvenience to your honeymoon will soon come to an end.'

Charlotte controlled her urge to shout. Instead her voice fell to a whisper. 'There aren't just two of us being inconvenienced Mr Streat.' She looked away. 'And I'm not referring to our best man, either.'

The pale, sun-bleached eyebrows rose... and his focus briefly alighted upon Charlotte's torso, as only a bachelor can. Then his mouth narrowed and there was the glimmer of a smile in its disobedient corners. Despite his best efforts it couldn't help but seep out and that told you everything.

'Assuming your husband is aware of this, then I can only imagine that it will doubly ensure his compliance with our requests, thereby greatly adding to your own personal safety, which I'm sure you welcome.'

Specious to the point of absurdity, thought Charlotte.

'Get me a doctor.'

Charlotte turned her head away and waited for Andrew Streat to leave.

Whatever it was down there, it was big. In rapid order the Bavarians had cleared a flat area the size of a squash court across, revealing a flat, smooth recessed surface, like the base of an empty swimming pool.

Three engineers with pickaxes now stood around the original inspection hole at its centre, while everyone else stood well back. On command they began. With each swing they dislodged fragments around the edge of the hole, widening the aperture, until it became big enough for a man. Once they had moved back, Siviloglu then went forward, a rope looped around his waist. He peered into the opening, shining a torch into the subterranean space. After a moment he stood up and turned to Drabble.

'Come, Professor, the moment of glory has arrived!'

AFTER THE FLOOD

Chapter Twenty-six

Drabble was lowered by increments into the void, dangling from the end of a rope looped under his arms. The limits of the torch that Siviloglu had given could so far find nothing to illuminate: this cave, assuming that's what it was, was large. It was also deathly cold – and after being out in the open for so long and constantly assailed by the elements it was also deathly still. In the unbearable quiet, Drabble could hear the creak of the hemp rope but the voices above now seemed eerily distant.

Drabble had been given a pistol, in case he disturbed a bear or some other predator that might be hibernating in the cave. That would be no way to conclude his honeymoon. So far, however, there was little sign of anything. Except the cold, which stung his face and began to penetrate his gloves and those parts of the body like his elbows where the fabric of his overclothes pressed against the bone. He cast the torch around: still nothing showed itself in the pitch black – the only light seeped in from above, from the dusk peeping through the increasingly small opening.

Drabble continued to descend. He must now be down at least twenty feet, perhaps more. Still his torch found nothing apart from black space to illuminate. Drabble didn't mind: he had been apprehensive before stepping down into the hole, but now he was here, he was in his element.

'Keep going!'

A head appeared in the opening. It was Sahin.

'Just attaching another rope, Professor!'

A minute later his descent resumed, as before inch by inch.

In Genesis God tells Noah to build the Ark three hundred cubits long, fifty cubits wide and thirty cubits high. A door was to be put in the side, and then there might have been a structure on top, a deck-house if you will, that was a cubit high. Assuming a cubit was a foot – or a couple of feet – then that would make for a substantial craft, but hardly big enough to accommodate fourteen of examples of each type of animal deemed clean by God and a pair of those that were not, for four months at sea. Where would the food go, let alone all the animals? But if a cubit were three or four feet, then we'd be talking about something absolutely enormous – with floors high enough for giraffe as well as elephants. The resulting craft would be something big enough for the Royal Navy fly aircraft off.

Just then the beam of his torch formed a broad circle.

'I can see the ground!'

A moment later, Drabble was standing on his feet and unlooping the rope. It was swept away. Drabble stamped the ground: rock solid, and he cast his torch around — the beam finding nothing but a dark, icy expanse without limit. The cold pierced his eyes, the chill indescribable. He felt it on his chest, through the layers of mountain clothing. This was ancient air.

Drabble looked up, with night falling the opening was fading from sight. It was no matter; they would shine a light down for him to find their way back but he decided it would be well to mark their way in case they got lost. Drabble took out his penknife and scored a deep cross on the ground… it didn't feel like timber. It was more like rock, almost, or compacted ice. But what would you expect after all this time?

He heard voices from above and looked up, seeing a light. Sahin was coming next. He bobbed down slowly, his torchlight roaming the cavern.

Drabble was no Bible expert but he knew enough to know that it was believed that the Book of Genesis, along with the first part of the Old Testament, was believed to have been written at least a thousand years before the birth of Christ – making it at least three thousand years old. And given that

AFTER THE FLOOD

the flood occurred long before this point – it was ancient news even at the time of Genesis being set down – that meant that any Ark was likely to be four or five thousand years old or more. So it was hardly surprising if the timbers had been altered in this time – petrified was the word, especially given the altitude and the cold.

Torchlight drenched Drabble's view. He shielded his eyes and looked up.

'Professor!'

Sahin's fur-lined boots lowered to the ground and he stepped out of the loop, giving the rope a double tug – it was swept up as before. He turned to Drabble and gripped his arm, breath clouding at this mouth. The man was transformed.

'If this is not the Ark of Noah, I do not know what is!' He lit a lantern and stood it by the cross that Drabble had scored into the ground. Next he pulled out a compass and began pacing into the gloom. 'Professor, wait here – ' he bellowed, following the beam of his torch. He counted out each stride, marking the distance. '...Twelve, thirteen, fifteen, sixteen ...'

They were being joined by another now – Hauptman, Drabble guessed. Sahin was still counting and already some distance off, but still going. This was a cavern, all right, and if it were a ship, it would be approaching something of improbable scale for its period.

Sahin cheered. 'A wall! I've found a wall!'

His footsteps continued for another few seconds and then Sahin turned, the glare from his torch now little more than a large bright dot in the distance.

'Forty-six!' he bellowed. 'Forty-six paces!'

And Sahin was not a short man.

Sahin lit a lantern, left it in place, and began to walk back. The newcomer, the German major, was stepping free from the rope.

Hauptman's eyes glistened as he looked about him.

'We have found it, Professor.' He grinned. 'Who could have imagined that it was so easy? I will get the Iron Cross first class for this!'

Drabble had a lit a lantern himself and now strode in the opposite direction from that which Sahin had taken. Like the guide, he counted out his steps – following his compass to ensure he was walking true, while also keeping a close eye on the ground ahead just in case of holes. The ground was solid though not quite flat – it undulated like the floor of St Mark's Basilica in Venice, another rather ancient surface, albeit one over water. After eighteen long paces, Drabble's torchlight made a small uneven circle on what could only be a wall or rockface. He reached the icy structure and about-turned, calling back.

'Twenty-five paces!'

So whatever this was it was some sixty yards across.

Sahin, having returned to the landing point, was now striding in a perpendicular direction – northwards – counting out loud excitedly. His direction took him further under the mountain, if Drabble's bearings were right. As Drabble joined Hauptman, the guide shouted out.

'Forty-four paces!'

Hauptman handed Drabble a lit lantern and he started off to the south, counting with each stride.

Drabble managed thirty-eight paces before arriving at a flat wall-like rockface.

The Book of Genesis said that Noah was told to fill the Ark with rooms, all noticeably absent here, unless of course, partitions had been destroyed. In the distance Drabble could see Sahin's torch moving back and forth as he approaching Hauptman. Another figure was now being lowered into the void. Siviloglu.

Drabble and Sahin met at the starting point, as the general arrived.

AFTER THE FLOOD

The small Turk looked at each of the four lanterns in the north, east, west and south in turn.

'Good,' he pronounced. 'Very good. Now, Sahin, let us establish the complete footprint of the structure. Hauptman – ' He removed another lantern from his pack and ordered the major into the darkness in what Drabble supposed to be a south-westerly direction. The German barked out his footsteps…

'Sahin,' the General handed him a freshly lit lantern. 'Go!'

As another member of the German party began to descend, Sahin headed off in a north-easterly direction. Almost of sight, Major Hauptman called out.

'Fifty-nine paces!' He swung his lantern. 'An icy wall…'

Siviloglu nodded.

'Good. Hold your position.'

'Twenty-three –' that was Sahin from the other end of the cavern.

'Now,' cried Siviloglu. 'Both of you walk in a clockwise direction following the perimeter until you have reached each other's present places…'

Even without this exercise it was apparent already that they were standing in a large and regularly proportioned rectangular chamber. Judging by the positioning of the lights, Drabble guessed that it might be perhaps sixty yards in width and perhaps double that in the other direction. So it was enormous, in other words. Whether it could be the remains of a monastery – such as the one that was destroyed on Ararat in the earthquake of 1840 that he had read about, or of some other structure, or indeed, an ancient ship mysteriously a long way from the sea, was open to conjecture.

A new arrival was just landing – Drabble recognised one of Captain Bloch's junior lieutenants – and unthreading himself from the rope. He then stood to attention.

'Herr General?'

Siviloglu nodded.

'Get more men down here. We need more torches, more lanterns – more pickaxes and we need the photographer.'

The soldier saluted smartly – clicking his heels – and immediately began calling up to the opening above. But Drabble didn't hear him finish: his attention was seized by Hauptman's voice: loud, shrill with elation and penetrating.

'General. Look! A door! There is a door!'

Siviloglu advanced a pace or two – and then halted to glance over triumphantly at Drabble.

'You still doubting me, Professor?'

Drabble's reply was lost to the booming sound of gunfire – from above. The sound was loud enough to make you duck. There was a cry and a moment later a man slammed to the ground next to them.

Drabble flicked off his torch and grabbed Siviloglu's shoulder.

'Come on!' He sprinted towards Hauptman as bullets strafed the landing area behind them. Hauptman, taking the initiative, strode towards them, firing up over their heads. The muzzle flashes of his pistol dazzled and his shots were deafening.

A wail came from above and another figure fell from the opening, striking the floor. Hauptman continued to fire up at the opening; he began shouting exultantly – with each shot his riding boots and flared breeches were silhouetted against the light. Sahin reached them as Hauptman's spent magazine rattled to the ground. The major reloaded.

In the distance – or muffled at any rate – there was the *rat-ta-ta-ta-tat* of automatic weapons from above, presumably German submachine guns, and the crack of rifle fire. It sounded like the Bavarians were mounting a counter attack. There was shouting but Drabble could make nothing of it.

'Hauptman!' Siviloglu barked. 'Move back! One grenade and we're all finished. Come!'

AFTER THE FLOOD

The Turk flicked on his torch and entered the doorway.

'Great Scott!' Harris pulled out his pipe and shouted over his shoulder at Fisher. 'It's like the ruddy Alamo down there.'

Flashes from the gunfight lit up the sky and the noise was incredible. Rifles boomed out and stray shots hissed overhead. Harris could see pretty clearly that an attack was under way on the Bavarian camp. Several dozen men dotted around the mountainside were firing down on the camp, but now that the element of surprise had been surrendered, the Germans were bringing their disparate positions under sustained machinegun fire. One by one the flashes from the hillside were falling dark as either the assailants were either killed or regrouping. Harris knocked his pipe clean and slipping it away. He took out a cigarette.

'Looks like the Krauts have got them on the run. That Johnny on the hilltop over there has gone, so's the one who was firing from over there.'

Fisher was now at his side, submachinegun in hand.

'Whoever they are, they could do with some help.'

Bit late for that, thought Harris, as the mechanical chant from the machinegun cut through the air – *cha-cha-cha-cha*…. He glanced over. Fisher was on the move.

'Just a second,' he remonstrated. Fisher paused. 'You're not expecting us to get involved are you? Those ruddy Krauts are trained killers, for God's sake. *And* they've got machineguns. We wouldn't stand five minutes up against that lot.'

The American was off. Harris swore under this breath – and scampered after Fisher.

Harris arrived at their camp, panting, to find the girl stabbing a magazine into the side of her German submachinegun. She cocked it, like she had been doing that all her life. The two guides were armed already – and draped

219

in bullets like Mexican bandits. Suddenly they really didn't look like donkey drivers; in fact, they looked rather too at ease. Fisher cocked his weapon and met Harris's gaze.

'You coming? Coming to help save your buddy?'

Harris exchanged a glance with the girl and received a terse nod.

'Right.' He took a last, long drag on his Craven A and threw it aside. Inside him, everything was rebelling – his stomach was clenched like a spaniel about to spring on a crippled pheasant, his throat was tighter than a cramping big toe. He had to will the tears from welling up in his eyes. He stilled himself.

Right.

Harris pulled out Yurttas's revolver and checked it was loaded. There were no excuses now.

'Righty-ho,' he bellowed. 'Let's make some sour Krauts!'

Drabble followed Siviloglu through the doorway-shaped opening. Overhead the sounds of gunfire were still clearly audible, and so were the cries of men – either dying or killing Drabble could not tell. Behind him came Sahin and Hauptman. As they entered the room they fanned out, their interwoven torchlights and shadows streaking across a broad undulating floor. This then was another large chamber, clearly, and just like the first, apparently featureless, yet too evenly proportioned to be cave.

And then they saw it.

Interrupting the beams of yellow torchlight was a foot – the sole and heel of a boot in fact, and then a second boot, tall and sheepskin-lined. Then the legs and a clothed torso quickly came into view. The figure was dressed like Sahin, a greying dagger even protruding from his whithered waistband. The guide was at the body's side first, his torch illuminating an unruly grey beard springing from a face which was half decayed but still very much a man. Sahin let out a low, guttural moan and appeared to lose his footing. He fell to his knees.

Siviloglu's voice cut through the air, 'What is it, Sahin?'

The Kurdish guide gave painful, wailing sob.

'Come on, Sahin, we don't have time to lose…' Siviloglu's voice tailed off as he reached Sahin's side and he looked down. 'Surely, it can't be – '

Sahin was mumbling, his shoulders heaving. 'I knew I recognised this place,' he sobbed. He cradled the grey face tenderly in his hands and cried out…

Just then they heard a loud thud from the first chamber. Someone or something else had landed. Siviloglu turned first, his torch following him. 'Hauptman, *the door*.'

The major moved fast.

'Sahin.' Siviloglu placed his hand on the guide's shoulder. 'We must go.' The guide, weeping profusely, shook his head, his hands still cradling his father's face.

Siviloglu turned to Drabble.

'Very well. Leave him. Let us go.'

Hauptman fired. The shot from his Luger shattered the air of the enclosure. And then a gunshot exploded close by – the bullet smash into the wall beyond, throwing out a splintering plume of ice and rock shards. A cry went up. Hauptman was down.

Drabble and Siviloglu broke into a sprint.

They charged towards the interior of the chamber – and there, *there* was another doorway. A boom shattered Drabble's eardrums and the wall ahead exploded in dust as another bullet struck. Drabble dodged left, careening into Siviloglu and the two of them bounded into the next chamber. On the far side of the door they divided – taking cover on either side of the opening.

Siviloglu drew out his Luger and shouted over.

'We have to stand and fight. Soon we will have nowhere to run to.'

He was right and Drabble knew it. Assuming his sense of direction was correct, they were now deep underground – certainly under many more metres of rock, ice and snow than before. The only way out was the way they had come. What was also certain was the whoever was attacking them would not see a shadow of difference between him and Siviloglu. They also did not seem very inclined towards taking prisoners. A beam of torchlight now strafed through the open doorway between them, bleeding out into the dark interior beyond.

Christ alive. Drabble took out the pistol he had been given when he was sent into the chamber and cocked it. He swore under his breath. He had no interest in killing a man, especially one who had no beef with him. Drabble called across to the Turk.

'What do you suggest?'

'*Shhsh*!'

They crouched in silence, their backs to the wall, listening hard. The gunfire above had stopped and in the strange quiet they could hear moaning – Hauptman, probably. But there was something else. Drabble concentrated hard… Yes. That was it. It was the intermittent, gritty sound of slow, deliberate footsteps. And they were getting closer.

Siviloglu pulled an object from his backpack – and struck a match, intensely bright in the pitch black.

A tapered fuse hissed into life. Drabble saw Siviloglu's face in the sparks and experienced a rush of admiration and horror all at once. Siviloglu was a veteran of Gallipoli; he wasn't going to go down without a fight, even if it meant blowing himself up in the process – not to mention Hauptman who was lying injured or dying in the next room. And then there was whatever had happened to poor Sahin.

But neither of them probably weighed very heavily in Siviloglu's considerations. The fuse burned furiously and Drabble reckoned there might be three or four seconds at

AFTER THE FLOOD

most before it was fireworks time. Sahin was right in the line of fire.

One.

Drabble realised that he couldn't let him kill Sahin. And certainly not like this.

Two.

Even Hauptman, no matter how much he despised him, deserved better than to be blown up like this.

And then there was their attackers. Whatever their motivation, it could not be worse than Siviloglu's. In fact it was liable to be a damned sight more noble.

Four –

Drabble pounced – hurling himself across the open doorway at Siviloglu. There was gunshot, deafening and a bullet tore past, thudding into an unseen wall. The wiry Turk collapsed under him, the stick of dynamite spun from his grip and flew through the air…

Harris, Fisher, Yasmin and the mountain guides skirted around the German camp keeping to the high ground, passing into the territory recently occupied by the attackers. That felt dangerous, but there was no other way to advance. Down on the plateau below the heavy German machinegun fell suddenly quiet. For ten minutes or more it had been pounding away at the mountainsides above the camp, but now the guns of the attackers had stopped firing, so they could see no one to fire back at.

The peace after the thumping seemed like silence. Although it was not. Men lay dotted and heaped here and there in the darkness, moaning. The dowsed embers of one of the campfires glowed. It was cold and the fresh breeze was keen.

A distinct shout went up, a German voice.

It was joined with replies, calling out for help. Slowly, from different positions, torches were illuminated and their beams streaked across the snowy slope, showing the dead, and blood stains in the snow. The German survivors began to come together and see to each other's wounds. Harris counted ten figures at most. Among them he could not make out Drabble. He wasn't here. Or worse he was dead.

As for the attackers; they had either been killed or driven off, or were regrouping to perform another assault. It was possible that they were satisfied with their work. It wasn't far-fetched to think that they would show themselves again now that the Germans had dropped their guard.

Fisher crouched down low next to him.

'We're too late.'

'Yup. I'd say those other Johnnies have had a bellyful.'

'There are still more Germans to kill,' hissed Yasmin. 'I need to make sure that Siviloglu is dead.'

Fisher rested a restraining hand on her shoulder.

'Easy. It would have been different if the Jerries were still fighting for their lives, but I don't fancy charging in there, all guns blazing.'

'And certainly not against that heavy machinegun,' agreed Harris.

Yasmin cast him a reproving glance, 'You lack courage, Hareez.'

He shrugged. 'That's as may be. I certainly have no desire to leave a party sooner than I need to.' She didn't look entirely satisfied but she lowered her submachinegun, which was a step in the right direction. 'Fisher, it begs the question. What *are* we going to do?'

Just then, they heard a series of metallic sounds – the noise of several rifle bolts being locked into place.

'HALT!'

Harris froze.

A matter of yards away, a fresh-faced German officer stood with a fistful of soldiers fanned out either side of him, each

AFTER THE FLOOD

armed with rifles aimed straight at them. The smirking commander addressed them in English.

'Drop your weapons and put your hands up.'

Harris flung down his pistol and his hands shot up. All done before he realised that no one else had moved. The donkey-handlers exchanged glances: their fingers were on the triggers of their submachineguns.

'Your weapons!' The officer jabbed the air with his Luger. 'Or we will shoot!'

'Christ be born,' squealed Harris, his hands touching Saturn. 'Do as he says. It's not the ruddy Sally Army!'

No one moved. The breeze suddenly stiffened and a piercing wind howled down the mountain bringing a flurry of snow. Fisher was the first.

Slowly, he took his left hand off his weapon and raised it, fingers spread. He bent down to lower the weapon. 'This is over…'

Just then, there came a great rumble from underneath – a sharp tremor, and the ground beneath them seemed to disintegrate. Yasmin opened fire as she descended into the abyss, blasts of her machinegun emitting a strobe of bright, dazzling light.

And then everything went black.

Chapter Twenty-seven

When Drabble came to his senses, he was coughing, retching. His eyes were streaming. The world was pitch black again and he shifted his limbs, realising that he was caked in a blanket of rock, sand, grit and rubble. A bolt of pain lanced through his head, causing him to flinch and he knew he was quite likely disorientated. What had happened?

Siviloglu's dynamite. Yup. Those last frenetic split-seconds before the moment that the world stopped were curiously both immediate and an age away. He recalled quickly deciding that chasing the loose stick of dynamite was a fool's errand. Then there had been more gunshots and as the noise reverberated in his eardrums and the acrid musk of cordite overcame him, Sahin had appeared, having apparently made very short business of the intruders.

The guide had all but thrown Drabble into the next chamber and they had both-half run, half-tumbled towards the first chamber to get as far away as possible from the explosion.

Then came the inevitable; a powerful rush of pressure shattering the world around them, one whose prelude was a sharp intake of air…

Slowly, Drabble tried to sit up, finding thankfully that he could, but not without grave discomfort. He counted his hands and feet – and moved them. *Good.* But he legs throbbed and he found that the simple act of breathing caused a sharp pain in his chest and side. And then his head was pounding, he realised. *Not good.*

Carefully Drabble lifted his legs and shifted the rubble from them. He felt a weight on his chest, perhaps he had landed badly. But he was all in one piece. Again. And he didn't seem to be bleeding.

AFTER THE FLOOD

Drabble got to his knees and straightened out his back. How long had he been out for? There was no light anywhere and he could hear no sound of others – no shouts, no gunfire, no footsteps, nothing. He eased off his backpack and took out a candle. He had a box of Swan Vestas in his pocket.

He stilled his trembling fingers to strike a match, succeeding on his fourth attempt. The flare was blinding and he coaxed the flame to the candle before it died. The small, fragile yellow light showed him to be surrounded by rubble – a black interior landscape of desolation.

He was cold, he knew, and he had to get out. He had to get out quickly, get down the mountain and get to Charlotte wherever she was – and then get her away. But first he had to establish what on earth had happened here. There was no chance, surely, given the scale of the explosion, that Siviloglu had survived. Surely the Turk was dead?

And that ought to make matters simpler. Although Siviloglu was the one who had known where Charlotte was. With him gone that left Celik, who would be up on the top somewhere, so Drabble would have to find him and obtain the information from him somehow. Assuming he was alive still.

All this was washing over him as started to move around the disordered chamber – along with a mounting sense of danger. He was, of course, now an illuminated walking target, inviting attack. It also dawned on him that survival against the elements was probably now a more pressing concern than survival in the face of any human enemies.

Debris lay everywhere, shards of rock or perhaps petrified timber lay scattered. He picked up a strong hard sliver – about ten inches long – deciding that it would make a crude weapon. He realised that he was lucky he might chance upon an electric torch or one of the lanterns. He desperately needed a better light. And what about Sahin? Where was he? He turned around, holding the candle low at arm's length.

Drabble's heart sank.

The poor devil had not got far. He was on his back, half covered in a layer of rock, ice and God knows what else. Drabble propped up the candle and carefully lifted away the biggest lump of debris on top of him. Sahin's eyes were open, staring death in the face. His hat and the hair on the back of his head was gone, replaced by a bloodied, charred mass from the ears on. Drabble exhaled, deflated, his eyes falling shut. So that was that. The fellow had died bravely and saved his life. He sighed.

Drabble discarded the shard and removed the curved silver-handled dagger from Sahin's belt. As he got up, he discovered he was standing Sahin's pistol, which he gathered up gratefully. A quick inspection told him it had three bullets. He stuffed the knife and into his pocket, keeping the gun to hand – at the ready. At this rate it was perfectly possible that Sahin might end up saving his life more than once.

Drabble looked back at the face of the guide, and crouching down, closed his eyes.

Another time, he thought. Another life. Thank you.

Drabble rose from his haunches.

Now the quest for a torch or a lantern had to take precedence. Then warmth. And then he had to work out how to get out and off this mountain. His own torch – as well as Hauptman's were in the first chamber somewhere, as were the lanterns.

Drabble approached the doorway, the flame of the candle bucking and flickering. The first thing he saw were the blackened remains of Hauptman, his hand melted into his Lugar.

AFTER THE FLOOD

Drabble told himself again that there was no way that Siviloglu could have survived this. But he had to be sure. The doorway to the next chamber had been brutally widened by the force of the explosion, and the air was bitter with the acrid tang of smoke. Siviloglu's body should be here somewhere, he told himself. Drabble ranged around the chamber, searching the floor with the small circular pool of light emanating from the candle outstretched before him.

But Siviloglu was nowhere to be seen.

The candle bent over and Drabble turned, his curiosity aroused. That was interesting: a draught, that draught he had first noticed when he put his eye to the inspection hole. It really was the faintest of draughts. But it definitely was there. He walked towards it, sheltering the flame with his hand and aware of the weak current brushing his face. It led him to the corner of the chamber, where the floor abruptly vanished in a black void.

A lower level? In the King James Bible God had commanded Noah to build the Ark over three floors. It scarcely seemed credible, but as he lowered the candle, steps came into view. And there was the draught again, most distinctly. There it was. His spirits rose. Where there was a draught there was the outside world.

Drabble descended, bending low, the candle stretched out in front of him, its tiny, vulnerable flame providing his only visual clue to this alien underworld. The rake of the steps was steep and they appeared to run along a wall, going down further than he would have imagined. Drabble arrived at another floor. Again it was solid and stonelike, just as one the above. He exhaled, wondering at what he could not see in the black void... This was not the time for historical appraisal, he reminded himself. He had to get out. He had to get warm. He had to find food.

Drabble held up the light to the wall. Was this pitch over gopher wood? He took out his knife and scored into the surface. As before it was hard as rock and seemed to powder like stone under the force of the tip of Sahin's blade.

But you would need a drill to make a decent dent in it. He sheathed the knife and held up the candle, and gasped. Beginning just above head height, the wall was strewn with inscriptions. He stepped back and saw it stretched high up to the ceiling. It was a language made up of a series of geometric shapes scratched into the wall; triangles, squares and rectangles in sequential frames, reminiscent of the Standard of Ur or the Rosetta Stone. But where the stone was but a few feet wide this was *enormous*. Drabble hurried along the wall as more of the inscription appeared from the darkness. Good God… His head began to spin – but it wasn't concussion this time. Drabble pulled out a notebook from his rucksack and began to take rubbings. If he lived, then he would get these to someone who could do something important with them.

Drabble snatched five or six pages' worth in sequential order before his enthusiasm wavered. There was just so much; the writing covered the entire
wall… where would you stop?

And he had more important matters pressing to attend to. He had to get out. He had to find Charlotte. Drabble filled one more page, and then put the notebook away, before he stood back to take in the wall one last time. It was breathtaking.

He heard a scrape behind him and spun round, holding out the candle. There was nothing there.

Then he heard another scrape and Siviloglu stepped into outermost limit of the pool of candlelight. The Turk had his Luger pointed at Drabble, but was in a bad way. His left arm hung limply at his side and his left eye was closed, blackened

AFTER THE FLOOD

and bloody. Like Sahin, a portion of the hair on his head had been burned off, scorched. His clothes were torn and tattered. He gestured towards the wall with the Luger.

'Do more.'

Drabble returned to the wall and didn't stop until he had filled the rest of the notebook with rubbings. Siviloglu watched.

'I was right to bring you along, wasn't I, Professor? Now – ' He jabbed his gun towards the dark interior – 'Let us try to find our way out of here.'

Drabble bent down for his pack.

'Leave the gun, Professor.'

Under Siviloglu's close watch Drabble's hand retreated from Sahin's pistol. He shouldered his pack and turned towards the draught, leading with the candle as before. They proceeded slowly. Siviloglu limped and was breathing heavily behind him.

'You need medical attention, General.'

'And I'll get it, once we're down the mountain.'

'Sahin and Hauptman are dead.'

'I assumed as much. They died bravely and for an honourable cause.'

Out of the darkness a room was appearing like the one above. They reached a wall and followed it till they found a doorway through to another chamber. There were no more inscriptions here. Drabble was sure that they were now under the chamber in which they had arrived.

'Go on – '

They followed the breeze. Drabble cradled the candle and slowly they progressed. With each step Drabble became increasingly aware that Siviloglu needed him alive, in order to get out. There was a chance that the German engineers had survived the attack of course. In which case you would expect them to mount a rescue effort, and perhaps they already were. But that was all speculation. As it stood, Siviloglu needed him, especially since his left arm appeared to be entirely useless.

Drabble, of course, also needed him, because only Siviloglu could definitely
tell him where to find Charlotte.

Drabble stopped and turned to face the Turk, who was two or three paces behind him. He squared his shoulders.

'Where is my wife?'

Siviloglu raised his Luger. He didn't need to say anything. Drabble stood his ground.

'I'm not going to help you get out, unless you tell me where she is. But if you do, I give you my word I'll help you get out of here – and down the mountain if necessarily.'

'Don't be absurd,' Siviloglu's tone was savage, but the man was plainly flagging. 'You're in no position to negotiate. Once we've completed the mission I'll tell you – just as I said I would. But only then – now move!'

Siviloglu jabbed the Luger threateningly towards Drabble, but he didn't move an inch.

Siviloglu's good right eye blinked. 'Very well, Professor. Your wife is on Büyükada. an island in the Sea of Marmara. She's perfectly safe.'

'Whereabouts on the island?'

'The Palace of Lemons, the summer retreat of the grand viziers.' He swallowed painfully. 'Now move.'

They found another staircase.

They descended carefully, the current of air stiffening. On reaching the floor below, the ground rose steeply up and they were climbing now, in the face of definite a breeze. The flame of the candle could not be sustained, but curiously it was lighter here, and then Drabble understood it. They were outside – under a canopy of thick, dark cloud. But then, in a

AFTER THE FLOOD

break, he saw a star glitter and the edge of the moon came into view, its light giving the world form and shadows. They had stepped into the night.

Siviloglu was breathing heavily behind him.

'Well done, Professor. Now, where's the camp?'

Drabble turned toward the opening and the higher ground. 'It'll be up there, somewhere. I can't see any lights from here, but we're probably too low.' He checked his wristwatch; it was nearly two in the morning. They needed shelter and food. Otherwise, they would perish from exposure. That meant they should either return inside the structure they had just emerged from or they should attempt to climb up and find the camp. All that was feasible, but they would now be close to the Ahora Gorge and in the dark a slip might be fatal. Unfortunately, Siviloglu had decided for him. He pressed the barrel of his pistol into Drabble's lower back.

'Go,' he snarled. 'Keep moving! Let's find the camp.'

Chapter Twenty-eight

When Harris came to, the first thing that struck him was the cold. He was frozen like an Eskimo's martini. And he was covered in snow, but not too much that couldn't get up, which he managed. Scrambling to his feet, it took him a moment to establish what he was looking at. There was fresh layer of snow over everything, and that's when he realised what had happened – an avalanche or something like that.

Christ alive!

Yasmin.

He gasped in panic and span about, his focus shifting across the white, lumpen landscape. In the bright moonlight he saw something, poking out of the snow… an arm? He plunged forward and started throwing out great handfuls of snow. It was Fisher. Scarcely conscious, but coming to. He had a gash across his forehead, and looked in profound need of a St Bernard bearing gifts.

'Harris?' he moaned.

'Where's Yasmin?'

Before the American spoke a word Harris saw her. A dark lump that could have been mistaken for a rock. '*Yasmin*?' Yes, it was her! 'YASMIN!'

He sank to his knees and scooped her up in his arms. 'Yasmin…' Her eyelids parted momentarily and then closed heavily again. 'No, *no!*' With enormous effort Harris got to his feet, with her in his arms and staggered several paces towards the German camp, where there was fire and food, and there would be a medical person or at least medical supplies. And, frankly, regardless of whatever happened before the gunfight and the avalanche that followed it, they were all survivors now. They were in it together.

'Come on girlie,' he panted. 'You can do it.'

AFTER THE FLOOD

Behind him he heard Fisher calling out for the guides.

'... Come on darling. You can do it.'

Harris didn't know where the strength was coming from but he was determined not to fail her. He crested the low rise and turned to see the outline of the German camp and a slope dotted with ominous dark lumps. There were no lights. He swore under his breath. Then he heard Fisher's hoarse cry.

'Harris!'

He kept going.

'Harris!'

He needed to get Yasmin warm. The Krauts had warmth. They were now a damned sight closer than their own camp. He ignored further cries and stomped out across the plateau, taking the shortest route to the German base. But as he approached the remnants of the tents and the boxes, all he saw were corpses of the Germans and equipment strewn about, empty machinegun casings here and there and streaks of blood. What life that survived the attack had evidently been swept away in the avalanche. Christ alive. The poor buggers...

Harris bottled the revulsion and turned away.

He had to get Yasmin to their own camp. It was further and it was a climb, but that didn't matter. He looked back and saw Fisher looming into view, with one of the donkey-men, still clutching his German army-issue submachinegun. Harris doubted they would need that now. He was exhausted but knew that Yasmin could not walk. He doubted that he could carry her the entire way, but he would try. *He would try*.

Soon Fisher and the guide caught up, and the three of them embraced, glad and surprised to be alive. Just then Harris saw a figure approaching a good hundred yards off – the second guide. The one with them leapt forward and cried out.

'Aziz!'

There was no answer. He cupped his mouth to bellow, when Fisher dived to his knees. '*Shsssh!*' He dragged the guide down and Harris collapsed with Yasmin still in his arms. Fisher hissed in his ear.

'Look! There's two of them.'

And one of them, Harris realised, was Ernest. No one else walked with quite that gait, even if they were trudging through the snow. Harris laid Yasmin down, pecked her on her cheek, and then scrambled to his feet – confirming that his eyes were deceiving him.

It ruddy well *was* Ernest. Harris broke into a stumbling run, heading for the approaching figures.

'ERNEST!'

Drabble spotted Harris just as he heard his name in the wind. Oh, no, he thought. *Don't do that*. Don't run towards me...

The gunshot went off almost in his ear, and Harris dropped to the ground.

Drabble snatched a glance back at Siviloglu before charging towards his friend.

'Harris! HARRIS!'

Breathing hard, Drabble arrived at Harris's side. He lay motionless, a black shadow spreading in the snow, haloing his head.

'Percy... *Percy*.' He bent down and lifted Harris up, pushing the snow from his face. The side of Harris's head glistened ominously in the moonlight. He was bleeding. Anything more than that was hard to see in the light. The halo was spreading.

'Percy!'

Harris opened his eyes and coughed, the effort wracking his body in pain. His voice was faint.

AFTER THE FLOOD

'Christ alive, Ernest, how many times do I have to tell you *never* to call me that name.' The blood trickled down his face pooling in his throat. He smiled. I think that fucker shot my ear off.'

Drabble pressed his handkerchief to the bloodied side of Harris's head, stemming the flow. Just then laboured footsteps approached and Siviloglu stood over them.

'The new Turkey has no need for effete pseudo-English aristocrats. In fact, nowhere does.' The barrel of the Siviloglu's Luger settled above Harris's head. 'Better to put him out of his misery.'

Drabble threw himself across Harris, shielding him just as the first shot boomed out above their ears. Then there were more. Drabble saw Siviloglu stumble backwards and his body jerk back and forth as the multiple impacts spouted blood from his torso.

Then as the echo of the gunfire faded the general's body seemed momentarily to defy gravity – before collapsing to the ground, all at once, crunching into the snow.

There was a moment of silence and then the sound of more footsteps approaching. Drabble saw an armed man in German army-issue fur-lined hat standing over Siviloglu's body. He gave him a kick and waited. When he didn't move, he spat on the corpse.

It was Fisher.

'Hello, Professor,' the American smiled, and stretched out his hand. 'With your help I think we can get Harris and his paramour to safety – and patched up. You never know, but there might be a few more hostiles loitering around these parts, and I don't know about you, but I've certainly had enough of all this for one night.'

Chapter Twenty-nine

Charlotte's breakfast trolley had long been taken away, taking the smell of baked eggs, fresh citrus and cinnamon with it, but the morning had not yet passed when a light knock at the door roused Charlotte from her thoughts. She rose from the sofa and stood in the centre of the room facing the door, ready to receive her visitor. It was two days since Streat's visit, when she had asked him to provide a doctor for her, and she hoped – she thought not unreasonably – that perhaps, now, the moment had come.

But instead of an honest-looking man of late middle age with a black Gladstone bag and stethoscope draped around his neck, it was Andrew Streat. The very last person she wanted to see. Again.

'I have good news – ' He showed her that thin untrustworthy smile of his. 'We are moving you back to your hotel, pending Ernest's safe return, which I understand is imminent. With luck he should arrive into Istanbul tomorrow on the express from Ankara.'

Ernest? Ankara? Tomorrow? Inside her Charlotte leapt for joy. On the outside she remain utterly impassive.

'How do you know this?'

'I received a telegram from Ernest this morning. Rest assured madam, he is on his way. Harris is with him.'

'You're positive that it's genuine?'

'I have no reason to doubt it.'

Charlotte stepped back and lowered herself onto the edge of the sofa. She was in shock, perhaps. Certainly, she did not quite know what to do with this information. Over the past week she had grown so accustomed to her incarceration that the very idea of it ending was hard to contemplate. She did not even quite register the import of Streat summoning the osteopath in to gather her things up into a bag. It was all puzzling. It was all too good to be true. All too sudden.

'And what of your *grand projet* – the plot which has occasioned all of this?'

'In abeyance, for now.'

'And you're letting me go? Just like that.'

'Absolutely.' He smiled again and his cheerfulness made it her skin crawl.

'You're not worried that I might go to the authorities and tell them everything you've done? That I might expose you?'

'You wouldn't be that stupid.'

'Oh really? I'm afraid you haven't got a clue how stupid I can be …'

His expression changed and he looked at her with such a baleful loathing that looked quite unlike himself. In that moment her vocal cords failed her and she took a faltering step backwards. She leaned on the armrest for support, suddenly feeling very afraid. She realised she needed to be away from him and said, 'If you'll excuse me for a moment,' before moving into the bathroom, to get her breath back. She then heard Streat say, 'There's a ferry leaving for the mainland in fifteen minutes that we can catch if we are quick. That will have us back in Istanbul for one o'clock. I'm sure you don't want to stay here a moment longer than you need to.'

The rust-streaked ferry with its dreadnought bow was already alongside, filling up with passengers. Smoke trailed from its twin white and yellow funnels. Streat and Charlotte boarded and sat in first class where they ordered a cup of sweet black tea. Charlotte looked out of the window at the cheerful blue sea, feeling anything but. She was still afraid of the man she had glimpsed earlier in her room. The truth was she would much rather have taken her chances on the small sailing boat alone than been here with Streat.

Her eye traced the white and brown buildings along the front, the palm trees, the sand. None of it felt real. It was not real, in fact, and she knew it because it wouldn't be so until she was away from him. And though he told her that she was on her way to Istanbul and to Ernest, she didn't believe it because she was still, in effect, in his captivity, in Streat's charge. And he was not to be trusted. Never.

Except, possibly, to do the worst. How could she know that he wasn't taking her to Istanbul to do something despicable to her there? Or for that matter, how could she trust that he wasn't going to do something despicable with her *before* they arrived? So, in going along with him was she therefore a willing party to her own demise? Unfortunately, it was too late. She could see that readily enough. After five days of imprisonment on this island, here she was.

Nothing this man said could be accepted at face value. What's more, she could patently identify him and she knew he was involved in whatever Ernest had been caught up in. She may not know the substance of the matter but Ernest would and between them they must therefore constitute a serious hazard to either all or several of the individual plotters as well as their wider objective.

The waiter arrived at their table with their tea. He whisked each glass off his high tray and set them down with a flourish. She hoped Streat would not speak to her and he hadn't yet. The first-class cafeteria was empty apart from them, and when the waiter departed they were alone. In a few minutes they were well away from the island and Charlotte glimpsed the large white mansion she had been imprisoned in as well as the small blue sailing dinghy. They drank the tea in silence and then, when they were finished, Streat suggested, 'Shall we take a stroll on deck?'

AFTER THE FLOOD

Something in the way he said it put Charlotte on edge. She most certainly did not want to take a stroll on deck with Streat. Not when one could be pushed off it quite so easily. But the look on his face told her that he would brook no disagreement.

'It is rather warm in here, isn't it?' she agreed, smiling. 'Yes, that would be nice.' She pulled on her gloves and glanced over her shoulder at the end of the compartment, where there was a ladies' lavatory. 'If you'll give me a moment…'

Streat rose to his feet and watched Charlotte walk unsteadily to the ladies' room. People often remarked about the sensation of being watched and Charlotte understood exactly what they meant. She felt acutely isolated, her knees knocking together beneath her skirts.

Entering the tiny lavatory compartment, Charlotte closed the door and locked it behind her, feeling the pressure lift. She closed her eyes and took a deep breath. What was she going to do now?

Charlotte was not going to be taken as a fool by anyone – and never had. And she had decided. No matter what he said, it was too fanciful to believe that Andrew Streat and his friends would let her go, not after what had been seen, said and done. That was too much villainy to be swept under the carpet and forgotten about. No matter what she and Ernest said, they would worry. And that worry would eat away at them irrevocably until they decided to eliminate it, and they would know that already. Don't forget that she had seen the old man. Oh yes, she had a good idea who the elderly gentleman with his paintbrushes was. The ex-Caliph – a man forbidden to set foot on Turkish soil, the ruling family having long been banished by Atatürk.

Charlotte knew too much.

It felt like a spike was pressing against the inside of her sternum. Something was turning somersaults in there, too. She could at least govern her face and, looking in the small mirror, she imitated how she would look when she sat back down in front of Streat, the corners of her mouth upturned in imitation of a smile. Yes, she could manage that.

She exhaled, flattened the hair at the side of her hat and prepared herself. Right. She could go through with this. She simply had to believe that Streat was telling the truth, presumably for once in his life. And if it came to it she would fight. She would scream. She would bite, kick and scratch her way to freedom. And she would keep away from the edge…

Charlotte flushed the lavatory and unlocked the door.

It immediately swept open, causing her to half fall backwards. Andrew Streat stepped into the closet and kicked the door shut behind him. Charlotte saw his eyes and screamed.

He lunged for her, his outstretched hands finding her narrow neck – silencing her. Charlotte lashed out at his arms, but they were suddenly so strong and she knew that this was how it was going to end. She could not breath. She wasn't breathing. She couldn't even cry out for help. She could not scream. She could not dislodge Streat's hands. She was weakening.

But she could kick.

Her foot connected with Streat's groin and, for a split second, she thought he might stop. She kicked out again. He grimaced, but the grip around her neck tightened. Her strength was fading and she started to feel smaller, like she wasn't there. Tears filled her eyes and a trickled down her face. Andrew Streat smiled, the tip of his tongue protruding from the corner of his mouth.

And then a man's voice broke the silence.

AFTER THE FLOOD

'Andrew...'

The word hung in the air and then Charlotte fell gasping to the floor. In the doorway she saw a pair of black trousers and a pair of worn black half-Oxfords. The baritone voice spoke again.

'Kindly take a step away from Dr Drabble, Andrew.'

Streat reached out.

'No, no, please... *Douglas*...'

The shot was no louder than an escaping champagne cork with a tinny, rather than explosive ring. Charlotte felt the force of it – close and lethal. She scampered out of the way as Streat slumped to his haunches and fell back, clutching his bleeding stomach. He began moaning pitifully.

The Reverend James stepped closer and took careful aim at the Streat's face.

Popsst!

Streat's head snapped back against the metal bulwark; a red dot, the diameter of a dab of lipstick, appeared on his forehead and began to ooze blood. The Reverend James slipped the gun with its long protuberant silencer into his coat pocket and offered his gloved hand to Charlotte.

'Dr Drabble –' He smiled and helped her to her feet as though he were welcoming a blushing bride out of her wedding car. 'It's a pleasure to see you again...'

ALEC MARSH

Chapter Thirty

The next day Drabble, Harris, Yasmin and Fisher arrived in Istanbul from aboard the Eastern Express from Ankara. Drabble and Harris checked out of the Pera Palace and were reunited with Charlotte at the parsonage. Then with Fisher and Yasmin, they held a celebratory supper, all with a studious avoidance of the topic of what had happened over the preceding days. They were drunk with relief and exhausted, and all in one piece, except for Harris who had been separated from a small but fortunately unimportant piece of his left ear.

After supper they assembled in the drawing room, where the Reverend James served madeira. The wiry parson seemed to be enjoying himself. His sunken, lined cheeks were flushed red and his small-calibre chitchat expertly kept the whole party moving along seamlessly. Nobody uttered Andrew Streat's name.

It was only then that the topic of the previous days arrived. Like a Venetian flood, once begun the deluge could not be stopped. Of the various details several were kept back: Drabble avoided discussing the underground chamber and most certainly did not share the fact of the rubbings he had made. Nor would he. Asked by Fisher what was down there, he simply described it as a cave. James had enjoyed that.

'O ye of little faith, Professor. Did you not see the giraffe and elephant footprints? What of Noah's holy binnacle?'

The spry parson continued.

'And who, then, were the people who attacked you up on the mountain – Mr Yurttas's friends?

Harris, who had been discreetly pressing his hand against Yasmin's bottom, spoke up.

AFTER THE FLOOD

'We think so. What I gathered from him was that he was a member of some sort of group – I imagined it was rather like some militant order of monks – whose job it was to protect the, er, the Ark. That's was Yurttas told me and I rather believed him.'

'And then, of course, poor Mr Yurttas was murdered.'

'Yes. Shot on the Erzurum train.' The parson frowned at Harris as he topped up his glass. 'In the head,' added Harris after a sip. 'He gifted me his pistol which came in jolly handy.'

Yasmin cocked an eyebrow at him. 'Yes, you shot me with it.'

There was a ripple of laughter, but the Reverend James was not finished.

'So you said, Harris, but *who* killed Mr Yurttas?'

Harris shrugged, 'Buggered if I know. Presumably some cringing cove from this Green Fez brigade.'

James nodded thoughtfully, 'The unlamented Order of the Green Fez. It was most fortunate that having eliminated Mr Yurttas that they didn't then take a pot shot at either you or Mr Fisher.'

Fisher, who had been smoking silently, spoke up. 'Maybe they didn't regard us a danger worth eliminating, Reverend.'

The Reverend James nodded, but his eyes remained mischievous. 'It's a possibility. It would be reassuring to know who did kill the poor man.'

There was a knock and the Turkish housekeeper entered and bent down to James's ear. He nodded.

'Show him in.'

He waited for the servant to leave the room before making an announcement. 'We are blessed, friends. We have a visitor from the local constabulary. Goodness!'

The door opened and Inspector Hikmet of the Istanbul Police strode into the room. As before he wore tall leather riding boots with flared breeches and an immaculate tunic with leather Sam Brown. His manner was stiff and formal. He declined a glass of madeira and remained standing.

This was not a social call, plainly.

'I regret to inform you that the body of a British subject was washed ashore on the Asian coast of the Bosphorus yesterday afternoon,' he declared. 'He had been shot twice.' Hikmet permitted this information to settle. 'The dead man's name is Andrew Streat. I'm aware that several of you knew him well. Reverend, please accept my condolences.'

Hikmet left the statement there, his gaze taking them all in one by one. Harris took a contemptuous puff of one of the Reverend James's cigarettes, and offered the box to Hikmet, who after a moment's consideration took one, before accepting a light from Fisher.

'If any of you has information about Mr Streat's final movements then we would like know it.' The inspector's eyes roved the room before his gaze stopped at Charlotte. 'Dr Drabble, I am delighted to see you reunited with your husband. I gather that you checked out of your hotel yesterday. Did you arrive back in Istanbul yesterday also?'

'That's right.'

'A man fitting Mr Streat's description was seen boarding the eleven o'clock Istanbul ferry from Büyükada with a European woman.'

'Really?'

'Was that you Dr Drabble?'

'Yes it was.' She spoke factually, as though owning up to nothing more than
a late library book.

'Did anything strange happen?'

'No, nothing that I recall. After we set off we had tea in the first-class lounge, and when we arrived at Istanbul I got off the ferry and he stayed on, in order to return to Büyükada.'

AFTER THE FLOOD

'And what were you doing with him in Büyükada without your husband on your honeymoon, if I may ask?'

She swallowed and frowned, as if this was a topic of regret, which of course it was but not for the reasons she was about to express. 'It's a sad story, and one I'm not proud of, Inspector. Suffice it to say, Andrew had developed an infatuation with me, and he was sure that I reciprocated his feelings. But he was wrong and eventually he understood that, which was kind of him.'

'Am I to understand that he took you there against your will?'

'Yes, that's correct.'

'I see. And then he decided to release you?'

'I think he wanted me to fall in love with him but when he realised that it was not going to happen he changed his mind about the whole thing. I rather got the sense that he rather regretted his actions, which is why I was happy to leave the matter as it stood.'

'And he wasn't worried that you would report him?'

'No, I gave him my word that I would tell no one about what he had done. I could see he regretted it.'

She bowed her head and Drabble, his arm already around her, drew her closer still.

Hikmet took a long drag of his cigarette, and accepted a brass ashtray from James. 'It's a very interesting story, Dr Drabble,' he cleared his throat. 'One I find most surprising, since Mr Streat was a homosexual.'

Charlotte exchanged a glance with Drabble and then looked up, her expression resolute. 'Nothing surprises me about men anymore, Inspector. They come in all shapes and sizes.'

'Yes, Madam.'

The policeman paused, presumably contemplating his next utterance. 'What I don't understand, Professor Drabble, is why a newly married husband would go off on a hiking trip to Mount Ararat during his honeymoon when he has just reported that his wife to be missing.'

Drabble spread his hands. 'I was beside myself and so decided to follow your advice, Inspector. You'll remember you told me to stay in hotel and await news? I'm afraid I'm not very good at doing that. So, Harris convinced me to go to mountains – as you may I know, I've done some climbing – and it was the perfect place to get away from it all. It probably sounds a little callous, but it was all I could do to take my mind off it.'

Hikmet nodded dubiously.

'And you, Sir Percival, are you also a keen Alpinist?' Harris nodded blithely. 'How curious that you did not travel together. You arrived, Professor Drabble, in the east of the country by unknown means, certainly not ones which I can verify, but you Sir Percival, travelled east on the train with Mr Fisher here.'

'That's right…'

'Where an eyewitness says that you both became acquainted with a man called Ibrahim Yurttas.'

Harris and Fisher stared fixedly at the policeman.

Harris reached for a cigarette, 'I don't recall an Ibrahim Yurttas…'

Hikmet accepted this with a nod.

'Mr Yurttas was found dead in his railway compartment with an armed assailant still present. The assailant was described as bespectacled, of fair complexion and having a light moustache; "an English gentleman who smelled of strong spirits" was what the witness said.' Hikmet paused dramatically, regarding Harris under lowered eyelids. 'Does that sound like anyone present here?'

Harris threw his arms up in protest.

'I don't know what you're talking about! Inspector –'

AFTER THE FLOOD

From his pocket, Hikmet produced a silk handkerchief, the very one that Harris had used to fill in the mouth of the railwayman who had found him in Yurttas's compartment. 'Recognise this, Sir Percival?'

'Never seen it before in my life.'

'How surprising,' sighed Hikmet, as he unfolded the handkerchief to show its monogram – P. L. A. H. 'Since it has your initials on it. Am I correct? Percival, Lancelot, Augustus Harris. Or am I to deduce that you must have been the victim of a petty theft or is this a sensational coincidence?'

Harris frowned at the handkerchief unsure of what to say.

'Did you kill Mr Yurttas, Sir Percival?'

'No! No, I swear it!'

The inspector cocked an eyebrow and waited.

It didn't take long for Harris to blurt out the truth.

'I was there – *yes*, I can't deny it, but I found the body. I didn't kill this Yurttas Johnny. He was dead already when I got to his room.'

'But why didn't you raise the alarm? That would be the ordinary and reasonable thing to do?'

'I-I was in a hurry to meet Drabble in the mountains. I-I-I didn't want to get tied up in local police investigations.' Harris tried not to sound pompous but failed utterly. 'I'd only met Yurttas briefly and he seemed a nice enough man but it was none of my business.'

'Oh, you met him, did you? What did you talk about?'

'I can't really remember. Just chit-chat. We had a drink together.'

Hikmet pecked at his cigarette.

'Do you remember threatening the railway guard with a gun? For an entirely innocent man, that seems rather dramatic, no?'

Harris hung his head, muttering. He managed a 'yes' eventually, but after that his words started to fail him.

'And what about you, Mr Fisher? Did you happen to cross paths with this Mr Yurttas on the Eastern Express to Erzurum?'

'I have no recollection of meeting a man of that name.'

'Yet the railwayman, the man who spent an hour or two with Sir Percival's handkerchief in his mouth, remembers you clearly. He described seeing an American newspaperman in the company of Mr Yurttas the very morning he died.'

Hikmet now turned on the balls of his feet to the Reverend James.

'Moving on, I have to ask you something, Reverend. Where were you yesterday morning?'

The cleric paused. 'In a meeting at the British Consulate. Ghastly appointments but unavoidable.' He smiled.

'Ladies and gentleman,' Hikmet stubbed out his cigarette and handed the ashtray back to James. 'I am aware of the existence of a clandestine organisation, the Order of the Green Fez – the reputed membership of which includes leading Turkish monarchists, whose leader is a man named General Mehmet Siviloglu, whereabouts is presently unknown. Intriguingly, it has come to light that Mr Streat was connected with this monarchist organisation and indeed the general himself, thanks to documents discovered at his home.' Hikmet let all this sit for a moment before continuing, 'Intriguingly, the general was seen at the Pera Palace Hotel on Sunday afternoon, the day Dr Drabble went missing *and* the day that Professor Drabble elected to commence a hiking trip to Ararat.' Hikmet surveyed the room, reading the blank faces around him. 'Has anybody in this room seen General Siviloglu since Sunday or know where might be found?'

AFTER THE FLOOD

There was silence and gazes remained unwavering. The only sound was the whisper of the Reverend James's cigarette as he drew exhaustively upon it. He knocked a half inch of ash from its tip and looked at the policeman earnestly.

Hikmet nodded and turned to Yasmin, who sat on the chesterfield beside
Harris, one leg crossed over the other – her elbow on her knee. Her cigarette burned at forty-five degrees from the nook of her first and index fingers.

'Miss Yildiz, you are a known associate of General Mehmet Siviloglu, are you not? In fact, I believe you are his mistress. When was the last time you saw him?'

Her long black eyelashes performed a delectable double flick, as if she had been asked nothing more important than to choose between Crémant or champagne.

'Last Tuesday,' she stated coolly. Blink. 'Yes. Tuesday evening. We made love in his office.'

The room fell silent.

'I see.' Hikmet nodded and after a pause turned to face his next subject. 'Mr Fisher. I gather you were stationed in the Soviet Union prior to coming to Istanbul for the *Times*?'

'That's right, for about five years in different places. I don't miss it.'

The inspector cleared his throat.

'I understand that you have fathered two children in Moscow, and that you also have a wife in Wyoming. Is that correct, Mr Fisher?'

A second or two passed. Then Fisher nodded slowly. Drabble thought he saw the colour of his face change, but he showed no obvious sign of surprise at Hikmet's statement.

Now Hikmet spoke slowly, his focus staying on the American.

'Have you ever passed information to agents of the Soviet state, Mr Fisher?'

'Are you kidding? I'm a newspaper man – I pass information all over the world, indiscriminately!' Fisher chuckled lightly.

'I'm sure that is true. What I'm interested in is your work for the Soviet Union.'

The chuckle bridled. 'This is ridiculous!' Drabble noticed an edge to Fisher's voice, quite at odds with his usual breezy *sang froid*.

Harris, meanwhile, silent since discovering that Fisher had met Yurttas separately the morning he had died, reached a resolution. Fisher had lied to him. More than this, Harris was gripped by the unassailability of the truth of it – and also by a wider question, one that had been eating away at him since arriving at Erzurum if not sooner: why had this man really joined him on the trip to Ararat to rescue Drabble after only a chance meeting? And how seamlessly he had arranged all the travel details and their rather implausible guides who were also surprisingly adept, it turned out, in the use of automatic weapons? There had to be an ulterior motive, he'd known it all along, but nothing had spurred him to give it voice. Until now.

Harris sprang to his feet and the words came out of his mouth before he time
to think.

'You killed Yurttas!'

The accusation hit Fisher like a slap across the face, upsetting his remaining equanimity. He sprang out of his seat.

'What?'

'You jolly well did it when I was having breakfast, when you popped out to get provisions. That's when you killed him.'

AFTER THE FLOOD

Fisher showed his teeth, his anger flaring. 'This is ridiculous. You can't pin this on me just because I met the guy *once*. You're the one who was covered in his blood! You killed him!'

Harris's brain suddenly caught up with the truth that had been in staring him in the face for several minutes now.

'So what was it, Fisher? Did Stalin want to get his hands on the Ark, or were you just out to stop the Germans getting it on his orders?'

'Very funny, Harris. You and your girlfriend here – not to mention the Professor – would be dead if it wasn't for us. You should be thanking us – not accusing us. And as for you Inspector, you're right. You'd probably have had a new sultan by now if General Siviloglu had got his hands on what he wanted on Ararat – yeah, and a grand vizier, I should add, who bows to Berlin!'

Hikmet pulled out his pistol.

'I think, Mr Fisher, that I'll take that as your confession.' The door of the room opened and policemen swarmed in to the room. Within moments Fisher had been removed from the premises.

Hikmet reholstered his firearm and gratefully received another of the Reverend James's cigarettes. He leaned into the flame from Harris's proffered lighter and a cloud of smoke settled between him and his audience, whom he surveyed gravely.

'Now… which of you is going to tell me the truth about what happened on Ararat?'

ALEC MARSH

Epilogue

Inspector Hikmet did not get it out of them, well not entirely.

Three days later Drabble, Charlotte and Harris returned to Serkeci station to board the Simplon Orient Express for London. The Reverend James, this time accompanied by Sir Terence Greenhalge, the Consul-General, and several hangers-on, came along to see them off.

'Well done, all of you,' gushed the diplomat, shaking their hands hard. 'Good luck to you!'

Well done for what, thought Drabble bitterly, but he shook the man's hand all the same. He even smiled.

Their service left on time and they watched as the train pass through the terracotta old city of Istanbul, before leaving the dreamy milky light over the Bosphorus and Sea of Marmara behind and slipping from the coast and heading inland. The newlyweds retired to their wagon-lit, Harris to the bar. It was only later, as Charlotte combed her hair, that it dawned on her what relief it was to leave.

'It didn't really hit home until the train left the station, and then the city itself.' She looked over at him with tears in her eyes. 'Now I can almost let myself believe it's all over.'

She buried her face in Drabble's shoulder as he took her in his arms and held her tight.

'Would you like to go on another honeymoon, to make up for this one?' She nodded, her eyes wet against chest. 'I'd like that too.' They broke apart, and she returned to combing her hair.

'Where shall we go?'

'Oh, I don't mind. A cruise down the Danube might be nice.'

AFTER THE FLOOD

'After this I was thinking somewhere extremely dull like Llandudno or Troon would do me.'

'Yes,' Drabble brightened. 'Troon sounds jolly.'

'And a lot of decent walks and not too many crazy foreigners.'

'Splendid.'

'When shall we go?'

'As soon as we can. If we leave it too long I won't be up to much walking.'

'Of course not.'

He leaned in and they kissed. Slowly, they folded onto the bed...

Then Charlotte paused and smiled, 'At this rate Harris will be half-cut by the time we get to the bar.'

'Better half-cut than cut-up.'

'Is he very sad to leave Yasmin behind?'

Drabble sighed, 'I'll say. Mortified as only Harris can be.'

'Even though she didn't have a castle and "two thousand prime foxhunting acres" – '

'Or a moat…'

Charlotte laughed. They resumed.

In the distance they could hear the melodious rhythm of the locomotive and through the windows lush forests were starting to show themselves at their best. In the morning they would be in Bulgaria, their Turkish sojourn would be well behind them and the night after that they would be in Paris.

Half an hour later than planned, they got ready for dinner. Drabble was lacing up his brogues when Charlotte sat down beside him on the edge of the bed. He looked up and saw she had the notebook he had filled with rubbings from inside the mountain. Charlotte arched an eyebrow inquisitively at him.

'I've been meaning to tell you about that.'

'You have?'

He smiled.

'Is it what I think it is?'

'And what would that be?'

She emitted a withering sigh.

'What are you planning to do with it?'

'Burn it, probably.'

'You can't do that!'

'I can, and it's probably the right thing to do. Under the circumstances.'

Charlotte thought about it for a moment and then began flicking through the book.

'But they're beautiful. And aren't you the tiniest bit curious to find out what they all mean?'

Drabble laughed.

'Not really. Anyway I think that's beside the point.'

He plucked the book from her hands – ignoring a howl of protest – stepped across the compartment and flung it through the slot of the open window. The train was crossing a viaduct over a deep gorge at the foot of which surged a tempestuous river. In a moment the book fluttered down towards the gorge before vanishing from sight.

'There,' said Drabble. 'And now it's time for a cocktail.'

AFTER THE FLOOD

Author's note

In November 1938 Mustapha Kemal Atatürk died of cirrhosis of the liver at the Dolmabahçe Palace, formerly the home of the Ottoman sultans, overlooking the Bosphorus in Istanbul. He was 57. The first public announcement that he was unwell – suffering influenza was what was stated – had come in March 1938, around the same time that a French medical specialist, a Professor Fissenger, visited Atatürk in Ankara and confirmed the diagnosis of his Turkish physicians. There had, however, according to Atatürk biographer, Andrew Mangold, been rumours of his illness from French sources as early as December 1937. After a period of rest and withdrawal Atatürk subsequently made a final public appearance in May 1938, whereupon one onlooker described him as having 'the skin of a dead man'.

Nearly a century later, Atatürk is still regarded as the founding father of modern Turkey. And unsurprisingly; Atatürk dominated Turkish politics and national life for two decades, becoming prime minister in 1920 and leading the country through its war of independence (against Britain among other countries). He was accordingly at the centre of the moves to abolish the sultanate in November 1922 – founded by Osman I in 1299 – and he became the first president of the newly proclaimed Republic of Turkey in 1923, a position he held until his death. He changed the country's alphabet, gave its people surnames, banned the fez ... he was a revolutionary. He also sought to take the modern nation of Turkey on a secular journey which involved, among other things, abolishing the Caliphate in 1924. Abdulmejid II, formerly a crown prince of the Ottoman Empire and first cousin of the last sultan, was the last caliph.

He would remain head of the house of Osman until his death in 1944, living out his days in Nice where he painted, apparently well. It's hard to understate the significance of these changes in transforming Turkey.

Today, if you visit the country, you're likely to see countless portraits of Atatürk in cafes, restaurants, offices and public places.

The timing of his death at such a critical moment in international tensions, then, is a principal strand of the story of *After the Flood*. As it turned out, Atatürk's long-time deputy, Ismet Inönü, would serve as Turkey's second president until 1950 and largely follow his course of sticking well clear of international discord (although Ankara finally declared war on Nazi Germany in February 1945). But it might not have been this way if another faction had taken control.

Another pivotal strand of the story, of course, concerns our continued fascination with the creation myths handed down to us through, among others, the Book of Genesis, notably of Noah's ark, a narrative that might have been written down in tenth century BC.

In his excitable tome, *The Lost Ship of Noah*, the writer Charles Berlitz detailed many of the attempts or apparent sightings of parts of the ship of Noah on Mount Ararat in the far east of Turkey. Among these is documented the reported sighting of a 'battleship' sized object on the mountain by a Russia aviator, one Captain Roskovitsky, in 1917, which was subsequently documented in an interview he gave to a magazine in California in 1939. It is stated that the details of his discovery and those of a subsequent mission to verify it

AFTER THE FLOOD

by Tsarist troops were lost during the Russian revolution of 1917, leading the article to report on rumours that it had come to the attention of Leon Trotsky, who suppressed it. The positioning of the Ark in this story is inspired by this alleged sighting but also others. And, of course, it was to Turkey and Istanbul that Trotsky was deported when he was exiled by Stalin in 1929, offering the opportunity for the connection to be made in this story. (Coincidentally, Trosky would leave Turkey in 1932, having spent much time on Büyükada in the Princes' Islands, where our would-be sultan is placed in this story).

I hope I have not played too fast and loose with the last Caliph, Abdulmejid II. I can only imagine that had the invitation been made, he would have been quite happy to have accepted the job of becoming the constitutional monarch in a post-imperial Turkey, if the country had decided upon that course upon Atatürk's death.

Apart from Andrew Mangold's magisterial biography, *Atatürk*, I drew on Patrick Kinross's *Atatürk: The Rebirth of a Nation* and Norman Stone's, *Turkey: A Short History*, which remains a superb introduction to the complicated history of this country. Charles King's *Midnight at the Pera Palace: The Birth of Modern Istanbul* was also invaluable for background on the city. For help with the sections on Ararat, apart from a good map of Ararat and Turkey, I also enjoyed Frank Westerman's *Ararat: In Search of the Mythical Mountain*.

The writing of this book would not quite have been possible without my having lived in Istanbul, which I did with my wife from January to December 2015. Time in that incredible city gave me time to get lost in its streets and alleyways and to see a little of the rest of the country, all of which was invaluable for bringing this story to life.

While living there I also made friends, including with the Ottoman historian, Dr Murat Siviloglu, now of Trinity College, Dublin. He told me a great deal about the country's history and was kind enough to discuss the pretext for this novel when I was first drawing its strands together. He was also generous enough to lend me his surname for the principal villain of the piece. (I didn't ask, I confess, but he was happy to agree. Among other names co-opted from life for this book is that of another friend, Andrew Streat, who likewise has taken no offence in having his name borrowed for this story.) People I had the fortune to meet while living in Turkey included Norman Stone himself, and Father Ian Sherwood of the Crimean Memorial Church, which is a stone's throw from the Galata Tower and was designed by G. E. Street, better known for the Royal Courts of Justice on the Strand. Both the church and the parsonage feature in this story.

If the reading of this story has inspired a desire to read more fiction set around this period in Istanbul, then you can't go wrong with Eric Ambler's *The Mask of Dimitrios*, which was published in 1939.

Among the final thanks, I should like to express my gratitude to my former agent, Louise Greenberg, for her enthusiasm and encouragement during the writing of this book. I would also like to thank my publisher, Richard Foreman, at Sharpe Books for his part in bringing the fourth instalment of the Drabble and Harris series to life. I must also thank my proofreader, Stephen York.

AFTER THE FLOOD

Final thanks and love go to Ashley, my wife, for her continued support and indulgence of my desire to write historical fiction, and to my sons, Herbie and Douglas for not complaining too much when I vanish to write.

Alec Marsh
June 2024
Manningtree, Essex

Printed in Great Britain
by Amazon